BLOOD TIES

Verónica E. Llaca

BLOOD TIES

Translated from the Spanish by
Mark Fried

First published in Spanish as *La Herencia* in 2021
by Planeta México

Published in the English language in 2024 by
Mountain Leopard Press
an imprint of
HEADLINE PUBLISHING GROUP

1

© Verónica Escalante Llaca, 2021
English translation copyright © Mark Fried, 2024

The moral right of Verónica E. Llaca to be recognised as the author of this work has been asserted in accordance with the Copyright, Designs and Patents Act, 1988

Mark Fried asserts his moral right to be identified as the translator of the work

Apart from any use permitted under UK copyright law, this publication may only be reproduced, stored, or transmitted, in any form, or by any means, with prior permission in writing of the publishers or, in the case of reprographic production, in accordance with the terms of licences issued by the Copyright Licensing Agency.

All characters in this publication are fictitious and any resemblance to real persons, living or dead, is purely coincidental.

Cataloguing in Publication Data is available from the British Library

ISBN (HB) 978-1-914495-19-9

Designed and typeset in Albertina by Libanus Press Ltd
Printed and bound in Great Britain by Clays Ltd, Elcograf S.p.A.

Headline's policy is to use papers that are natural, renewable and recyclable products and made from wood grown in well managed forests and other controlled sources. The logging and manufacturing processes are expected to conform to the environmental regulations of the country of origin

HEADLINE PUBLISHING GROUP
an Hachette UK Company
Carmelite House, 50 Victoria Embankment, London EC4Y 0DZ

www.headline.co.uk   www.hachette.co.uk

To Ana, Luisga, Montse and J.P., who have flown the nest and are multiplying as I write.

To Luis, always.

To all who have known depression and anxiety.

Anxiously we nurture one yearning: the need to know,
Not where we're headed, only that we are headed somewhere.
Once we arrive, we remain anchored for a time,
Until we again grow desperate

        Ramón Córdoba, *Cada perro tiene su día*

The poor man, knowing he could not fool
an ogress, took his enormous knife
and went up to little Aurora's room

        Charles Perrault, "Sleeping Beauty"

The wind buffets the body, plays with the chestnut curls, seems to infuse them with life. Observing the scene, a man exhales a lungful of smoke that is quickly dispersed by the breeze. He drops the butt, rubs it out carefully with his shoe, then picks it up and puts it in his pocket. Approaching the teenager, he tries to smooth her hair, but the wind won't let it lie. He raises the camera, brings the body into focus. A few seconds later, out pops a snapshot. The streetlamp flickers suddenly and the wind stirs up a few leaves and deposits them in the girl's lap.

The man moves away, climbs into his car, and is lost in the night.

FIRST FRAGMENT

Once upon a time, there was a woman the press called the Hyena-Woman. Infant Annihilator. Witch. Child-Chopper. Butcher of Little Angels. Monster. The Ogress of Colonia Roma.

Julián and I called her Mother.

Her name was Felícitas Sánchez Aguillón.

Your grandmother.

I'm not sure what motivates me to tell you the story of my mother, our story. No-one recalls her life except in fragments, nothing but snippets of the play in which we were obliged to act.

I ought to tell you the story from the upper balcony, far from the front row and hidden in the crowd, nowhere near the stage on which I played the son of a murderer.

She was born in 1890 on what was then Cerro Azul hacienda, a perfect name for the cradle of a fairy-tale princess, not for the birthplace of an ogress.

In that hamlet, deep in the region of La Huasteca, where a wave of the hand chased away both flies and heat, people cultivated corn, beans and lethargy as a way of life. The workers on the hacienda, most of them Huasteca Indians, were so oppressed by the conquistadors that they fell prey to the stupor and enervation fostered by a climate that rendered poverty more intense with every urge to move. No wonder this part of the north of Veracruz became known as

Sleeping Beauty. It's a coincidence that continues to amaze me: Perrault's story "Sleeping Beauty" gave us literature's first ogress.

The mother of Felícitas, my grandmother, had some mental defect at birth, which prevailing ignorance took to be the exhaustion common among her relatives. At the age of fifteen, with a mentality of seven and the ripe body of a woman menstruating every twenty-eight days, she was raped by a cousin. From which act my mother was born. Then mother and daughter were enclosed in a corral by order of the master, who was offended by my grandmother's groans and moans, which rose above the birdsong, the quacking of ducks, and the howling of coyotes.

No. It wasn't like that. I'm imagining. I'm making it up.

My grandmother gave birth squatting over a blanket spread across the dirt floor, then lay down with the infant on a filthy reed mat and slept as the blood drained from her body. The next day she was dead. The girl grew up naked on that same peed-on, shat-on mat, raised by my great-grandmother, who supported the two of them by begging, and once in a while offered her a bottle, but never picked her up...

That wasn't it either.

I'm trying to invent a past of which I know nothing. I know nothing of my mother's birth, her childhood, her adolescence, or a large part of her adulthood. I have a general picture of the extreme poverty of the hamlet where she was born, on that hacienda perched atop an enormous underground lake of oil, whose owners were dispossessed with an iconic turn of phrase: "Either you sell to me or I'll buy it from your widow." Peasant farmers were obliged to become oilfield workers who dug wells, laid railroad lines, built housing and roads, as the population multiplied and the hamlet became unrecognisable.

Her family certainly had never imagined that this hot country, isolated from the world by voracious and exuberant nature, surrounded by mountains and beset by temperatures that made the hours stretch and melt, would become a bustling town.

When I decided to research my mother's roots, I tried to make contact with members of her family. I was able to find her birth certificate in the civil registry, as well as the names of my grandparents, but I had let so much time go by that I could not locate a single living relative. Lacking information and imagination, I cannot recount how she managed to become such a freak.

Sociologists like to list the ingredients that mould a murderer, as if it were a recipe: a failed family environment, violent and alcoholic parents, maybe a close relative with mental illness. Serious abuse in childhood, physical and psychological. A negligent mother, uninterested in physical contact or affection. Various traumas besides child abuse: bullying in school, drugs, sexual disorders. Let's add to that inherited traits, the roulette of genetics. There ought to be an alarm bell that rings every time such a monster arrives in the world, so we can keep an eye on it or dispose of it immediately. Maybe my grandmother foresaw her daughter's future and was trying to save her when she gave her that happy name.

My mother never grew more than a metre and a half tall with a broad face, outsized hands and feet, eyes bulging from their sockets, and a pronounced crocodile jaw. In the early morning mists, her carnivalesque body and diminutive stature must have made her seem like a hallucination, an ogress even before she became one. Or maybe she always was.

In 1907, at the age of seventeen, in the midst of the Huasteca oil boom, Felícitas left Cerro Azul to work in Xalapa, the capital of Veracruz State; a cousin had recommended her for a maid's job in the home of a physician. Since the doctor's wife found her size, her irritable temperament, and her habitual silence intimidating, the doctor put her to work in his brand-new clinic, where among other ailments he attended to births. She studied assiduously under the doctor's supervision, without ever guessing what a prosperous business she would have twenty years later. And one day she exchanged her coarse cotton clothing for a nurse's uniform and her sandals for shoes. In fact she developed a fascination with footwear.

I confess – and here I pause this, what? biography? – I confess I have uncovered a rather dark motive for writing the story of my mother's life: to justify my own actions to you. I write to expiate, to extirpate.

After a year at the clinic, Felícitas was bringing children into the world. After two years she returned to her home town. Twenty-four months of nursing instruction and experience made her an authority in a place where people rarely got through primary school. She herself never got beyond third grade.

While the winds of the Revolution swept the rest of the country, geography protected La Huasteca, where the rising number of barrels extracted daily, with the encouragement of the dictator Porfirio Díaz, marked the rhythm of the town's growth. Foreigners, mostly American, arrived, some with their families, as well as people from other parts of Mexico, all working for the Compañía Huasteca Petroleum Company. Growth meant more births for Felícitas to attend to, children of the new families, as well as the progeny the oil workers sowed all over what people now called the Gold Belt.

Our lives must be written on some part of our bodies in a language we cannot yet decipher, in the lines of our hands, the whorls of our fingerprints, the wrinkles, moles, or freckles on our skin. I think about the trunks of trees, a ring for every year, wide or narrow depending on whether it was rainy or dry. Some of my mother's rings must be wider than others, especially the one that ought to come with background music or sound effects to announce that everything is about to change. A man entered her life.

*

Carlos Conde was a well worker in San Luis Potosí when he came to the attention of Edward Dawson, an oil company contractor. My father made an effort to stand out. Rather than wear an enormous sombrero like most Mexicans, he preferred a modest hat. He learned some rudimentary English and imitated as best he could an American style of dress. Son of a single mother, he laboured from the age of fourteen in the mine at La Concepción, until a fire in the shaft closed it down. By that time the oil boom was under way and he found work with Dawson's drilling company. When Dawson moved to Veracruz and settled there with his wife Dorothy, the American took Conde along.

In November 1910, at the outbreak of the Revolution, Dawson ordered Conde to find a midwife, since Dorothy was already in labour. The baby had come early, and disruptions caused by the war meant no foreign doctor could possibly arrive in time. Dorothy Dawson took one look at my mother and sent her away, insisting that no Indian was going to touch her. However, the accelerating contractions left her no choice. Felícitas took charge. It was a complicated birth, and the baby, a girl, lived only a few days.

When my mother returned home, she looked in the mirror and felt very Indian, outrageously so. She did not like the feeling. Taking a pair of scissors, she lopped off her long black braid.

From that ill-starred birth, something strong and healthy was born: Carlos Conde's somewhat morbid interest in the midwife. He appreciated her skill and assurance in attending to a woman who did not speak her language and who scorned her for who she was.

He began to visit her, drawn by the force of the black hole that was my mother, unaware that nothing, neither matter nor energy, not even light, could escape it. Felícitas, hardly accustomed to male visitors, did not wish to receive him in her room. So she put on the shoes she had bought in Xalapa and let herself be swept away by someone's unexpected interest in her. I do not understand what flowed between my parents, whether it was love or even related to love. What did exist was an unofficial partnership, an obscure arrangement.

The first in the chain of events that decided my parents' fate involved a woman, barely out of girlhood, who refused to keep the baby daughter born to her after she was raped by one of the oil company men. "I don't want her. Sell her, find another mother, another family, do whatever you want with her. I'll pay you to get rid of her." The mother was a dark-skinned Indian, but the baby had white skin and blue eyes like all the American engineers working there. Carlos Conde offered her to Dorothy Dawson, and to his surprise she bought her. Word got around and other women, each with reasons of her own, came to the door and paid Felícitas to dispose of their babies. My parents found the infants new families and sold them for a price.

Felícitas and Carlos were married on June 6, 1911, the year the Mexican Revolution brought down the Díaz government and the Mexican oil market along with it. Rail lines were sabotaged, trains were destroyed, and many foreigners fled the country. The Dawsons remained and raised their daughter — half gringa, half Mexican — in La Huasteca, where possibilities still seemed limitless.

One morning in May 1914, days after U.S. forces disembarked at the port of Veracruz, Felícitas gave birth to a girl, my sister. In La Huasteca, anti-Yanqui sentiment was stronger than revolutionary fervour, and those with guns were bent on driving the foreigners out. Rather than an army, the movement consisted of isolated bands of thieves who roamed about robbing and threatening the towns and oilfields. Five men with pistols and machetes showed up at my parents' door in the middle of the night, pulled my father from his bed, and beat him to a pulp. The men were drunk, but they knew my father worked for Dawson. "So you like sucking gringo prick? You bastard, your bitch is gonna like mine."

He tried to get up, blood pouring from his forehead. He never saw the quick and precise movement that fractured his right arm. He fell to the floor, curled around that arm, and a kick to the face knocked him out. Darkness. He did not see when they attacked my mother, nor did he hear her screams or the howling of the men. When he came to, she was sitting amid the tangled sheets, her face swollen, scratched, and bruised. In her arms she was rocking what looked like a crumpled blanket.

He crawled to her side, bleeding profusely from where the bones had come through his skin. She raised her eyes, then looked down at the bundle. A little leg slipped out from between the layers of cloth. What happened after, I never learned. How they reached the rudimentary clinic for oil company employees, or when they returned home, or where they buried their five-month-old daughter under shovelfuls of silence and horror.

Twenty-seven years later, lying on the floor next to the bars of her prison cell, my mother screamed that they had to let her out, so she could care for her daughter.

ONE

Friday, August 30, 1985
05.00

The wind will not let her sleep. It creeps into Virginia's dreams and flutters about her ears like a pigeon in the sunlight, sounding like a death rattle. The nightmare seems to issue from the bodies she handles at the funeral home. It has been five years since she married the owner of Funerales Aldama and still she is not accustomed to death.

She reaches for the clock on the bedside table, groping carefully so as not to wake her husband, and pushes the button in the middle, which casts a bluish light on her face. Five in the morning. Fearful of the nightmare's return, she gets up, throws on a sky-blue bathrobe over her nightgown, and goes into the bathroom. When she lowers herself onto the toilet, she realises her underpants are damp. That happens with a bad dream. "One of these days I'm going to wet the bed," she thinks as she changes into dry underwear.

After brushing her teeth, she looks in the mirror, fluffs up her hair with her fingers, then tiptoes down to the funeral home on the first floor. In the parlor, where the caskets are on display, she runs her fingers across the surface of one and thinks it will take all morning to dust them. She unlatches the front door and heads outside with a broom, intending to sweep up the dirt and litter that the night winds have blown onto the sidewalk.

Above the door hangs a sign: Funerales Aldama. The street lamps begin to fade with the first rays of the sun. She lays the broom down when she discerns a shape leaning against the wall of the building, directly under the window.

Approaching slowly, squinting to bring into focus the girl sitting on the sidewalk, she reaches out and shakes her shoulder. The girl does not respond; she looks asleep. Drunk, Virginia thinks. As the sun rises higher, Virginia crouches to get closer and confirms what she already knows. She sees dead bodies every day, but never here outside the building.

Concentrating on the violet face of the dead girl, she does not hear the footsteps of a neighbour behind her.

"Virginia!" the woman cries, making her start and tumble backwards. The neighbour rushes to help, and Virginia hurriedly straightens her nightgown to hide the underwear she just put on. She points and the neighbour stifles a scream, hand on her mouth, eyes on the girl, who is seated with her legs spread apart, her hands on her big pregnant belly, her gaze vacant, mouth open, long brown hair entangled, and her make-up a smeared mask that accentuates the rictus.

Their cries alert the homes nearby. Virginia's husband is the first to arrive. He grabs hold of his wife's arm, helps her up, and she takes refuge in his arms.

"Call the police!" Señor Aldama tells the neighbour's son, who has come to get his first close look at death.

TWO

Friday, August 30, 1985
06.35

An hour later and five blocks away, Leopoldo López, the proprietor of Funerales Modernos, emerges from his office, coffee in hand. He spent the night here, since it was impossible to pry the widow from the man lying in chapel number two. Neither he nor anyone else could get her to leave before four in the morning.

He sets to work. He opens the lid of the coffin to make sure the man is as he was the day before, albeit a bit stiffer. He arranges the flowers, sets up the coffee machine, exchanges dirty cups for clean ones, places new tissue boxes on the tables. Then he sprays the room with lavender air freshener, opens the windows to let the air tainted with sorrow escape, and crosses himself before the figure of Christ hanging on one wall. As he lights the candles, he hears screams in the street and banging on the door. Shaking out the match, he runs to the entrance, where his assistant is crying, "She's dead! She's dead!" Her tone is so sharp that Leopoldo reaches for the hearing aid in his right ear and turns down the volume. The woman seizes his arm and pulls him to the body of a teenage girl seated on the pavement with her legs spread and her head leaning against the wall where it says, "Funerales Modernos". He knows immediately what he has before him. With the employee hanging on to his arm, he goes inside and calls the police.

Leopoldo López then steps back outside, approaches the body, begins to squat, and his knees crack. His brow furrows in pain.

Steadying himself with the tips of his fingers on the sidewalk, he observes the dead girl, whose hands rest on her thick midriff. He reaches out to touch the hole in her forehead, between the eyebrows.

"Don't do that!" The warning comes from the owner of the corner store, drawn by the shouting. Leopoldo has trouble getting to his feet. "Don't touch her, Don Leopoldo. You might leave fingerprints on her clothes and they'll accuse you of being the murderer."

Leopoldo nods. "Can you leave fingerprints on clothes?" He eyes the girl's red skirt and the single shoe she is wearing.

"Sure, I saw it on television," the store-owner says. "The girl was pretty, what a shame."

"She was an adolescent, practically a child."

Leopoldo turns up the volume on his hearing aid and hears a siren in the distance.

By mid-morning the bodies of the two murdered girls are stretched out on steel tables in the morgue.

At the Public Prosecutor's Office Virginia and her husband repeat what they have already declared several times. Never having set foot in such a place, Virginia finds it impersonal, frightening, stuffy, noisy, grey. She is aware of a hum that seems to grow more intense by the second.

"Why did you go out so early?" she is asked for the umpteenth time by the man who identified himself as Agent Díaz. "Did you hear anything strange during the night? Did you see anyone near the body?"

"No, I saw no-one. It was dark," Virginia says yet again. She is exasperated, tired, sweaty. They gave her no time to shower; she was barely able to change out of her nightgown and robe. She hates going out like this, without make-up, and most of all she hates the humiliating rush of heat that will not abate no matter how much she fans herself. "It was just getting light when I stepped outside."

A couple of desks to her left, Leopoldo López and his assistant, who is clutching her handbag, speak with another man, who identified himself as Detective Rodríguez. Out of the corner of his eye Leopoldo watches Virginia, whose shrill voice obliges him to lower the volume on his hearing aid yet again.

"What time do you usually go to work?" the detective asks Leopoldo.

"Six in the morning. When I have to work late, I sleep at the office. I keep a sofa-bed there and a change of clothes."

"What about you?" he asks the assistant.

"At seven. Today I arrived early because the boss stayed over. I wanted to help him straighten up the room before the mourners came back. They must be so upset. The Mass was supposed to be at ten and it's nearly noon."

The detective gives a slight nod and returns his gaze to the papers on his desk.

"What time did the last person leave?" he asks Leopoldo, his blue Bic pen hovering.

"About four in the morning."

"And the body of the dead girl wasn't there?"

"I don't know. I locked the door right away so dirt wouldn't blow in. There was quite a wind."

"And the people who left didn't see anything?"

"I don't think so. They hurried to their car. The wind had stirred up a lot of litter and dirt."

"So you didn't hear anything strange?"

"I wear a hearing aid," pointing to his right ear. "I don't hear well."

The officer nods again, rubbing his chin. He makes a note: "Witness deaf."

They are finally released at two in the afternoon with a warning that they might be summoned again if a further statement is required.

Leopoldo López has known Virginia and her husband for years. For a time they were arch competitors, but they soon realised corpses were never in short supply.

Outside, Virginia lights a cigarette. "It must be someone wanting to give funeral homes a bad name," she says in a low voice.

"Who would kill two girls just to make a funeral home look bad? By God, woman, don't say such stupid things." Señor Aldama plucks the cigarette from his wife's hand and takes a drag.

"I don't know. Someone." She retrieves her smoke. "I can't get the image of the girl out of my mind."

"You've seen dead bodies."

"This is different."

"It's no different, just another cadaver."

López says, "I'm on my way. I have a dead man locked up in the parlour." He raises his arm to hail a taxi and gets in.

"He's annoying," Virginia says and tosses her butt. "Let's go."

SECOND FRAGMENT

Midway through 1923, two things occurred in my parents' lives. First, a couple came to the door, the woman eight months pregnant and bleeding heavily. Felícitas had her lie down and shortly thereafter the woman breathed her last, having given birth to a stillborn child. The husband ran out and returned a few minutes later with his two brothers, all three of them armed with machetes and eager to destroy whatever they could. The neighbours intervened and threatened to call the police. The attackers swore they would be back to kill my parents.

The second event came in response to the collapse of international oil prices, which caused a drastic cutback in production. Carlos Conde lost his job. My father's arm had never really healed, he could barely use it, and Edward Dawson could easily find an able-bodied and ambitious worker to replace him. My parents decided to move to Mexico City.

It took several weeks, but they found an apartment beside and above a store at 9 Cerrada de Salamanca. Felícitas had never imagined such a place: ceramic tile floors, white-painted walls, access to a yard. There were two bedrooms and a living room on the second floor, and on the first, beside the store, a bathroom and a kitchen with a gas stove — no need for a fire — plus a pantry that was bigger than her room at Cerro Azul. The previous tenants had left a few things behind, including a table and a mattress that became the couple's only furniture. The steady stream of automobiles, streetcars, trucks, pedestrians, and cyclists provided a strange and exciting soundtrack for their new life.

Felícitas had wanted to move to Xalapa, a place she knew. She had never been outside of Vera Cruz, yet here she was, far from Cerro Azul, one more stranger amid the nearly one million people living in Mexico City. Her husband had convinced her by extolling the opportunities in a place where so many pregnant women weren't able to pay for a private hospital or gain access to the public system. "We'll set up a clinic," he promised.

In this exercise of the imagination I'd like to set aside my feelings so I can get inside my mother's skin, understand her story. I have scrutinised my heart and I am certain that in the very beginning what I felt for her was love, the way all children feel love for their parents. It's something close to a reflex, but in my case the reflex soon atrophied, and today it is entirely absent.

The building was in the poorest part of Colonia Roma, at a distance from the avenues lined with mansions — French, Colonial, Arab, Neo-Gothic, Romanesque — inhabited by a social class unheard of in Cerro Azul. The landlady did not want to know about their plans, and warned only that the neighbours had better not complain.

When Felícitas walked the streets she must have felt out of place among the women in high heels and skirts or dresses so unlike the coarse embroidered cotton she wore. Her first purchase was a pair of black shoes with heels, although she had to content herself with the only pair that matched her outsized feet. She wanted to blend in, to be seen as just another woman in the big city.

Who was her first client? How did she make a name for herself? Let's imagine a woman from one of the nearby homes whose labour came on early, bringing profuse bleeding and such pain that she cried out in the early hours of the morning. The desperate husband took to the street shouting for help. Carlos Conde was already pounding the pavement on his daily search for work. The money they had saved would not last and with his mangled arm finding a job was not easy. He heard the shouts, turned, and lengthening his stride, brought his wife to attend to the woman in labour. A healthy baby was born, a girl. Word got around, there were no other midwives in the neighbourhood, and it was not long before a second woman called, then another, then more. The money kept the roof over their heads, and Felícitas soon went about in new clothes and new shoes.

Through her clients, word also got around that she could procure babies. And thus, three years after their arrival in the capital, in 1926, my parents once again began to trade in children.

Then a boy arrived they could not sell. Days passed and the baby was hungry, soiled, wet, and bawling. They could not find a buyer. Demand does not always keep pace with supply.

Wails and more wails.

One morning, Felícitas picked him up from the box where they kept him and took him into the bathroom beside the kitchen. The infant struggled, anxious to latch on to a breast he could suck. She pressed both her thumbs against the throat of the newborn, who continued to cry. She pressed harder and the baby waved his hands and gasped like a fish out of water.

Silence.

Felícitas laid the tiny corpse on the cold tiles of the washbasin. For a few minutes she stared at the body. Then she balled her huge hands into fists and sighed.

A year earlier, that is, two years after my parents arrived in Colonia Roma, a woman with a stylishly short haircut, wearing a narrow-brimmed hat and a skirt that came to the knees, her eyebrows neatly plucked and darkened with eyeliner, her rosebud lips bright red, got out of a black 1925 Chevrolet on my parents' block. She was the first of what my father called "well-off señoritas" to seek out my mother, the first of many. She looked in both directions before opening her cigarette case and lighting up. Her hands were trembling and she had a hard time putting the flame to the tip of her cigarette. She coughed and told the driver to wait, inhaled deeply to steady her nerves. A light breeze erased the hieroglyphics of the smoke. She adjusted her hat and began to walk, eyes on the ground, attentive to the rhythm of her steps, concentrating on the sound of her heels striking the pavement. Now and again she raised her gaze to measure the distance to her destination. She walked past the store and stopped in front of the door to number nine, took a last puff on the cigarette, let the butt fall and rubbed it out with her shoe, perhaps with more force than was necessary, as if she were also extinguishing the urge to do an about-face and go home.

Unexpectedly, a hot fat tear slid down her cheek and dropped to the pavement. Straightening herself, she pulled a handkerchief from her bag and blew her nose. Then she tugged on the brim of her hat, cleared her throat, and knocked. She heard footsteps approaching. She nearly turned and fled, but she got a grip on herself.

"Is this where the midwife lives?" she asked quickly, before she could change her mind.

As an answer Carlos Conde opened the door a bit wider and pointed to a couple of chairs in the hallway that served as a waiting room. The woman sat down gingerly, her handbag in her lap. She smoothed her skirt with both hands to ease her doubts and stared at the floor tiles. Felícitas soon appeared. The woman leapt to her feet, her heart beating hard, the blood like ice in her veins. She opened her mouth to introduce herself and immediately thought better of it, stuttering out the first name that came into her head. She would have preferred something entirely made-up, but her nerves betrayed her and she gave the name of her sister-in-law. Felícitas nodded. The woman felt herself shrinking until she was shorter than the midwife's metre and a half. She had trouble controlling her trembling fingers, which seemed unwilling to pull an envelope from her bag.

"I want you to remove the child I'm expecting."

"You're awfully skinny to be giving birth."

Carlos Conde grabbed the envelope and took out the money.

"I want you to remove it," she repeated in a whisper. "I want an abortion."

"I don't do abortions."

The woman took out another wad of bills and hesitated, unsure who to give it to. Carlos Conde held out his hand, then counted the money in silence, while she sat down, fearful that at any moment her legs would fail her.

"How far along are you?"

"I think four months."

"You waited too long, I can't guarantee either the result or your life."

"I can't have this child."

"She will do the job," Carlos Conde intervened. "A job is a job," he said to his wife.

The woman got to her feet. Felícitas observed her silently, measuring her from head to toe, with particular attention to her shoes.

"Where did you buy them?"

"In Paris."

"They're pretty."

The woman nodded and said nothing. She followed the midwife, feeling that she was entering one of Dante's rings of hell, Felícitas as her Virgil. She swatted away such thoughts and concentrated on her husband, her family, her life at the side of one of the men running President Calle's government. "I don't want any more children," he had told her. "So what do you want me to do?" "That's your problem, four children is enough. No more."

Instinctively, she brought her hands to her belly, closed her eyes, and said goodbye to the child she was carrying.

Although she could not know it, that day she launched a new line of business for Felícitas.

THREE

Friday, August 30, 1985
09.00

With the final images of her dream dissolving behind her eyelids, Elena Galván reaches out to touch Ignacio Suárez. Her fingers find only the cold white sheet. She had been dreaming about her dead brother Alberto; they were children in an unfamiliar and decrepit house, and before waking up she managed to hear the echo of his laugh. Squinting, she half-opens her eyes only to snap them shut against the wounding light that reminds her of the two bottles of red wine they drank the evening before. She shades her face with one hand and forces her eyes open.

"Ignacio? What's wrong?"

He is seated on the edge of the bed, his back to her, elbows on his knees, face buried in the palm of his left hand. His naked body trembles from his agitated, uneven breathing. Elena pulls herself over to him and the bed creaks. The furniture of her room in the family hotel has not been changed since she was a teenager. These old boards have supported various mattresses, several lovers, peaceful nights, bad dreams, and for the past three years the tender pleasures of Ignacio's caresses.

Feeling Elena's fingers outline the half-moon scar on his right shoulder-blade, he gives a start and runs a hand through his silvery hair. Then he covers his mouth, as if to trap any words that might escape from between his clenched teeth.

The sheet slips off her when she embraces him from behind, pressing her naked breasts to his back. "Come lie down, let's stay a bit longer. My head aches, two bottles was too much. Do I have to beg you?"

Elena slides her fingers down to his penis. She fondles his flaccid member, but he pushes her away and gets to his feet. "Two girls got killed," he says, and without even glancing at her he takes a step towards the window.

"What? Those things you write give you nightmares."

"No, Elena, look," he says, and he holds out two photographs. "Someone slid these under the door. I don't know when. I found them when I went to the bathroom about twenty minutes ago."

Ignacio lays two Polaroids on the bed. Elena leans over to pick them up and her nipples graze the comforter. Her long black hair, closing like a curtain, hides her face for a moment before she leans back against the dark bedstead and tucks a lock behind her ear. She watches Ignacio step again to the window, observes his naked body, the old man's ass she enjoys kidding him about. She likes that ass and she likes the rest of his mottled body, which she has explored with her palms, her eyes, her tongue, learning its ins and outs by heart. In no hurry, she lowers her eyes to the photographs. She has never liked instant cameras; the pictures are never as good.

"They're dead," Ignacio says.

She squints trying to see the faces. "'Look me up,'" she says aloud, reading the words scrawled in black on one of the shots. "Who . . . ?"

She can find no words to frame her question. The snapshots fall from her fingers as she covers her mouth with both hands.

Sitting down beside her and picking up the photographs, Ignacio sees, not the images in his hand, but others from a past that bleeds into his present and colours the life he has tried so hard to write about without equivocation.

"We ought to ask if anybody saw who left the pictures. It must be a joke. Who would think of doing such a thing?"

Ignacio shrugs and shakes his head.

"Do you recognise either of them?"

"No. But I know who killed them . . . It's a message for me, Elena."

"Huh?"

Ignacio remains silent. Elena picks up the photographs and looks again. Each girl is sitting with her legs spread, hands on her belly. Since they were taken at night with a flash, no surrounding details are visible. You can barely make out the kerb or the walls they are leaning against.

"Isn't this like the murders in one of your books?" she says, holding the pictures like a pair of murdered queens in a deck of cards.

"I think so. I'm an idiot, I should have seen this coming."

Ignacio paces the room, first to the window, where the shade seems to tremble at his approach, then to the door, then back. The hotel room is much too small for his anxiety.

From a shelf, a dozen books watch their author's comings and goings. Elena made him sign each one with a different dedication. Eight of them feature José Acosta, the iconic protagonist in Ignacio's fiction and a detective certainly capable of finding whoever it was who slid the photographs under the door.

"I've got to go."

"Where? I'll go with you."

"No, I need to go alone."

He grabs his trousers folded over the back of a chair, uncovering the shirt he buttoned carefully the night before to keep it from wrinkling. He dresses in a hurry. She leaps out of bed and reaches for her dress on the floor next to her panties, her bra a bit farther away near the chest of drawers. Ignacio leaves, still buttoning his shirt, shoes and belt under his arm.

"Ignacio, wait!"

Elena runs after him in her sea-blue floral dress, but no underwear.

"I'm going to kidnap you," she had told Ignacio when he walked in the previous afternoon. "We're going to disconnect from everything," she insisted, kissing him on the lips while slipping one hand inside his trousers. He did not resist. They shut themselves into Elena's room, unplugged the telephone, and hung a "Do Not Disturb" sign on the doorknob, so that none of her employees would interrupt them.

Now Elena runs barefoot across the main courtyard. A surprised guest jumps aside to let her pass. At the hotel entrance, she hears Ignacio honk the horn of his grey 1984 Fairmont.

"Elena, listen carefully," he says when she reaches the car door. "If something happens to me, I need you to take all the red notebooks and papers out of my room, all the boxes I would not let you open. Take everything you think might be important and hide it. Don't give anything to my children or my ex. Here's the key to the desk drawer, hide everything that's inside."

"Ignacio, Ignacio! You're talking as if you aren't coming back. Wait!"

"Elena, I can't explain now. I have to go. I might not be back for a few days. I need to find him."

"Ignacio. Hang on. Who do you need to find? Where are you going? Let me go with you."

Elena barely manages to sidestep the back tyre as the car speeds away over the cobblestones leaving a cloud of dust behind it.

FOUR

Friday, August 30, 1985
21.47

Leticia Almeida's mother Mónica rises slowly from the chair she has occupied for hours awaiting the release of her daughter's body. Some time has passed since she last insisted on being with her girl. The shaking sobs have subsided, giving way to an occasional off-key moan that slips through her nearly closed lips. Her husband has not let go of her cold hand; he caresses it nervously with his thumb. They cannot tell which of them is holding up the other.

"I'm looking for some relative of Leticia Almeida," a masculine voice had said over the telephone. The call came in at five-thirty-two in the morning. Ricardo Almeida, Leticia's father, had picked up the receiver and looked at his watch, something he cannot explain, as if he had somehow known the reason for the call, and that he ought to register the precise time at which he was told of his daughter's death. Leticia had not come home from school and no-one knew where she was. In direct proportion to the minutes passing, her father had become infected by his wife's anxiety. Their daughter had told them she was going to sleep at the home of her friend Claudia Cosío, but when they called the Cosíos they discovered neither of them had slept there.

"She always lets me know," Mónica kept repeating. "She always tells me where she is."

Three times he stopped his wife from going out into the street to look for her. "Where are you going to go? We're better off waiting here."

They sat in the kitchen, on Lety's bed, in their bedroom, in the dining room. Distress latched on to their breasts like a blood-sucking tick, making it hard to breathe, injecting them with an urge to move that only increased the level of their anxiety.

"Stop moving, take it easy, sit down," her husband said. "You're making me nervous."

"We have to call the police," Mónica said again and again.

"She and Claudia must be somewhere nearby," Ricardo tried to reassure her. "Let's give it a little more time."

He poured two glasses of the cognac he saved for special occasions, the only thing on hand, which he knocked back without tasting. His wife reproached him, saying he needed to be sober if they had to go out and search for their daughter.

"Yes, I'm her father," he said to the man on the telephone, who without any preamble told him that he had to come to identify the body of a girl who might be his daughter. He listened to the address and wrote it on the pad, as if it were any old message. His hand did not shake as he wrote, he remained calm during the call.

"Who was it? What did they say? Ricardo, tell me!"

His soul slipped out of his open mouth, his heart lost its rhythm, he could not find enough air to pronounce the name of their daughter.

"It was Leticia, right? It was Leticia," his wife said, shaking him by the shoulders, while he gasped and moved his head from side to side.

At the morgue, seated across from them with his head in his hands, is Mario Cosío, Claudia's father. A scene much like what had happened at the Almeidas had occurred at the Cosíos, only there the mother answered the telephone and could not write down the address on the message pad because the receiver fell from her hands as she screamed, "No! Not Claudia!" Her husband picked up the telephone.

He already knew the address because a year before he had been there to identify the body of his younger brother, who had been killed in an accident.

"What happened?" their eldest son asked his mother, who continued calling her daughter's name. "Papá? Who are you talking to?" The son tried unsuccessfully to grab the receiver. "Papá, who was it?"

"Stay with your mother," the boy's father said while his arm slowly dropped to his side. He had the impression that the hand holding the telephone was not his. He let the receiver fall to the table and did not hang it up.

"Mamá, Mamá. Calm down. Mamá, what's going on?"

His mother went quiet when Mario Cosío said, "I have to go see the body of a girl at the morgue, because they think it could be your sister."

"I'll go with you."

"No, you stay here," he told him, and he took his wife by the shoulders and pushed her towards the door.

"How long are you going to keep my daughter in there?" Leticia's mother asks once more. The odour of her perfume saturates the room along with the clacking of the typewriter.

"I don't know, señora. They've said you can go. I'll let you know when you can come to pick up the body."

"Leticia! My daughter's name is Leticia Almeida!"

"There's no point staying here, it's hard on everyone, on you and on us."

"Hard? I make things hard for you? I interrupt you?" Standing beside the desk, her hands on a pile of papers, Mónica exclaims in a loud voice, "My life just got interrupted forever."

Ricardo Almeida takes her arm before she can sweep everything from the desk onto the floor. The secretary leaps to her feet, upsetting her chair. Leticia's father hugs his wife, his arms like a straight-jacket, but he can scarcely keep her upright. It seems to him that his wife has become thinner over the past few hours. She collapses, unable to control her sobs. He would also like to dive deep into his sorrow, to drown in the tears he is holding back. "You have to be strong for your wife," he keeps repeating in his mind like a mantra. He wants to believe those words, wants to convince himself he can be strong, but he knows the phrase is a lie. It's a delusion to believe anyone is capable of sustaining another when faced with the unthinkable. He smooths her tangled hair. In normal circumstances — if what people call normality exists — she never would have left the house without brushing her hair or putting on lipstick. She even keeps a mirror in a small table by the front door, along with some blush, lipstick, and a hairbrush, in case she needs a touch-up before going out.

"Easy, my love, easy. We're going to go where you can rest. The señorita is right. You'll be able to wash up and eat something."

"Let me go. Don't tell me to calm down. I'm not going to calm down. I want my daughter and I want her now. Do you hear me? I want my daughter this instant!"

Mónica de Almeida throws off her husband's arms and strides towards the doors that lead to the mortuary.

"Señora, you cannot go in there." One of the officers posted by the entrance, alerted by the shouting, seizes her arm.

"Let me go!"

"Señora, as I said, you cannot go in there."

She struggles to escape his grip. Pain spreads up her arm into her shoulder, her breast, across her abdomen, and breaks her in half. The officer holds on to keep her from falling to the floor, and her husband manages to catch her from behind.

Another man, dressed in grey and reeking of sweat, approaches the officer and beckons him over. The men confer while the couple make their way back to the chairs, where Claudia Cosío's father sits, observing the scene in silence. He knows that he too ought to demand the release of his younger daughter's body, but he hasn't the strength to get to his feet. Señor Almeida helps his wife lower herself into the black plastic chair, which creaks as if protesting the weight of her sorrow and desolation.

"You will be able to have your daughters in a moment," the officer says with his hands on his hips. "To take possession of the bodies, you will need to sign a few documents and call the funeral home."

THIRD FRAGMENT

Let's pick a date: November 1931. Salvador Martínez, a plumber carrying his toolbox, knocked at 9 Cerrada Salamanca. My parents had called him to fix a problem with the pipes: a blocked toilet, the usual. Upon entering the house, a horrible stench reached him. Accustomed as he was to most odours, this one struck him as far worse than any he had ever encountered. Carlos Conde welcomed him and took him to the bathroom.

"Our toilet is clogged," he explained.

Salvador Martínez raised the lid and had to cover his mouth and nose. His mouth filled with a bitter taste. He clenched his jaw to keep from vomiting on the tile floor.

"Is this your first job?" Felícitas, leaning on the doorframe, watched Salvador concentrate on controlling his stomach.

"No," he mumbled, stepping towards the toilet and peering down to inspect the floating mass. "How long has the bathroom been like this?"

"Since yesterday."

Salvador stirred the water with his plunger, then bent to pump vigorously, spattering his forearms. When he pulled out the tool, with it came what at first he thought were bits of toilet paper. But when he looked closely, he jumped back and threw the plunger at the wall, where it left a dark brown stain before falling to the blue-tiled floor along with a tiny leg stuck to its rubber lip.

"What . . . ?" The plumber stared at the amorphous lumps floating in the toilet. Rapidly, he picked up his toolbox, leaving the plunger behind. Felicítas blocked his path.

"You can't leave, you haven't finished the job."

"I don't do this sort of job."

"How much do you want for it?"

"Let me by."

Salvador heard his tools clanking in the box. He raised a hand to push Felicítas aside when Carlos Conde reappeared behind his wife.

"Move over," the plumber insisted.

"Friend," Carlos Conde pointed a finger at him, "you were recommended by a buddy who was in jail with you, and he knows all about how you . . ."

"Never to a child!"

"That buddy told us about someone getting killed."

"Are you threatening me?"

"Here we don't threaten, we do business." Carlos Conde held out a fistful of bills, which Salvador Martínez took. "And we pay well."

Salvador examined the money in the palm of his hand, calculating the total without unfolding it. When he looked up, his eyes met Felicítas' icy stare, boring into him like a viper's fang.

"So?"

Salvador Martínez looked again at the bills, then at the blue tiles where the little leg lay, then the toilet. He stuffed the money into one of the pockets of his overalls and, avoiding the tiny limb on the floor, picked up the plunger. He leaned over the bowl and said, "I'm going to need other tools."

Some time later, in March of 1932, Salvador Martínez brought his sister-in-law, Isabel Ramírez Campos, his brother's widow, to work for my mother. He told her my parents needed a cleaning woman, the wages were good, and it would help her pay the bills now that her husband was gone. Felícitas showed her the closet where she kept the cleaning things and curtly told her to figure it out on her own, because she had a lot of patients to attend to that day. "The señora is a midwife," Salvador had explained. "She needs someone to do the cleaning and cooking." Felícitas explained how much she would be paid and what would be expected of her. As she spoke, Felícitas looked her up and down, wondering whether to tell her to clean the room where she attended to her patients, and decided not to give her any warning.

Isabel put her handbag on the floor, tied on an apron. Mop and pail in one hand, duster in the other, she was crossing the apartment when she heard a sound underneath the table where we sometimes ate. Squatting, she discovered a child hiding between the legs of one of the chairs. On hands and knees she crawled over to the boy, who hugged his knees and watched her approach, wide-eyed and wordless. "Come with me," she said, and she reached out her hand. The child did not move, a statue glued to the floor. Isabel touched his shoulder and felt the boy's teeth sink into her forearm. She lost her balance and banged into the chair. "Let go," she said, not raising her voice much, as the burning pain spread up her arm. "Let go," she said again. She wriggled a bit closer in the tight space and stuck the fingers of her free hand into the child's mouth to force his jaws open.

"Let her go," I ordered my brother from behind a chair. "Let her go." I ducked under the table and grabbed Julián by the hair and pulled until he released Isabel. She got up immediately, hugged her wounded arm close to her body, blood seeping from the toothmarks. Underneath the table Julián and I punched each other. I was six and he was four.

That was our first meeting with Isabel, one of the clearest memories I have from my childhood. Isabel with her black eyes, her long braid wrapped around her head, and a dimple in her right cheek.

"Cut it out! Stop fighting!"

Felícitas entered the room. We froze. She grabbed Julián by the arm. "What's wrong with you?" She shook him like a rag. With her other hand she slapped him across the head, then threw him to the floor. I tried to sneak away, but Felícitas caught me by the foot. "Take your brother to his room and neither of you leave it until I say so," she said.

"Yes," I mumbled.

I rose slowly and helped my brother to his feet. I was crying. While Julián made no sound, he did give my mother a look that made Isabel shudder. Julián wiped his lips, stained with Isabel's blood and his own, on his sweater, and we disappeared down the hallway that led to the bedrooms.

"I don't think I'm going to stay at this job," Isabel muttered.

"That we shall decide at the end of the week," Felícitas said. She smoothed her hair with one hand and her clothes with the other. "I have a patient, we'll talk later."

Isabel ran to get the things she had brought and went to the front door. It was locked.

"Forgive my brother," I said from behind.

Isabel turned. I took her by the hand and led her away from the door. I wanted her to stay.

"What's your name?"

"Manuel."

I walked her to our bedroom. At the threshold, Isabel came to an abrupt stop. I tugged her and she tried to find a place to step. The floor was awash in dirty clothes, garbage, papers, shoes, newspapers.

I didn't see Julián coming, but he grabbed one of her legs and kept her from moving.

"Julián, let her go."

He raised his face, looked Isabel in the eyes, and made a grimace imitating a smile. Isabel tried to do the same. She squatted to face him. Julián took the arm he had bitten and touched the toothmarks.

"He doesn't talk," I said. With other people, Julián almost never spoke. Between us we had a made-up language using signs and the few words he could say. He had some sort of speech impediment, which was never taken care of.

Isabel's eyes again met Julián's. His gaze pierced her heart like a thorn. She brought her hand to her chest and looked away, while he crawled up on the only bed in the room and began playing with a doll.

Isabel patted my head and surveyed the room. Again, she brought her hand to her chest as if it hurt. Then she bent over and started picking up the clothes and piling up the rubbish.

Diario de Allende
August 31, 1985

MACABRE MORNING

by Leonardo Álvarez

The community of San Miguel awoke to shocking and macabre news yesterday. The body of a young girl, barely seventeen years old, was found a few steps from Funerales Aldama. Virginia de Aldama, the owner, spotted the corpse about six in the morning and alerted the authorities.

Agents from the Public Prosecutor's Office arriving on the scene declared the girl dead and called for detectives. An hour later, a second female body was discovered only a few blocks from the first, leaning against the wall at Funerales Modernos.

Both young women were in the same posture: seated with their legs spread, as if about to give birth; each had a pillow tucked under her clothing, giving them the appearance of being in an advanced state of pregnancy.

The bodies remained at the morgue until autopsies were complete. Just before midnight they were transferred to Funerales Modernos, where a crowd had been gathering since the news broke that the visitations would be held there. Floral arrangements filled both chapels.

At the site where the body of Claudia Cosío Rosas was found, candles, flowers, and messages accumulated throughout the day. The same occurred where the body of Leticia Almeida González was discovered. Both were students in their last year of high school.

Most people interviewed said the terrible events made them feel outraged and indignant, and, above all, fearful that they might be repeated.

Ricardo Almeida, the father of one of the victims, said he would focus first on giving his daughter a proper burial and only later would he demand the capture of whoever was responsible. For their part, the Cosío Rosas made no comment.

Today, at seven in the evening, their bodies will be interred in the Municipal Cemetery.

FIVE

Saturday, August 31, 1985
18.00

From her chair beside the bier, Mónica de Almeida watches four men lift the casket so effortlessly she thinks it must be empty and she's inside a bad dream, a long, eternal nightmare.

"Is my daughter still in there?" she says, and her voice sounds strange to her own ears.

"Sure," one of the men says, unable to repress a half-smile. One of the other pallbearers gives him a kick.

Mónica notices neither the mockery nor the kick. She is absorbed in thinking about the lightness of the box and the absence of her child. She wonders if she is still the mother of that weightless body. Her eyes follow the four men, then she gets to her feet and stands next to the one who made fun of her.

"I'll carry her too," she says, placing her hands on the oak coffin.

"Let the men do their job." Her husband hurries over and tries to pull her hands off the lid.

"Stop, Ricardo, leave me alone. I want to go with Leticia!"

"Mamá!"

"I want to go with her," she says to her son. She places a hand on the boy's right cheek.

Up to now her son has managed to contain his grief, not wanting to further upset his mother to whom they had had to give a tranquilliser the night before. Mónica wants to explain to him why she has to go with her daughter: she needs to atone for herself, to beg forgiveness for not taking proper care of her child, for having allowed a demon to murder her. She feels so guilty. When she was pregnant with Leticia, she nearly miscarried and had to stay in bed for six months to not lose her. How short a time among us, she thought when she first saw her in the casket, looking as if she were asleep, and so pretty Mónica found it hard to believe she was dead.

"Let me help too." Her son moves in beside his mother and covers her hands with his own.

Last night at the funeral home, when it was nearly eleven, Claudia's mother Martha went up to Mónica, who was trying to say the rosary but kept forgetting the words and could not put together a complete Ave Maria.

"It was your daughter's fault!" Martha screamed, and she pushed Mónica off her chair. Mario Cosío held his wife from behind to keep her from pummelling the grieving woman.

"Forgive her," he said, pulling his wife away. "Please forgive her."

"It was Leticia's idea! She was crazy! It's her fault that my daughter — my daughter! — is dead!"

Many hands hurried to raise Mónica from the floor.

The funeral home was packed with mourners and gawkers, all of whom remained silent, either staring at the floor or the ceiling or the flowers perfuming the atmosphere with their aroma of death. None of them could look directly at the families' sorrow. Any murmurs were pleas to the universe — to their god, that puppet-master who at a whim cuts the strings in order to fulfil his quota of blood — pleas that he be satisfied with the two dead daughters and not take anyone else's.

Martha de Cosío escaped her husband's grip and rushed over to the pine casket where her daughter's body lay unaffected by her parents' bickering. "Leave me alone," she begged her husband, who had again taken her elbow and was squeezing it too hard.

"It's time to take you home," he said, his jaw set, yanking her arm the way he did every time she refused to do his bidding, to be willing when he pulled off her clothes, his breath stinking of alcohol and tobacco, and sometimes other women. Martha would close her eyes. Her life veered between what she avoided seeing and what she was obliged to watch.

"Leave her alone, let go of her," Mónica de Almeida shouted, planting herself in front of Señor Cosío.

"Don't stick your nose in our business," he threatened, maintaining his grip on his wife.

"Stay with my daughter, don't leave her alone," Martha begged, while her husband hauled her to the car.

Now Mónica stands behind the hearse as they load her daughter's casket, and she will not let them close the back.

"Can't I ride with you?" she says to one of the men in black, the tall thin one with bony white hands who has already told her twice that he has to shut the loading door.

Leopoldo López, the funeral director, emerges from amid the reliquary and approaches them.

"I want to go with her."

"I'll take charge," Leopoldo López says as he slides behind the wheel of the hearse.

"But . . . ," another of the men in black objects.

"The señora will go with her daughter to the cemetery."

SIX

Saturday, August 31, 1985
22.00

Esteban del Valle, his lab coat bloodstained and his safety glasses perched on his head like a tiara, takes a gulp of Coca-Cola without lifting his eyes from the body in front of him. He is the pathologist at San Miguel's General Hospital and the forensic medical officer for the Public Prosecutor's Office.

Esteban has not slept in two days. In the background a radio broadcasts the Third Annual Government Report, read aloud by President Miguel de la Madrid Hurtado:

> In response to vigorous popular demand, we have made substantial improvements in the justice system and carried out a broad national programme of public safety to purge, modernise, and professionalise the police.
>
> We have acted in an unprecedented manner in the fight against drug trafficking.
>
> We have worked equally hard to prevent drug addiction and offer rehabilitation to those who suffer from it.
>
> Moral renovation has been our permanent commitment and our steadfast norm.
>
> I know very well there is still much to do, but the downward slide has been reversed.

> We shall persevere in the moral renovation of our society: the nation itself depends on staying the course and making renovation irrevocable.

The wind woke him up the night the girls were murdered. He had forgotten to latch the kitchen window and a gust sent it crashing against the wall. The noise brought back a memory of his father near death, rapping his knuckles on the chest of drawers to awaken him. Once again Esteban saw himself at fifteen, in the chair beside his sick father, in the house where he still lives. His mother and sisters had abandoned them a year before, perhaps a bit longer. Esteban, the eldest, had remained because he understood his father and shared his preoccupations. His father was a physician, his mother a housewife. Not long after Esteban uttered his first words, his father set himself the task of educating him in medicine and human anatomy. As a result, whenever Esteban suffered a scrape or cut, he told his friends he had an abrasion, his bruises were hematomas, his legs lower limbs, and his arms upper limbs.

His father had one overriding obsession: he was convinced that "life force" could be measured, verified, weighed. He wanted to locate the vital energy in nature, the driver of the universe. He conducted experiments with animals, killing them in his son's presence, in a laboratory he built in the garden so as to work away from prying eyes. He spoke his thoughts aloud in front of Esteban, who repeated his words at school. His teachers could do little to protect the boy from being bullied by his schoolmates.

"You must observe and measure my death," his father told Esteban when he learned he had leukemia. His wife accused him of not wanting to get better, just so he could feel the footsteps of death in his own body. That's why she and the girls departed. They had begged him to seek treatment. "Life force you find by living," she told him.

"I will not be a witness to your suicide." For friends and relatives, ignorant as they were of Esteban's real role as lab assistant, his decision to remain made him an exemplary son.

By the time the banging on the chest of drawers occurred, the agony had lasted for weeks. Helping, annotating, accompanying, Esteban had barely slept and had lost all notion of time. Every few moments his father the guinea pig dictated the changes he felt in his body. Esteban weighed him, measured him, photographed him. And despite the dozens of Polaroids, he did not manage to capture the loss of vital force, nor did he notice at which point the pictures he was taking were of a corpse.

Fifteen years after his father's death, Esteban observes the body of the writer Ignacio Suárez Cervantes and feels incapable of beginning the autopsy. He stares at the swollen face, bruised, dirty, stained with dried blood, unrecognisable. Twice before he has lived through the trauma of having a friend on his table, and never has he known what to do: should he speak to him? Say goodbye? Ask permission before cutting him open?

According to the report from the traffic police, an ambulance picked Suárez up at the site of an accident involving a grey 1984 Fairmont, plate LKM265, owned by Ignacio Suárez, and a 1982 Renault 18, plate GTR892, owned by Víctor Rodríguez Acosta.

Suárez was still alive while two paramedics struggled to staunch the flow of blood from his many injuries. He went into convulsions and died before reaching the hospital, which is why they brought him directly to the morgue.

Esteban had met the writer three years before, when his childhood friend Elena Galván introduced them. Ignacio needed to check a few facts in the manuscript he was working on, to make sure his story held up from a medical point of view. A devotee of crime novels,

Esteban was delighted to assist, and his name appeared in the book's acknowledgements.

He recalls their first conversation, when he asked Ignacio to meet him in this very room. "No matter how tough writers of noir fiction may think they are," he had told him, "they wilt when they see a real cadaver." Suárez's aplomb surprised him; he seemed unbothered by the smell of death, which is the first thing that scares the weak of stomach. Esteban makes a habit of handing out Vick's Vaporub to medical students on their first labs, so they can spread it under their noses, including those who pretend to be brave and stand in front of the others. One of the brave ones once vomited all over a corpse and had to clean it up. But not Ignacio Suárez. He strode in wearing a white lab coat and asking for a pair of gloves so that he could touch.

His curiosity satisfied, Ignacio invited Esteban to supper and ate a huge steak that was practically raw. The pathologist liked the man with an iron stomach, who listened and asked good questions about a subject most people find difficult.

After gulping more Coca-Cola, Esteban puts on his latex gloves. He places his tools within reach, lowers his safety glasses, and makes the first cut in the body of his friend.

FOURTH FRAGMENT

My brother Julián almost never cried, even as an infant. He would simply lie there until my mother remembered to give him a bottle. I don't recall him ever complaining, though for my own survival I have forgotten many episodes of our childhood; in fact I have only a few isolated memories.

Whenever I try to remember I feel I'm sinking into shifting sands and can't catch my breath. It's fear. It's that dark place my mother shut me into, the same place where she hid the children and babies people brought to her, and where she murdered I don't know how many.

I find it hard to imagine my mother giving birth. I thought of writing "having a child", a phrase applicable to a mother who takes part in the lives of her children, who lives with them and for them, and sees life through their eyes. "Having a child." When those children go off to live their own lives, such a mother feels blinded. She has nothing to do, and her life is in the hands of a stranger: herself.

My mother was the opposite. If she had made some connection with us, perhaps none of what occurred would have taken place. Maybe she would still be alive. The basic problem with our relationship was that we never had one.

I dig into the shifting sands to seize another recollection. I was seven. Howls woke me very early. I had seen the cat two days before and had left a bowl of milk hidden amidst the shrubbery in the yard.

I refilled it every time I found it empty. I got out of bed as fast as I could before my mother heard. She did not like animals. I retrieved the bottle of milk from the refrigerator and ran to where I'd hidden the bowl. It was not there. The night was cold and I only had on my underpants and undershirt. I lay on the ground and looked under the bushes, calling the cat in whispers.

I heard it again, at the back of the yard. My mother was there, leaning over the washstand, her hands underwater. "Mamá?" She did not hear me. I thought of forgetting about the cat and escaping to my room. She had warned me many times: Do not set foot in either of the rooms at the back of the yard or go near the washstand. Then I saw her pull something from the water using both hands, it looked like a little ball, and it slipped out and fell with a splash. I heard her curse. On tiptoes I watched her pull it out again.

"Mamá?" I forced myself to look. The bottle slid from my hand and shattered on the ground, splashing me with milk and shards of glass.

"What . . . ?" She turned towards me.

"Is it . . . the . . . ?"

"Yes, it's the damned cat, look what it did to my arms."

Floating on top of the water was a newborn kitten.

"Take it out," she commanded. I shook my head. "Take it out," she repeated.

"No," I whispered, on the point of crying, or perhaps I was already crying. She bent down and thrust the mother she had just drowned at my chest, obliging me to hold it. She pulled out the dead kittens one by one and piled them on top.

"Walk." She gave me a shove. "You gave her milk, didn't you? That's why she stayed, it's your fault she gave birth here, it's your fault I had to drown them."

I managed to count five kittens at a glance, not as in school where sometimes I used my fingers. We reached a cardboard box; my mother grabbed them from me and threw them in. She made me carry it to an empty lot, where we left the kittens on a pile of garbage.

"I don't like animals," she said on the way back. "Now, get lost. Go to school."

I shut myself in the bathroom, still carrying the phantom weight of the cats in my arms, and opened the bath faucet; the water was cold. I undressed in the tub and scrubbed myself with soap to get rid of the smell sticking to me. Even today, as I am remembering, my body seems to stink of dead cat.

Two years later, I could still hear the cat howling every night, as if it were lost in the labyrinth of my ears, unable to escape. I buried my head under the pillow whenever the ghost of the cat visited me, its body soaking and its gaze vacant.

"I can't stop hearing the cats," I told Julián one day. I said it to get the thought out of my head, to let it go. I had never told him about the cat or the kittens, and I reckoned he would not understand.

"I hear them too," he answered slowly in his new-found voice that had Isabel so excited and our parents so unmoved. It was thanks to the insistent coaching of our daytime substitute mother that Julián learned to speak.

"You hear them? Did you see the cat and the kittens Mamá drowned?"

Julián shook his head, signing with his hands that I should shut up and listen.

Howls.

I held my breath, every pore of my skin transformed into an ear, so absorbed I could hear the beating of my heart and Julián's.

"What are you doing?" Isabel entered our room, as she did every morning. The two of us gave a start. "Why are you still in your pyjamas? You're going to be late for school. What's wrong?"

"Nothing," Julián answered with astonishing composure, while I got up from the floor with a shake of my head, unable to explain myself.

Julián's intelligence was unusual. He distrusted everyone and spent all day at school alone. In the schoolyard during recess, he killed ants, spiders, whatever insects crossed his path. I tried and failed to disappear in the crowd. It was obvious Julián was a child of the fairy-tale Ogress, and through my veins ran the same accursed blood.

That day after school we ran to our bedroom. Julián seemed to have forgotten about the howling. I asked him to sit still so I could try to hear it again, but at that time of day, the noise of traffic and people obliterated the necessary silence.

We spent the rest of the afternoon either doing homework or out in the street. I always kept Julián with me so he would not be in reach of our parents. Isabel wanted us out of the house as much as possible for the same reason. She took us to the market or to see her son Jesús, who spent the whole day with his grandmother. In the evening, before leaving, she would insist that we stay in our room until the next day.

At last it was dark. Isabel tucked us in — my brother and I still slept in the same bed. She blessed us and said the Prayer to My Guardian Angel.

I waited a while before opening the window onto the yard and gesturing to my brother to come closer.

"I'm sleepy," he mumbled in his off-key voice.

Finger to my lips, I cautioned him to stay quiet. Peering out, listening hard, I saw my mother cross the yard with one of her patients. My mother looked up and my heart stopped. I ran to bed and got under the covers, terrified that she might have seen me. Next thing I knew it was the middle of the night.

An icy breeze was making the curtains move about like ghosts desperate to escape. The wind blew papers from the bedside table onto my face. Half-awake, I got up to close the window and heard the howls. I froze, holding my breath, nearly holding my heartbeats. I dropped to the floor and crawled back to the bed.

"Julián," I whispered. "Julián."

He was seven, and the only time he seemed his age, the only time he dropped his sullen scowl, was when he was asleep. That was the last night I saw him sleeping deeply. After that, his sleep was light, alert, and his face was set in a grimace at all hours.

A drowsy Julián got down on the floor with me and we crawled to the window. We heard the few vehicles on the road at that hour, some far-off laughter, words carried by the diminishing breeze. The curtains swayed gently. Then the mournful howls reached us.

"Maybe it's another cat, if they find it they'll drown it. We've got to rescue it."

"Let it die."

"No!" I whispered. "Come with me to look for it."

Julián shook his head.

"Please."

He shook his head again and crawled back to bed. "Close the window, you're going to wake them," he ordered.

"Please."

The howls echoed in my head. I went to Julián and pulled on his arm.

"Alright." He shook off my hand. He did not like to be touched.

With infinite care, we went down the stairs. We opened the door to the yard no less cautiously. The wind had picked up, cold. We edged towards the rooms at the back, the one where Felícitas saw her patients, and the other where we believed tools were kept. The howls became more mournful in the moonlight. The sound was coming from the tool room, but the steel door was locked. I tried to see in the window, but it was too high and the glass was frosted. My hands and knees were trembling, and my movements became clumsy.

"I'll get a knife from the kitchen, maybe we can spring the lock with it," I said, pointing at the keyhole.

I did not give Julián time to answer. Urged on by the need to save whatever was inside, I ran to the house and yanked open the door. The wind pulled it from my grasp and it banged against the wall so hard the glass shattered.

Julián took off and passed me, racing up the stairs. My reaction was not so quick.

As I went up after him, the ogres' door opened.

My thought was to get into bed and pretend we were asleep.

I could not close the bedroom door. My mother had the knob.

"Fi, Fa, Fo, Fum," says the ogre in Jack and the Beanstalk, "I smell the blood of an Englishman."

Fi, Fa, Fo, Fum, she pushed on the door, knocking me to the floor.

"What are you up to?"

She grabbed me by the foot.

"Nothing, no-thing..." I stuttered.

She pulled me towards the stairs, and Julián made for the door. My father grabbed him and heaved him over his shoulder as if he were a sack of flour that wouldn't stop wriggling.

"They were in the back room," my father yelled. "I saw them out the window."

"Stupid brat!" she screamed and gave Julián a slap so hard that he went still.

I thought she had killed him. Had she killed him at that moment, it would have been for the best, for him, for me, for everyone. So I believe today.

My mother gripped me by one arm and whirled me around. Now I was the one who went still. She had that effect on me, as if she had a switch to turn me off.

"So you want to see the room?" she roared, and she dragged me down the stairs. My father had gone on ahead, hauling Julián. He opened the door of the tool room, and I saw him throw Julián onto the floor from his full height.

Carlos Conde slammed the door and locked it. I tried to hold back my sobs, I could barely breathe. My mother opened the door to the room where she attended to her patients. "If you're so curious to know what goes on in here, you're going to help me clean up."

She had me by the collar of the sweater I sometimes wore over my pyjamas. She turned on the light, so bright I had trouble seeing. In front of me was a table, and shelves with jars and objects I did not recognise.

Now, trying to recall what was in there, my mind mixes it with the image of the place in shambles, once Julián had destroyed everything after Felícitas died.

"Clean," she ordered. She thrust a rag into my hand and dunked it, hand and all, into a pail of water.

"Clean!" She shoved me at the red stain covering part of the table.

I drew a frenetic circle on that dark, viscous substance.

"Wet it!"

Felícitas plunged my hand into the water again, manipulating me like a doll.

I scrubbed the table and returned to the pail. The water got redder.

I let it happen.

"Stop crying," she commanded, and she squeezed my fingers harder.

Then, in a clumsy movement, I kicked over the pail.

"Get out of here!" She shoved me towards the door.

I ran to the back gate. It was locked, but my mother did not come after me and did not call me again. The moon was high, the nearby houses nearly all in darkness. The noise had set a dog barking, then another dog, and another, until the night was filled with barking.

My father was inside the house by then. I tried the door to where Julián was. Impossible. I sat on the ground and leaned against it. My mother came out of the other room and paused a second to look at me. When I think of that moment I believe she considered consoling me. But ogres don't hug. I kept my eyes down, shrank into myself, and hid my face between my knees. There I remained until dawn.

"It wasn't a cat," Julián told me in the morning, after my father unlocked the room and I ran to him. My brother was on the floor, his eyes swollen with tears, his nose dripping mucous, his hair a mess.

"It was a baby." He fell silent.

I went to the box next to Julián, but before I could look inside my father stepped in and picked it up.

"Fuck it all," he swore and he strode out, box in hand.

I tried to help my brother up, but his leg hurt too much. My father returned and plucked Julián off the ground as easily as he had the baby in the box, and took him to the doctor.

Julián's left leg was in a cast and he walked with crutches. The sound of his new way of walking spoke for him: I learned to recognise his mood by how hard he slammed the crutches on the floor. In school I carried his backpack, his books. I tried to read his mind, to anticipate what he wanted. I used crutches too, but mine were made of guilt and regret, heavier and more clumsy than Julián's. I stayed with him during recess, listened to him chew the sandwich Isabel made us every morning, always strawberry jam with butter. I borrowed books from the school library and read them to myself while my brother stared into space. Whenever my anxiety got the better of me and his silence overwhelmed me, I read aloud and loudly. Julián neither approved nor disapproved. Reading saved me. The invisible strings of my voice held me up.

I kept asking Julián what happened inside that room, but he

ignored me. Then, one night he woke me at midnight, driven by some urge to talk, no matter how accustomed he was to saying nothing.

It was dark in the back room when he opened his eyes, he said. His head was aching, and his body too, although the worst was the shinbone that broke when my father threw him down. He made a huge effort to sit up, and tried to orient himself. He saw the faint glow coming through the window and dragged himself towards it. The door was locked. That was when he heard a sound very much like a howl. He felt along the wall for the light switch.

Inside a cardboard box was the animal that had started it all. Rage made him forget his pain. He crawled to the box, opened it, and saw, not a cat but an infant. The smallest baby he had ever seen.

It stank.

The sounds were not howls, but human cries.

Sensing Julián's presence, the infant renewed its complaints, crying louder still. Perhaps it was trying to say, "Save me." But my brother just covered his ears.

"Shut up!"

The pain in his leg was driving him crazy.

"Shut up," he said again in his off-key voice, roughened with tears and rage.

He grabbed the baby and began to shake it, squeezing it by the ribs.

"Shut up!"

Julián shook it again and squeezed harder.

"Shut up!"

After a while, when he was certain the baby had indeed shut up, he put it back in the box and curled into a ball.

When the cast came off, I expected to see Julián walking as before. He never did. His left leg refused to recover the rhythm. He limped and so did I, although mine could not be seen; a mental limp, if you like.

It was 1936 and the world was on fire: the Civil War in Spain, the Berlin Olympics, the Hindenburg's maiden flight. I tried to take care of my brother and the months slipped by. Then Guernica was bombed and the Hindenburg exploded, foreshadowing the disaster soon to follow, which would sow all Europe with corpses. In our house there were dead bodies too.

One afternoon my mother called to us. She and my father took us to the yard. She handed me a spade and ordered me to dig. It wasn't hard, since it was where they often buried remains. After a few shovelfuls, my mother handed Julián a bucket. "Empty it into the hole."

I thought I caught a glimpse of a tiny head.

"Throw dirt on it," she told me.

That was the beginning of our participation in the family business.

A week later, we went with my father to leave bags in vacant lots. I began to work out who came to give birth and who to have an abortion. I hated the aborters and I hated the ones who left their babies behind.

By then I was ten, Julián eight. We were kids who made the remains of other kids disappear.

Isabel hugged us more and began to give us Bayer Tonic, maybe in the fond hope it would fortify not only our bodies, but our souls.

Diario de Allende
September 2, 1985

WRITER IGNACIO SUÁREZ CERVANTES DIES

by Leonardo Álvarez

Mexican writer Ignacio Suárez Cervantes has died at the age of fifty-nine following a head-on collision. The accident occurred Saturday night on José Manuel Zavala freeway shortly after six p.m.

Emergency services brought the injured parties to the hospital, where the writer breathed his last.

Suárez's remains were taken to Gayosso Funeral Home on Félix Cuevas Boulevard in Mexico City.

The Secretary of Culture and numerous personalities from the artistic, cultural, and political world have expressed their condolences.

Ignacio Suárez leaves a vast literary oeuvre that won him several prizes. He also wrote film scripts, the most recent being "Blood Game".

His work appeared in literary magazines and he wrote a weekly column for *La Prensa*, the daily that was his journalistic home from the beginning of his career.

His noir novels, featuring the memorable Detective José Acosta, established him as one of the giants of the genre.

May he rest in peace.

SEVEN

Wednesday, September 4, 1985

07.23

Elena examines herself in the mirror. She spies a white hair and pulls it out; two chestnut ones come with it. She smells of nerves, of bed, of sadness, the scent of a body battered by anguish, incredulity, mourning. Ignacio was buried two days ago and she has not emerged from her room since, despite her aunt Consuelo's cajoling.

After the writer had driven off, Elena asked her employees about the photographs slipped under her door. In vain. Then she searched for Ignacio in places he frequented. Also in vain. Hotel work helped distract her from the pain in her chest and an inner trembling that grew more agitated every second without news of Ignacio.

In the evening she shut herself into room number eight, which the writer occupied half the year. She sat on the bed and began to turn the pages of a red notebook lying on the sheets. He always wrote in these red notebooks, which for him were sacred. It was not easy to decipher his diminutive penmanship on the tightly-lined graph paper. She went to the desk, picked up a pen, and committed the sin of invading his sacred terrain.

Idiot.

Stupid.

Where are you?

Shit. Shit. Shit.

She nodded off at the desk, and by the time she roused herself it was late at night. She went out, her clothes wrinkled and her hair mussed, to ask the night watchman, "Did he call? Did he come back?" The man answered with a shrug. She did not sleep the rest of that night. The following day, hotel work kept her occupied, but her thoughts were with Ignacio. She called his house in Mexico City, but no-one answered. She drove San Miguel's streets looking for his car. She called the Red Cross, the hospital, the police.

It was 8.26 on Saturday night — she knows the exact time because she looked at her watch on average three times a minute — when her mother's twin sister Consuelo ran to find her, shouting that they had to go to the hospital because Elena's stepfather José María had had an accident. Elena barely had time to grab her purse.

"What if Ignacio calls?" she hesitated before stepping through the door. "I can't go out."

"Are you nuts?" Consuelo hurried her and grabbed the car keys from her hand.

At the General Hospital the doctor on shift explained that José María was being operated on for internal bleeding.

"Is he going to die?" Consuelo asked.

The doctor, a young man who had just finished his training, took a moment to respond. "It's serious, he's been badly injured, but he's alive. The man who was with him died."

"Who was with him?" Elena asked.

"I don't know. They brought in the driver of the other vehicle too, a kid."

"Elena."

Elena turned and found herself face to face with Esteban del Valle, the forensic pathologist she had introduced to Ignacio.

"What are you doing here?"

"José María had an accident, we just got here; from what they say it looks serious." She moved her cheek close to Esteban's for a kiss, and smelled the formaldehyde impregnating his clothing and skin, part of his personality.

"Ignacio is with me," he interrupted her.

"With you? Here? What are you up to? I've been looking for him all day." Elena turned and walked quickly towards the morgue; she knew the way.

On one occasion she had accompanied Ignacio there. Despite the hospital rules forbidding it, Esteban had allowed them to be present during an autopsy. Ignacio had bet Elena she wouldn't be able to stand it even for five minutes. But she went right up to the dead man and made a cold and conclusive diagnosis: "He looks like he's made of wax." It wasn't her first encounter with death. When she was only ten, she had found her grandfather in a field, dead of a heart attack. Years later, she spent what seemed a very long time staring at the cadaver of her brother Alberto, after his multiple handicaps did him in. She had been very curious to see a body to which she had no ties of affection. What she could not stand was the place, the temperature, the bloodstains, the white and green tiles, the sensation of being in a crypt, all of which made her intensely aware of her own mortality. The death of her loved ones had filled her with sadness, but that unfamiliar, unrelated dead man spoke to her of the end of life. It made her think, "We come into this world just to grow old and die, that's all," and the thought churned her stomach. She felt so awful that Ignacio swallowed his urge to poke fun and spent the afternoon consoling her.

"What is he doing here with you?" she asked Esteban as he stepped ahead of her.

He put his hands on her shoulders and said very slowly, "Ignacio is dead. He was with José María in the car."

"Ignacio? No, it can't be! He's got a very common face, maybe you're confusing him with someone else."

"It is Ignacio. I had just gone up to call you from the office. I was about to begin the au— the procedure, when I thought that maybe you didn't know. I didn't want to call you from the extension in the morgue. And then I heard your voice."

"I want to see him."

"You can't, it's not allowed," Esteban said.

"I want to see him, Esteban. I want to see him."

Now, after a long while staring at herself in the mirror, Elena returns to the bed, picks up the red notebook she pilfered from Ignacio's room, which has accompanied her like a security blanket for twenty-four hours, and writes:

I never imagined I would see you on a table, see your body, your dead body. It was you and at the same time not you. Naked, swollen, injured, undone, absent, and so dead.

I answered questions and took care of the hospital paperwork until your ex and your sons turned up. Esteban called them. He said he had to tell your children you had died, even if they weren't close to you. I didn't realise who they were, I was so caught up in my own feelings, until I heard one of your sons say your name. I sat in my plastic chair, a mere spectator from that moment on. I witnessed the comings and goings of your children, the exaggerated and inappropriate sobbing of your ex, the condolences directed at her. My anger grew and overwhelmed my sadness. For as long as it took her to drive the 245 kilometres from Mexico City, you were my dead man. When the hospital released your body, they appropriated you, took you away in a hearse. No-one told me where, nor did I ask. I couldn't, I felt out of place. You belonged to them, not to me. The next day I decided to follow you to the capital. It was Esteban who told me what funeral home, but he didn't want to come along.

What was I in your life? A six-month's lover? What of you belongs to me? Maybe just this notebook. You bastard. They pushed me aside without even a glance. I stepped out of the way, I didn't feel I had the right to ask for anything.

During the Mass, your ex-wife sat in front of the coffin, flanked by your two sons. For the years we were together, I avoided thinking about her and I nearly managed to convince myself she did not exist. She wailed so outrageously that the priest had to raise his voice to make himself heard above the sobbing. She likes to call attention to herself, doesn't she? I sat next to a stone column, hidden behind a wall of people dressed in black. The place was full of journalists and artists of all sorts; actresses and actors in your films; painters, publishers, sculptors; and of course most of them were writers. I was the nobody, maybe the only one who will tell you what your funeral was like. Does that matter now?

The priest said he had known you for many years. I'll never know if that's true, I'd never met him. My place is here in the parallel universe where you lived six months of the year, more than two hundred kilometres from a world that is not mine. I confess I'm trying to control myself, although maybe now you have access to my thoughts and you know I'm furious.

Idiot. You are an idiot. You and José María are both idiots. What were you doing with him?

All through the Mass your ex kept blowing her nose, honking so loudly that everyone could hear, and then she stuffed the dirty Kleenexes in her bra. One of your sons kept patting her messy hair. He kept that up, stopping only during the Our Father because he was holding her hand.

No.

I lie.

She is not ugly. She did not blow her nose or put the dirty Kleenexes in her bra. In fact she didn't even cry. For the entire ceremony she sat unmoved. The priest was able to speak without raising his voice. Now you know. I was the one who cried. I was the widow, not her; she didn't shed a single tear for you.

When the priest finished at last and people were leaving, I went up to the coffin and was tempted to knock and ask if you were there inside, since the only indication was your photograph on the lid.

We headed off to the cemetery and it started to rain. Of course somebody said the heavens were also in mourning, the stupid things people say when death overwhelms us. At the cemetery, colourful umbrellas clashed with the rest of the scene. It looked as if we were in a black-and-white film, the technicolour got switched off when we came through the gates. The paths soon became rivers of mud that drowned our shoes. No-one knew where you were to be buried. After an accident they don't let you cremate the body; it has to be left intact for seven years in case they need it for the investigation (if you were wondering why they didn't incinerate you). At last we were shown the way.

Your children and your ex stood in front of the hole, and it seemed to grow wider.

One of the workers announced on a loudspeaker that the grave was ready. I looked around to see where you'd be coming from. I haven't told you that the funeral home looked like a flower shop, there were so many arrangements. They brought them all to the cemetery and most were laid out on the surrounding graves, there wasn't enough space for them all. Someone had the idea of handing out white flowers, maybe we were supposed to leave them on your coffin, very Hollywood, although not at all the style of the Panteón Francés in Mexico City, where everyone is cheek by jowl.

As your casket arrived, a bolt of lightning lit up the sky and a peal of thunder announced your descent into the earth. It was very theatrical. The rain got heavier and several people opened their umbrellas again, while the gravediggers let you down with ropes. There was no graveside speech, nor could we toss in a handful of earth. When they finished setting you down, they got straight to work shovelling. Somebody threw a flower into the hole filling up and swallowing you, your last stop on a trip to nowhere. The rest of us followed suit. The atmosphere eased up enough that a friend of your ex's, who stayed at her side throughout, had an attack of nervous laughter, hysterics, which made everyone smile. The deluge limited our farewells to wishing you a quick bon voyage, *hopefully we'll see each other again.*

Elena takes her time closing the notebook. Having spilled her guts, she feels she is nothing but an empty shell. She leaves the red notebook on the bed and drags herself to the bathroom, where she opens the shower faucet, and contrary to habit steps in before the water heats up. Cold water bounces off her shoulders, neck, back, breasts. Her weary skin feels a bit of relief, as if she were crying from every pore. She shampoos her hair, her eyes closed, and thinks about José María, who is in an induced coma. She hasn't gone to see him. Rinsing herself, she feels she is getting rid not only of the oils on her scalp, but the fog that since the day Ignacio died has kept her from thinking clearly.

EIGHT

Wednesday, September 4, 1985
12.38

Elena has been sitting in a chair beside José María for more than an hour. Hypnotised by the nearly imperceptible rise and fall of his chest, she has taken on the rhythm of her stepfather's breathing. She examines his face, stained, bruised, swollen, scraped, and spattered with the warts and moles accumulated over twenty years of marriage to her mother. While stroking his hand, she becomes aware of the odour of his body, mixed in with hospital disinfectant.

"What happened?" she asks in a low voice so as not to awaken her aunt Consuelo, who is napping in the other chair. José María does not respond.

Consuelo has been going back and forth to the hospital every day since her brother-in-law was admitted. For years she has cared for her twin sister Soledad, and now for José María as well. She has also taken charge of the hotel since Elena abandoned everything after Ignacio's death.

"Did he wake up?" Consuelo asks, startled, rubbing her eyes. She runs her fingers down her cheek and tries to get to her feet.

Elena shakes her head. "Wait, don't get up so fast, you'll get dizzy."

"When did you get here?"

"An hour ago."

"Are you going to stay for a while?"

"No, I ought to get back to the hotel and catch up on things that need doing."

Consuelo leans over José María, pulls up the sheet, and caresses his sparse white hair. She kisses her brother-in-law on the forehead and gives him a couple of pats on the chest. "Wake up," she whispers in his ear, then turns to Elena.

"I'll be there in an hour, I'm going to stay a while. Yes, go to work, it's just what you need to start feeling better. I'm so glad to see you out and about." Consuelo pats her cheek, then hugs her. "Go, go, and stop in to see your mother, we've left her on her own with all this."

"With all this," Elena repeats, thinking she will never see Ignacio again.

She leaves the building and gets behind the wheel of her car. In the hospital she had managed to hold back her tears. Now the knot in her throat makes it hard to breathe. She leans her head on the steering wheel and the car rocks to the rhythm of her sobbing. Once she has herself under control, she wipes her face on the sleeve of her sweater and pulls out of the parking lot.

At the hotel the receptionist stops her. "You have a visitor, he's been waiting over an hour," she says, and she points.

"Esteban, what a surprise."

Elena hurriedly leads him to her office, where she chases off one of the chambermaids dusting her desk.

"I told you not to move any papers I leave here. They might be important," she scolds.

"And if I don't do it, you'll tell me I only clean the surface."

"Leave us alone," she says, indicating the door.

"I'm not finished."

"You can do it later."

"Not until tomorrow. Today I won't have time to come back."

She shakes her dusting cloth, filling the air with motes that glint in the light.

"Go, and close the door behind you."

Elena waves Esteban to a chair. "What's up?"

"How are you, Elena?"

"Awful, truly awful. I can barely get out of bed. I still can't seem to take in what's happened. I keep hoping he'll walk in the door." She brings her hands to her eyes and tries to control the storm gathering within. "I've just come from the hospital, José María's still in a coma. Jesus, I can't stop crying."

The pathologist sits silently beside her. Gingerly he reaches out, but quickly repents and folds his hands in his lap. Elena gets to her feet and disappears into the bathroom, leaving Esteban to pace the room nervously. He too feels intensely sad about the loss of his friend.

"Forgive me, Esteban. Today I made the effort to get up, but to be honest the only thing I want to do is climb back into bed, take something so I can sleep, and wake up in a week or two or a month, when I feel less sad."

"I understand, no need to excuse yourself. I'm sorry to be bothering you. I came because I have something for you. I didn't want them to take it. I thought you would want to have it."

Esteban pulls from his trouser pocket a chain with a medallion.

"Ignacio's chain . . . " Elena brings her hands to her face and tears roll down her cheeks.

"Forgive me," she says, wiping her eyes.

"Which saint is it? Do you know?"

"No, Ignacio said it was the patron saint he would have to explain himself to."

"A writer's thing, I suppose."

"Esteban, I have to tell you something important." She pauses for a long moment. "The day before Ignacio had his accident, early in the morning, somebody slid two photographs of the murdered girls under the door."

"What?"

"He showed them to me after I woke up. I couldn't make out the faces. The pictures were taken from a distance with a Polaroid. On one of them somebody had written: 'Look me up.'"

"Look me up?"

"Ignacio was really upset, he said the murders were a message for him."

"Where are the pictures?"

"I don't know, he took them with him."

"Maybe they're among the things they found in his car, I'll look into it. What else did he tell you?"

"As he was leaving he said if he didn't return I should hide all his belongings and not let anyone take them, not even his children or his ex-wife."

Esteban paces back and forth, rubs his hands together, and takes a pack of cigarettes from his shirt pocket. "May I?" he asks, and she shakes her head.

"There's no smoking in the hotel."

Esteban puts the cigarettes back in his pocket and continues to pace. "Elena, listen, you can't tell anyone what I'm going to tell you. When I was examining the bodies of the murdered girls, two judicial police came in and stopped me. Somebody from the government must be involved or some big-shot in business, somebody with clout in the city or the state. The same thing happened a couple of years ago when they took away the body of that young man who'd been raped and tortured, remember?"

Elena shakes her head, tapping her fingers impatiently on the desk.

"The murderer was the son of a cabinet minister. They sent him abroad. The victim's family demanded justice, but since the order came from the governor nothing could be done. I think in the case of these girls they're not going to look for the murderer, because they already know who it is, at least that's how it seems. I'll find out what I can about the photographs and let you know."

They leave the room and walk to the lobby, each absorbed in thought. "Thank you," Elena says, bringing her cheek close to Esteban's and smacking a kiss in the air. After watching him get into his car, she hangs the chain around her neck and feels the medallion nestle on her chest.

FIFTH FRAGMENT

Writing about yourself can give you a martyr complex, and that's something I want to avoid. As a child I liked to imagine myself a warrior in the adventure stories I became addicted to. I read Emilio Salgari, Stevenson, Mark Twain. I dreamed of becoming Prince Sandokan, the Count of Monte Cristo, Errol Flynn in "Captain Blood". Immersed in a story, I could forget that I spent my life crisscrossing the city carrying burlap bags filled with foetuses. I could imagine myself doing all sorts of things. I told myself lies, and in time lying became my way of life. I became a professional liar, a writer.

This morning I visited Julián to pin down a few memories. He has a different idea of what happened. There is no absolute truth about our childhood. Memory plays tricks. Life is the story you tell yourself, which is why I like fiction. Life is an immense vacuum we attempt to fill and made sense of, right up to the day death takes us by surprise. Then nothing matters, not how you lived, or what you lived for, what you remember, or how you remember it.

At the beginning of September 1940, I was fourteen and I had drawn up a plan to get my parents arrested. In my imagination the plan was perfect; in practice it had its flaws. I would leave the bags nearer and nearer to our house, one block at a time. I thought that would alert the police.

I was emptying a bucket down the drain when I heard

knocking on the street door. Felícitas was with a patient. I ran to the yard to leave the bucket next to the washstand, so I could rinse it later.

The knocking came again. Unbuttoning her bloodstained housecoat, my mother came out of her examining room without closing the door behind her. I could see the patient was asleep, there was a lot of blood. Maybe Felícitas had been unable to wake her. I don't know how many women died in our house, perhaps more than one, since my mother's methods and skills were likely insufficient for emergencies and unforeseen complications.

Felícitas rinsed her arms off at the washstand, smoothed her hair, and went into the house to answer the door.

I got there first and opened it. It was two police officers.

"Yes?" I started trembling when I saw them.

"We've come to ask a few questions. Are your parents home?"

I nodded. The bags, I thought, they're here about the bags. "My parents are here," I invited them in.

The men followed me into the hallway, where my mother stood calm as could be.

"Señora, we've come to ask you a few questions, because we've received a report about a bag found a block from here full of abnormal things."

"Abnormal?"

"We don't want to frighten you," the second officer piped in. "They were human remains, foetuses to be precise."

"Jesus!" she exclaimed, bringing her hands to her mouth, then sinking into one of the chairs where every day women waited their turn. She was obviously unsettled, having believed the bags had been left far from the house.

"My mother..." I began to say, but the words stuck in my throat. "She's..."

"My wife has a heart condition and I believe your visit has upset her," my father interrupted.

"Mamá, are you alright? Are you sick?" Julián said. I hadn't noticed my father's or brother's arrival. Julián spoke up to cover for Felícitas, and what he said confirmed us as accomplices.

The officers excused themselves and asked us to get in touch with them if we noticed anything unusual. My father and Julián and I accompanied them to the door, then retraced our steps. Felícitas screamed and leapt at us, wielding the shovel we used to bury foetuses. Carlos Conde stood behind her.

"Idiots! Where did I tell you to leave the bags?"

Julián pushed me just in time to keep me from getting hit and we both fell to the floor. We got up quickly and tried to run to our room, a bad idea. We should have run into the street after the policemen.

My father grabbed me by the shirt collar and held me back. Julián, of course, could not run fast because of his leg. My mother swung the shovel but missed him. Julián ran to hide in the same room where years before my father had locked him up. Meanwhile, I slipped my father's grasp and made for the street door, but I fell face first when the shovel came down again, making a half-moon cut on my right shoulder-blade.

"No, Julián!" I managed to hear Isabel's cry before losing consciousness.

When I woke, my face was against the floorboards and my head was bleeding. I felt woozy.

The images I recall are very blurry.

A woman came out of the room where Felícitas attended to her patients. There was no sign of my parents. Julián had a wound in his forehead.

"Take us to the hospital," Isabel begged the woman, whose name we learned later was Eugenia Flores.

Eugenia Flores swayed as she walked. We got into her car and the driver took us to Juárez Hospital, where they dressed our wounds and saved the woman's life.

Eugenia Flores paid all our medical bills. When Julián and I left the hospital, we went to live with Isabel in the room she rented in a tenement at 119 Calle Mesones, where she and her son slept in one bed, Julián and I in the other.

NINE

Wednesday, September 4, 1985
18.33

Elena Galván sips her coffee and watches a swallow trace a pentagram in the sky, then alight on a wire. She takes another sip and brings her attention back to her mother's bedroom. She puts her mug on the table — home to medicine bottles, a jewelry box, an ashtray, and a Lladró figurine with cracked arms — and strokes her mother's head. Consuelo is busy trying to feed her twin.

"Auntie, can you believe it?" Elena says in a whisper so that Soledad will not hear and get upset. "Esteban told me they probably won't investigate the murder of those teens because somebody important might be involved." Elena had wiped away her tears before entering her mother's bedroom. She feels fragile, as if she could crumble at any moment. This is the first time she's seen her mother since Ignacio died.

"Esteban shouldn't tell you such things. They must be police secrets, and it might put you in danger." Consuelo raises a spoonful of soup to Soledad, who is in her wheelchair staring at nothing. Consuelo puts the spoonful of green mush in her mouth, then rubs her cheeks to help her swallow. "Do you think we ought to get her a stomach tube? The doctor said it was a possibility."

Soledad opens her enormous eyes. It has only been a few weeks since she regained control of her eyelids, kindling José María and Consuelo's hopes. Elena thinks hope is a place full of traps and dead-ends, a trick of the mind to keep the heart beating.

"Auntie! You can't talk about that in front of her." And to her mother, "We aren't going to put anything in you, I won't allow it." Elena strokes her head. "Don't worry, Mamá. Eat up."

Soledad exhales a guttural sound and dribbles a bit of mush.

A year and two months and twenty-one days ago, something burst in Soledad's brain while she was leaning over the washstand bleaching sheets. The washstand is deep enough that when Elena was a child she liked to take a dip there on hot days. Soledad was fortunate that the gardener heard the splash and pulled her out before she drowned. The theory of a ruptured vein came from the doctors, using a lot of complicated terms and Latin words. After weeks in the hospital, they sent home a woman lost to herself and disconnected from the world.

It took Elena months to get over her anger about her mother's condition. She blamed the doctors for having poked tubes into her, instead of letting her die, reducing her to a state more vegetable than human. She wanted to sue the hospital, but how could she, given that she had to care for her mother and run the hotel. Soon, she learned how to speak to her mother and answer her own questions, or be satisfied when anybody nearby answered, usually Consuelo or José María.

Posada Alberto had been the home of Soledad and Consuelo's parents, whom the girls called Chole and Chelo. Soledad and her husband turned it into a rooming house, then into a cheap motel. Once Elena was old enough to realise what was going on behind the closed doors, her parents went back to taking in boarders, so the children wouldn't grow up in the midst of urgent love-making, although it took some time before the regulars stopped ringing the bell. Elena spent her adolescence among the guests, labouring as chambermaid, scullion, waitress, and receptionist. Consuelo, who moved there when her husband died a year after her wedding, became a nanny and second mother to Elena and her brother Alberto.

"Have you decided to empty out Ignacio's room?" Consuelo asks in her ear before raising a glass with a straw to Soledad's lips.

Ignacio Suárez rented his room by the year, even though he occupied it for only six months. It was his second home.

"Not yet."

"You ought to, so we can use it."

"Yes, I know. I'll get to it when we finish with Mamá."

"I'll take care of her, do it right now. Don't put it off any longer."

Consuelo had shared motherhood with her sister, then divorce, then the hotel business. Now she has become her full-time nurse and translator, who answers what Soledad cannot.

Elena leaves her mother's room and crosses the courtyard, holding the key in her sweaty palm. She knows every detail of Ignacio's room. She herself supervised its cleaning, never moving books or notebooks. The one time she rifled through his papers and clothing, Ignacio noticed and threatened to move out. "I've got a photographic memory, and I take in details no-one else could recall," he told her, while returning books to the exact places from which she had moved them.

Now she opens the door wide before stepping inside. She feels a knot in her throat and coughs to get a grip on her nerves. She flips the light switch. The room is no longer the same as it was less than a week ago. Even though half the year it was unoccupied, now it feels truly empty: furniture, books, papers, clothing, shoes, cigarettes, ashtray, tape recorder . . . everything exudes abandonment. Even the paintings, masks, and devil figures on the walls — which Elena never liked — look as if they have been abandoned. She heaves a deep sigh, closes her eyes, and puts her hair up with the tie she always wears on her wrist like a bracelet. When anything makes her nervous, she likes to gather up the cascading locks which reach to the middle of her back and which she tints to maintain their chestnut colour.

Ignacio had arrived three years before. He parked his car downtown and asked a policeman where he could find a room. At that very moment, by a caprice of destiny, Elena was crossing the street laden with shopping bags, and the officer pointed at her back. "That woman and her family run a hotel." Ignacio watched the ponytail dancing to the rhythm of her footsteps. He liked it and ran to catch up. "The policeman told me you have a hotel," he said to her in the middle of the street.

Trying to hide her surprise, she answered, "Yes, a small place, family-run."

"That's just what I'm looking for, although I will never go looking for your family." He gave her a wink. "Let me help," he added, taking hold of a bag of fruit. "May I give you a lift?" Ignacio pointed to his car. As she settled into the passenger seat, he said, "Do you usually get into cars with strangers?"

"No, but I have to get the groceries home, and you'll save me the trek."

Elena approaches the unmade bed. The sheets are rumpled, the way he left them. On the bed is the book Ignacio was reading, open at page 152, where the writer had made some notes in minuscule capital letters. A black pen lies across the page. She sits on the bed, picks up the book, and reads what he wrote: "To live is to drown in mud. Leaving is nearly as desolate as staying." Astounded, she looks up from the page. The words seem like a premonition.

She puts the book down where it had been, as if at any moment Ignacio and his photographic memory might reappear. She caresses the pillow, which still retains the impression of his head, then lies down and fits her own head in the hollow.

She kicks off her shoes, removes her trousers, and slides under the sheets.

She buries her nose in the pillow, impregnated with the smell of Ignacio, filling her lungs and her being with these lingering traces of him.

Her right hand slips under her blouse and between her breasts, then down to her right thigh. A quick intake of air and her hand, which suddenly seems independent of the rest of her body, begins caressing her pubis through the silk panties. She shudders slightly at the touch.

Her hand again seeks out her thigh, her groin, her lower abdomen. Now under the silk panties, her fingers sweep through her pubic hair, timidly rub her labia, then her clitoris, which responds decisively. She caresses her sex for a few seconds, strokes it, kneads it, presses it, massages it. Her body tenses and her breathing quickens, as does the rhythmic movement under the sheet smelling of Ignacio, an odour which excites her to the point of orgasm. A moan escapes her lips, practically a sob, her back arched and remaining so for a few seconds, while a warm tear slides from her closed eyes. Unhurried, she opens her eyes and lowers her back, vertebra by vertebra, reclaims her hand and draws it away. She burrows into the pillow and is soon asleep, surrounded by the aroma of Ignacio and watched over by the book at her side.

TEN

Thursday, September 5, 1985
00.01

Esteban del Valle has pictures of the bodies of Leticia Almeida, Claudia Cosío, and Ignacio Suárez spread out on his desk. He sips his long-cold coffee and picks up the photograph of Claudia Cosío's face. With a magnifying glass he examines the small hole in the middle of her forehead. "Two millimetres," he says out loud.

Most of the homicide victims he sees are farmers killed in machete fights over land, or drunks arguing in bars, or women murdered by their husbands or other family members, children beaten by their parents.

This is the first death that seems so planned. Nearly a work of art, he thinks, regretting the thought immediately.

He rises and goes to the display case where he keeps his collection of pistols. He turns the key and opens the door. He could do this with his eyes shut, so well does he know the location of each of the forty-eight weapons. He takes the Kolibri, a miniature given to him by Ignacio Suárez himself as a thank-you for his assistance. It fits in the palm of his hand and is in perfect condition, cleaned and oiled like all the rest. Every two weeks he spends a day maintaining and polishing his weapons.

He and Ignacio shared a love of guns. Ignacio was the only person to whom he showed these pistols. He invited him to supper and instead of setting out plates and utensils he laid out a banquet of guns.

Ignacio wanted to handle them all. Esteban smiled, feeling proud and satisfied. Then they went out and ate shrimp soup at the bar they often frequented.

"I've got a present for you," Suárez told him one day, arriving back from Mexico City with a small case and a copy of his novel *Death by Kolibri* — in which the murderer gives his victims one shot in the forehead using a pistol identical to the one Esteban now holds. "It was designed by an Austrian watchmaker, Franz Pfannl," Ignacio explained after Esteban opened the present and laid eyes on the Kolibri. "No pistol has a smaller calibre, 2.7 mm, semi-automatic. Only about a thousand of them were made, all in 1914. This is one of them."

When he examined Claudia Cosío's corpse, Esteban noted that the hole in her forehead, a circular abrasion with the skin scored at the edges, looked very much like a bullet-hole, except there was no exit wound and no burn marks. He immediately thought of the Kolibri and figured the bullet was lodged in her brain. He recalled that the pistol did not have the power to send a bullet all the way through a skull, even though it did in Suárez's novel, a mistake the writer did not wish to correct despite Esteban pointing it out.

But he found no bullet in Claudia's brain.

The murderer had mounted a scene very much like the crimes in another novel of Ignacio's, *The Saints*, which was lying now beside the photographs on the desk.

"At least he closed your eyes," he says to Claudia's picture.

He points the Kolibri at the girl's forehead. The pistol is so small he has to hold it with his thumb and index finger.

"What happened?" he wonders aloud.

The only other person with a pistol like that was Ignacio himself. Ignacio could not have shot the girl. And where is the bullet?

He opens Ignacio's book to the scene he underlined, in which Detective José Acosta contemplates the body of a woman positioned just as the girls were.

A crowd had gathered by the time Detective José Acosta arrived at the scene of the crime. Two patrolmen were trying to hold the onlookers back. The victim was a woman about 35 years old who lived nearby.

The detective had to elbow his way through the crowd while at the same time directing the agents accompanying him to cordon off the scene and send all those people home.

"It's the 'Saints' killer again," a man shouted at him. "That makes three. How many more women have to die before you catch him?"

The detective forged ahead without answering. The body was leaning against the wall of a funeral home, just like the two previous victims. He felt for the victims, and his thoughts were entirely focused on finding the murderer. Suddenly a face swam into his mind, the man who shouted at him had also been among the onlookers at the previous crime scenes.

"Hold that man!" he shouted, turning around.

But the man was gone.

"Find him," he ordered his subordinates.

He went up to the body. It was in the same position as the other two: seated, legs apart. With a pen he poked the false pregnancy, a pillow once more. She was missing a shoe and her tight skirt had been slit up the middle to spread her legs. Her hands were on her fake belly. He squatted and found the same strangulation marks. Her red lipstick and rouge helped hide the body's purple tint. The murderer had applied the make-up after killing her. The hole in her forehead was clean, bloodless, perfect. She was wearing earrings, a necklace, a gold watch. The killer wasn't a thief.

"Why would he want to make her look pregnant?" he asks himself, while the officers came up to inform him they had lost the man.

"He vanished," one of them said.

Esteban closes the novel and picks up the photograph of Ignacio. "You and I were in the same business," he says. "You told stories about dead people and I tell the stories the dead tell me. I gave up my father's search for the invisible forces of life in order to seek the visible causes of death."

One day a man who had died in the ambulance came back to life just outside the hospital. Esteban was there. According to the paramedics, he was clinically dead for two minutes. Esteban asked him, "What did you see? Is there anything on the other side?" The paramedics told him not to bother the patient, but the man did answer: "White," he said. "There is a marvellous white."

"Really? Just white? Nothing else?" he asks the photograph of Ignacio.

He again picks up the unloaded Kolibri, aims it at nothing, and pulls the trigger.

SIXTH FRAGMENT

Dozens of men and women in black were pushing and shoving me. They knocked me to the ground, which was covered in tiny sharp stones that dug into me like thorns. I leapt up, panic gripping my soul.

To escape.

Rushing off, I remembered Julián and went back to find him, not knowing where I'd lost him. Julián couldn't run fast, his bad leg like a bag of sand he dragged around that grew heavier with every step.

I found him surrounded by people shouting, "He's here! Your son is here!"

My mother's voice ever closer: "I'm going to kill you both!"

I elbowed my way to him, lifted him up, and slipped my arm around his shoulders to help him run.

My mother's shouts closer still: "Julián! Manuel!"

His useless leg held us back.

"Please, Julián. Faster, make an effort. Help me!"

I looked into his eyes. They were empty, hollowed out like caves. Maggots wormed out of them and dropped on me and crawled all over my body. I threw him down and when he hit the ground he shattered like a clay doll, a piñata filled with maggots that curled and squirmed in the dirt.

"Julián! Julián!"

The maggots turned into minuscule babies. Human embryos crawling out of my brother's body and onto my feet. An army of them.

"Julián! Julián!"

I tried to brush them off and what fell to the ground were tiny dismembered limbs, bits of broken bodies clinging to my clothes.

"Julián!"

My shouting broke through my dream and awakened Isabel, who ran to the bed my brother and I shared, where I was struggling to rid myself of the baby parts, which were not on my clothes, but inside my cells, in my memory, in my soul.

"Get them off me!" I screamed at Isabel, who was trying to hug me. "Get them off me!"

I flailed my arms and legs.

I tore off my pyjamas. I was crying. Trembling.

Julián and Jesús were awake now, frightened.

"It's alright, Manuel. Easy now, there's nothing there. It was a nightmare."

The images faded bit by bit as I lay curled in a ball on the floor, a puppet without strings. A ferocious sobbing took hold of me. Isabel sat beside me, hugged me, then took me into her lap as if I were a small child. "Easy, everything is alright. Everything is alright. It was just a dream."

Julián and Jesús said nothing. Isabel was a ship buffeted by the storm of my sadness. She rocked me, stroked my hair, my face; she held me close.

She stayed with me in the same uncomfortable position until the sobbing ebbed. The ghosts of dead children receded, but I could still feel their tiny fingers on my skin.

She took me by the arm back to the bed and lay next to me until she was sure I was asleep. She put her hand on my forehead, on the wet hair stuck to my face. I was not asleep. I would never sleep again.

Ghosts are the shadows of the dead that belong to us, and those babies would stay with me forever.

This occurred a week after we moved in with Isabel and her son Jesús. He was ten at the time. The doctors at the hospital had asked us what happened, how we got our injuries. We did not say a thing.

"An accident," Isabel kept repeating, "it was an accident." She did not want trouble, and she especially did not want to reveal our complicity in my parents' affairs. She too might go to jail. Who then would look after her son?

My brother went back to being mute.

Our parents never looked for us. That was a relief, and a disappointment. Deep down I wanted to hear them beg forgiveness, say they missed us, show some sign of regret, of affection. It's stupid, I know.

Julián and I survived our parents. We took up a new life as part of the family of Isabel Ramírez Campos.

We got to know the neighbours. An elderly couple named Almanza seemed to be at least a hundred years old. All of their children had died and they believed God had forgotten them. Lupita was a prostitute with the name of a virgin. She would bring clients to her room once in a while, but no-one told the landlords because she was the one who contributed the most for our Christmas celebrations and the party on the day of the Virgin of Guadalupe. The Ramírez were a family of ten, and you could always find one of them under the stairs or in the back yard or at the washstands, even up on the roof.

The tenement still exists, still with the same twenty-two rooms made of red volcanic stone painted grey, each thirty-five square metres. At the entrance a black candelabra hangs from the long wooden beams, as well as a pair of crosses put up by the Augustines in the eighteenth century.

This is where we began to feel free. We still carried buckets, this time filled with merchandise that we sold to stores along the avenue.

We got whatever jobs we could: Julián was a shoemaker's assistant in the market, I worked at a fruit stall.

Isabel did not let us drop out of school. We went in the morning, and in the afternoon we earned our keep.

Sometimes I would slip away and spy on my parents' house from one of the entranceways across the street. The dead-end street was quiet, except for the activity around my mother's door. The neighbours complained about her and were convinced she practised witchcraft.

They hired a new woman to take Isabel's place.

Almost every day my father would head off in his Chrysler to dispose of bags.

Now that I mention my father's car, I can almost smell his cigarettes: Elegantes. "Blonde tobacco," he told me once as he disappeared behind a cloud of smoke.

"You look like a train," I said. I must have been six or seven. He smoked and I breathed it in, trying to absorb as much as I could. I liked the combination of those two words, the closest thing to a friendly remark he ever made to me. "Blonde tobacco" was like a couple of pats on the back. "You've got to smoke with style," he said another time, as if he were a movie star.

I was fourteen the first time I smoked a cigarette. Ramón García Alcaraz was leaning against the tenement stairs. I had seen him there before. He worked as a crime reporter for *La Prensa* and was away most of the day. There he was, smoking beside the freestanding grey stone staircase in the courtyard that divided partway up to reach both rows of second-storey rooms. He had one foot up on a ledge, his right hand in his trouser pocket. His black hair was curly and he had a scar over his right eyebrow. The story of the scar wasn't much, an unfortunate encounter with a doorframe.

"You're one of the kids that moved in with Isabel," he said pointing at me with his cigarette and blowing a cloud of smoke that disappeared in the breeze.

"That's right, I'm Manuel." I reached out my hand.

"Ramón García Alcaraz."

I shook his hand in silence, not knowing what else to say.

"Want one?" he asked, and he held out the pack. I clumsily took a cigarette and unbidden my father's words came to mind. I would try to smoke with style.

Ramón lived in a room on the upper floor. In the tenement everyone's business was public knowledge. It was not a place for keeping secrets.

"What's your story?" he asked, bringing his lighter close. I inhaled hard and could do nothing but cough, my lungs and throat aflame. Ramón laughed.

"You've never smoked, you ding-dong." His laugh sounded like a birdcall. "At least warn me."

Ramón had started out at *La Prensa* as a messenger boy when he was fifteen and worked his way up. Now twenty, he lived with his mother and grandmother; his father was in jail for robbery.

"My story?"

"Yeah, tell me who you are, where you're from, what you do."

I cleared my throat a few times, calculating whether I could take another puff without looking really stupid, and buying time to make up a story.

"We all start out like that. Coughing, I mean. Tobacco is a metaphor for life: it's expensive, it makes you dizzy, it tastes awful. But once you discover its pleasures, you can't let it go. It becomes your buddy, your accomplice. You think you're enjoying it, but the fact is it's killing you, just like life. The best puff is the first, maybe the second, but after the third you just smoke to get it over with because it's got you by the balls. The first is yours, after that the cigarette is smoking you."

While he talked I struggled to finish the cigarette. Then, as if I hadn't heard a thing he said, I took another from his pack.

"You're insisting. Good. Don't let life beat you," he decreed, holding the lighter in front of my face.

I felt really dizzy, seasick, but this time I didn't cough.

"Why are you and your brother living with Isabel?"

"Our parents went to Veracruz and left us with her until they get back." I blew out the smoke and spat the words out hoping to avoid another question.

"Slow down, don't inhale so much or you're going to throw up. Take it slowly, like life. If you wolf it down, it'll give you indigestion."

I nodded and inhaled more cautiously.

"I don't believe your parents are on a trip."

"Why not?"

"Because in my line of work I've learned how to tell when someone is lying."

"It's no lie," I said, and I threw the butt on the ground.

I watched my shoe rub it out, so I wouldn't have to look him in the eye. He glanced at his watch and said goodbye. "I've got to get back to the paper. I'm on the night shift."

He gave me a couple of pats on the shoulder and shook my hand in his comforting grip. He ruffled my hair and said, "See you later, kid."

I remained nailed to the spot, stinking of tobacco.

Still dizzy, I watched Ramón leave the courtyard, saying goodbye to each of the neighbours he passed. He bounced a little with every step, as if his shoes had invisible springs. I really wanted him to be my friend.

ELEVEN

Thursday, September 5, 1985
07.03

Elena opens her eyes. She has slept through the night. Having closed the curtains when she first entered Ignacio's room, it is rather dark. The book beside her falls to the floor and now she is wide awake. She smooths the sheet as if caressing the room's former occupant. It feels like centuries since she was last here at night.

"Ignacio is dead," she says out loud, forcing herself to confront the reality that hits her when she turns on the bedside lamp. She gets up quickly, still wearing her blouse from the day before. Slipping on her pants and shoes, she gathers a few things and leaves the room carrying all the red notebooks. She looks both ways in the hall, fearful of being seen, a habit she picked up when she did not want her mother to know about their relationship. She returns with a cardboard box, which she fills with his folders, manuscripts, letters, and other papers, planning to look through them later on, far from the gaze of the Moloch figurine on the bookshelf. They had made love in this room only a few times, because she did not like feeling watched by his proud collection of devil statuettes, paintings, books, and photographs. "Demons and deities of Avernus," he called them.

She remembers the day he arrived for his first six-month stint.

"Why are you so intrigued by the devil?" she asked while helping him unpack.

"I like him."

"How could you like him? Aren't you afraid of him?"

"No, this is just a statuette, a representation of evil. It's practically a self-portrait of our species."

"What?" Elena ran her finger over the figure of Moloch.

"What motivates man is fear. That fellow has been our motor, our protector."

"How's that?"

"Imagine primitive man confronting all sorts of threats: wild beasts, predators with fangs and claws. Without that internal alarm we never would have made it. Fear is the emotion that perpetuates the species. Do you know who we humans fear most?"

Elena, doubtful, pointed at a little figurine of Satan.

"No. We're afraid of other humans, because we know what we're capable of. Demons are just images men make to dominate others. The Church attracts many more followers out of fear of hell than love of God."

She listened without taking her eyes off the Moloch statuette, half bull, half human, barely thirty centimetres tall.

"But evil exists."

"Of course, but it has a human face, not a devil's."

The memory of that scene subsides when she opens the desk drawer and finds a set of keys held together by a black cord. She sticks them in the box and again the devil-figure catches her eye. "No, I won't take you with me," she says. "Not you or any of the others. I'll deal with you later."

After hiding Ignacio's belongings, just as he had asked, she showers quickly and begins her workday.

José María and Consuelo gave up their hotel duties when Soledad came home from the hospital, leaving Elena in charge of the business. She began to make changes, refurbishing the rooms, rearranging the furniture, modernising the washrooms and the swimming pool. She increased the capacity of the restaurant and replaced the heavy curtains and tablecloths with more contemporary ones. The hotel was closed for four months, inundated by an army of plumbers, masons, carpenters, electricians, and gardeners. Though bothered by all the hubbub, Ignacio remained throughout, insisting that his room be left as it was. "You can redo it after I leave or when I die," he told Elena, unaware of what the near future held. He allowed her only to change the door and paint the exterior walls.

Two decades earlier, on April 30, 1964, Soledad was washing the hotel linens. She always washed them herself. Everybody thought it was an obsession with cleanliness, but it was her means of escape. Soaking, bleaching, scrubbing, rinsing, and wringing them out, then hanging them up to dry, gave her time to be apart from others and sort out her thoughts. It was like a moving meditation in which she scrubbed away stains and worries, rinsed laundry and fears — many of them about her son Alberto. By the time she hung up the linen in the sun she had found some peace of mind. Joining the corners of the dry sheets with a perfect fold dispelled the last of her anxieties.

The sky was clear of clouds, which pleased her because the bright sun would keep the sheets white. She was still rinsing the linen when she heard Consuelo shouting to her to run to her son's bedroom. Alberto had been born with a stump for a left arm and a defective heart. "Thalidomide," Soledad would answer guiltily whenever anyone asked about it. "I took Thalidomide when I was pregnant." He nearly died at birth and remained in hospital for a long time. His heart sometimes beat too fast, sometimes too slow, but against all the doctors' predictions it had never stopped.

At that time the effects of the drug were not known. A few years later, a doctor asked her, "Did you take Thalidomide?" She had forgotten the name. The doctor reminded her: a drug for nausea during pregnancy. Then she remembered.

"Yes, that was it," she nodded, not realising that the revelation would change forever how she looked at her son. Guilt would eat away at her, and she would dedicate the rest of her life to her boy, forgetting all else, including her husband and Elena. She tried to repair the damage — to become his missing left arm and compensate for the irregular beats of a heart that might stop without warning.

Soledad ran to her son's room, where she found Consuelo trying to revive him. Seeing him collapsed in her twin's arms, Soledad saw herself holding the lifeless body of her child.

After a doctor confirmed the death, Soledad left the house and walked to Calle Del Llano, where she stopped at number seventy-three. She rang the bell and pounded the knocker until the door opened. "I need to speak with my husband," she said to the woman. And before her husband could say a thing, she announced, "Alberto is dead. He's at the house."

Once she had consigned her son's ashes to a shelf, she asked her sister to pack up her husband's things and send them to his lover's house. Without consulting anyone, even though no-one would have dared to contradict her, she had a "For Sale" sign placed at the entrance to the hotel.

José María appeared on July 26 that year. Born in San Pedro Manrique, in the Soria region of Spain, he had recently moved to San Miguel because Miguel was the name of his son, who had just died at the age of fifteen from cancer. The cancer had turned up without warning in the form of a tumour on the boy's thigh, a bulge that might have been a boil. José María and his wife had less than a month and a half to say goodbye to their son. They were alone then, with nothing but their sadness to share; their love was spent. An acquaintance who had sought his fortune in Mexico told José María about a town in the middle of the country called San Miguel de Allende. José María then spoke the words that had been floating between himself and his wife, waiting for one of the two to do so. "I'm leaving you after I do the Fire Walk one last time. I'll do it for me and for our son."

The Fire Walk was a family tradition, a ritual which all males performed for the first time at the age of fifteen on Saint John's Eve: walking on a bed of oak-wood coals in front of Virgen de la Peña church. On June 23, twenty days after the death of his son, José María tried to lengthen the five seconds it usually takes to walk over three metres of red-hot coals by imagining he was carrying his son, as he had every year since the child was four. The townspeople applauded José María with tears in their eyes, and some swore they saw the child clinging to his back. He did the walk dry-eyed. He had kept his emotions in check since the funeral; the closest he came to crying was a runny nose from a cold.

In San Miguel, he came across the "For Sale" sign outside Consuelo and Soledad's big house. Soledad let him in and showed him around.

"This is the tree where my son Alberto liked to play. These are the swings where he would spend hour after hour. This is the spot where he liked to hide. Here is the stable where we keep Lulú, the cow. Alberto loved her and that's why we didn't sell her. She's old and she'll die soon, but we don't want to put her down. Alberto couldn't milk her, he had only one hand, but he liked to rub her back while somebody else did it. He would stick his head underneath to get some of the warm milk in his mouth, and it would splash all over his face."

José María interrupted. "How long ago did he die?"

"It's been nearly three months," she said and right then Lulú mooed as if she had understood every word. Soledad was not crying because she felt she had no right to cry. Lulú moved her head from side to side, and the bell Alberto had hung around her neck rang out. Now Soledad's tears flowed freely.

"I'm sorry, so sorry," she tried to say, her head resting on José María's chest. She had not noticed when the weight of her sorrow made her embrace him. And it took her a few minutes more to realise the trembling she felt was not from her own sobs, but from his. Moaning now and then, they hugged each other until the storm of sorrow began to abate, although tears kept falling intermittently all afternoon. That evening they told each other their stories while working their way through several bottles of wine in Soledad's room. Defeated by the exhaustion of grief, they slept in the same bed.

"I want you to be my partner," he proposed a week later. "Don't sell your business."

Wordlessly, Soledad nodded in agreement.

TWELVE

Thursday, September 5, 1985
09.00

She feels like an intruder at her own desk. All the papers and business cards seem foreign, unfamiliar.

"You have to stop being a zombie," she had told her reflection while applying mascara. "Don't cry today," she said out loud, pointing the brush. "This stuff is not waterproof. No more drama."

"Some people here insist on going into Señor Ignacio's room," says an employee rushing into her office. "I told them they're not allowed, but they say because they're relatives they have the right to take his things."

Elena hurries out to meet Ignacio's ex-wife and sons. "Good morning," she holds out her trembling right hand. "My name is Elena Galván and I am the manager of the hotel."

"We know who you are," the woman responds, her arms crossed, making no move to extend her own hand. She is wearing a black skirt that reaches below the knee, stiletto heels, a white long-sleeved blouse. "We came to pick up the belongings of my children's father."

Elena opens her mouth, but one of the sons, Andrés, intervenes. "Forgive my mother, she is still very upset by Papá's death."

Elena nods and leads them to room number eight. Andrés walks beside her, saying nothing. She keeps her eyes on the floor, with an occasional sidelong glance at the group. The sound of the woman's heels on the ceramic tiles fills the silence.

"I am in the midst of a divorce," Ignacio had told her the night they first slept together. "My wife and I have been separated for some time, but we've begun the paperwork."

"I'm not asking anything of you," she said. "I'm recently divorced myself."

"Maybe you're the nudge I need to get the thing going," Ignacio said.

She did not like feeling responsible for a separation, and now faced with his ex-wife she feels guilty and ashamed. She gives her head a shake to chase off the memory.

"Here it is." Elena opens the door and stands aside to let them in. Instinctively, she moves to follow, but Antonio, the elder son, puts up his hand. "We'll take care of this," he says, closing the door in her face.

An hour later a couple of knocks interrupt Elena from the bills she is distractedly going over. "Yes?"

More knocks.

"Elena? It's Andrés. I've come to say goodbye and to thank you. We're leaving."

Opening the door she catches sight of the ex-wife climbing into a black car at the entrance.

"Everything alright?"

"Yes, fine. I wanted to ask you about my father's red notebooks. We found very little. Weren't there more things in the room?"

"No. We haven't been in there since the accident. We assumed you would come and we didn't want to touch anything. Besides, we wouldn't have known what to do with it all."

"You don't have to pretend. We know about your relationship with my father."

Elena avoids his dark eyes, takes a step backward, and stumbles. He comes up to her and points to her neck. "That's my father's medallion."

She closes her fingers around it. "Ignacio gave it to me."

"That's really strange. He never took it off."

She shrugs without letting go of the medallion. Antonio blows the horn to hurry his brother.

"Forgive my mother. She could never deal with my father's fondness for women. We'll never understand why they took so long to separate."

"Women?" the question slips out.

"Women."

"Do you need anything else?"

"Nothing, thank you. I'm sorry we left things a mess. Here's my card with my co-ordinates."

Elena nods.

Andrés takes Elena by the shoulders and plants a kiss on her left cheek. She does not manage to respond.

"Andrés Suárez, psychiatrist," Elena reads aloud.

SEVENTH FRAGMENT

The year 1941 began with an unfamiliar calm. Julián spoke more; he had his fourteenth birthday; he grew a couple of centimetres in three months. Ramón got me a job as a gofer, a messenger boy, at *La Prensa*. I was almost through high school and I wanted to be a journalist like my friend. I bought myself a suit, a shirt and tie, and that's how I dressed every day for work.

Without intending to, I spent less time keeping an eye on my parents' place, although I still went at least once a week. The store on the street level, La Imperial, was run by Don Francisco Páez, who my parents did not like because they wanted the space. My parents rented another storefront on Calle Guadalajara and opened a variety store they called La Quebrada, which they used as a cover for their real business, buying and selling children.

Ramón and I were smoking his unfiltered cigarettes on the stairs. We listened to the unending chatter of the women at the washstands, nearly all of them with kids hanging on to their aprons. They were so unlike my mother. They gave advice, they laughed. Sometimes they cried and their tears would fall into the water where they rinsed their clothes.

Ramón broke the spell. "I need a good story," he said.

"There are lots here."

"Here?"

"Here," I said, getting up and throwing my arms wide. Ramón looked around. He pulled long and hard on his cigarette and exhaled calmly, emphasising his words with curls of smoke. "Washstands are a metaphor for life. If we could hear the sound of time passing it would be a lot like burbling water. We're aquatic beings, like dirty clothes being soaked. We grow like fish inside the uterus and though we insist on becoming terrestrial our lives revolve around water. Heaven must be a liquid place where our souls can float."

I could almost see his words stirring the surface of the washstands.

"People don't want to read about metaphors, they want stories," he continued.

"Like what?"

"Crime, murder. People like to learn about other people's misery, so they can believe their own turn on the wheel of fortune is not so bad."

"There's plenty of misfortune here. One of Señora Yolanda's sons got stabbed to death and they never found who did it. Doña Aurora's husband was working as a bricklayer and fell from the fifth floor at a construction site."

"Yes, yes, I know those stories."

"So?"

"I need something sensational, though maybe the right word is 'sensationalistic'. Something that will draw the morbid interest of the readers and turn a tragedy into a spectacle."

"Really?"

"That's the business, Manuel. Writing up the crime of the season. Upset the readers, give them something to talk about at dinner, at work. I heard my first crime story when I was six years old."

He held out his pack of cigarettes. I sat back down beside him on the stairs. Ramón then unfolded his tale with all the dramatic pauses it required.

"My father told us about what he'd read in the paper: Miss Mexico had murdered her husband, a general in the army. They called her a self-widow. My mother leapt into the conversation, waving her dish towel, saying the woman was shameless. When I started working as a reporter, I dug up the story. María Teresa Landa y de los Ríos was eighteen when she became Miss Mexico in 1928. Her first scandal was posing in a swimsuit, that's why Mamá said she was shameless."

Ramón's smile lingered on his lips, where he placed an unlit cigarette which rose and fell with every word. "María Teresa was a schoolteacher, she spoke English and French. She wanted to be independent, which caused a huge scandal. She was studying dentistry and she swore women were as capable as men. But she never graduated. Instead, she eloped with General Moisés Vidal Corro, who was seventeen years older than she was. They lived in Veracruz for a year, like your parents. Maybe your folks met the General's family, since he was from there."

I tried not to avert my gaze. "I don't think so."

"When they came back to Mexico City, they moved in with María Teresa's parents, but the general wouldn't let her go out or read the newspaper, because a married woman should not be exposed to crimes and indecencies. On Sunday, August 25, 1929, María Teresa woke up late and went down to the kitchen to get some breakfast. Her husband wasn't around, but on the kitchen table was his Smith & Wesson and the newspaper open to the headline 'Señora María Teresa López de Vidal Corro accuses her husband, General Moisés Vidal Corro, of bigamy.' The bastard had married two women with the same first name. What's more, he had two daughters with the other woman. When I interviewed her, she told me she was convinced he had left the pistol there so she would kill herself. He thought his little woman would read the news and be so distressed and desperate she would put a bullet in her head, solving his problem. It didn't turn out that way. She waited for him, wearing the blue kimono she slept in. 'I married you for love,' she said. 'What you did to me is not right.' And she shot him dead."

Ramón had made his fingers into a pistol. Now he blew imaginary smoke off his index and middle fingers, and lit the cigarette that had been hanging from his lips. He took a puff, then pointed his fingers at his temple. "Click. She'd emptied the weapon on him and couldn't end her own life when she tried. She threw herself on the general and got his blood all over her kimono. She spent a few months in Belén prison before the trial. In court she wore stockings and a black silk dress, taffeta hat, and a demeanour that she hoped would awaken the jury's sympathy. She'd lost several kilos in jail and with that wan appearance, plus the speech her lawyer gave, she got off. That was the last jury trial held in this country. She didn't give another interview until she spoke to me, which she did just to demonstrate to women everywhere that, no matter what, life goes on."

Night had fallen. Ramón got to his feet. I observed his long, lean figure. His brown face seemed paler in the darkness. He brushed off his trousers and smoothed his unruly hair. "I'm going to bed. I've got to take advantage of not having to do the night shift to hit the hay early."

He climbed the stairs. I heard him whistling, and then greet his mother and grandmother before closing the door.

I remained on that step for I don't know how long. Until some neighbours made me get up because I was in their way.

At midnight I got out of bed. I couldn't sleep. I slipped out of the room and up the stairs, and knocked on Ramón's window, calling to him in whispers. His sleepy face appeared behind the glass, then he opened the door.

"I know a woman who kills children," I told him.

"What?"

"I know a woman who has killed a lot of babies." I kept my voice low so the words would not echo off the walls and find their way into some other room.

Ramón came out in underpants and a white vest. "A woman child-murderer?"

"She's a midwife and sometimes she kills newborns and other times she does abortions."

I couldn't look him in the eyes or let him look into mine, or he might discover I was speaking of my mother.

"Where does she live? Who is she?"

"If you want to know more, you should ask the owner of the store beside the woman's house."

"How do you know this? You didn't wake me up in the middle of the night to tell me to look for a storekeeper."

"Speak with that man. His name is Francisco Páez."

I ran down the stairs. He caught up with me at Isabel's door. "What more do you know? What's that woman to you?"

"Tomorrow I'll show you the place, but please don't ask me for anything else."

I slipped away and climbed into bed with my heart intent on cracking my sternum. My face was bathed in sweat. I dreamed my mother was chasing me with a knife.

In the early hours of April 6, 1941, Hitler turned his fury on Yugoslavia for having left the alliance with the Axis. That military offensive, which lasted four days, would be known as Operation Punishment. There was no declaration of war. The civilian population of Belgrade was taken by surprise. It was Palm Sunday and thousands died in the bombings. Smoke from the burning city could be seen for many kilometres. That day I too began my very own Operation Punishment, a surprise attack on my parents.

At seven in the morning Ramón was ready. Fear had me by the throat. I wanted to cry. Scream. Change my mind.

But I showed him the store, La Imperial. It was open, as it was every day of the week.

"I'll wait here," I told him. "I don't want to get involved."

He crossed the street, introduced himself to Páez, explained that he was a reporter for the crime page of *La Prensa*, and that he had heard about charges the man had pressed. At first, Páez wanted to throw him out, but Ramón told him he might be able to help get the police to take action.

Páez and Ramón agreed to meet on the following day.

While thousands of Serbs were searching for their relatives amidst the rubble, hoping against hope, and the Luftwaffe once again punished the Royal Yugoslav Air Force, I went to work at the paper. All morning long, news came in about the German offensive, but that meant little to me. I was trying hard not to think about the bomb that was about to blow up my parents. My mouth was dry, my head heavy, my hands trembling. I couldn't concentrate. Two or three times I tripped in the hallway, and even came close to knocking somebody down.

In the afternoon, when I returned to the tenement, Isabel was not yet back from her job. I lay down pretending to be asleep. I didn't want to face either Isabel or Julián.

Isabel worked for Eugenia Flores, the woman who took us to the hospital the night we left my parents' house. Because of the botched abortion, Señora Flores spent several days on the very edge of death. She had lost a lot of blood, and because of a runaway infection in her uterus they had to give her a hysterectomy. Isabel watched over her while she was in hospital, and when Señora Flores was allowed to go home, she took on Isabel as a maid. Her husband, Congressman Ramiro Flores, was out of the city, travelling with President Manuel Ávila Camacho, when the operation took place, and he never learned the real reason why his wife had to have it.

On April 9, 1941, *La Prensa* dominated the newsstands with an eight-column headline that rattled the kind hearts of the city's inhabitants:

SENSATIONAL DISCOVERY
A MIDKNIFE CUTS NEWBORNS TO PIECES

The typo was not intentional, but it was a journalistic coup and the edition sold out quickly.

> A sewer pipe in Colonia Roma was blocked by two tiny legs and wads of bloodstained cotton.
>
> It is believed that a woman who disappeared from a store on Calle Guadalajara was the one putting human embryos in garbage cans.
>
> *La Prensa* (Mexico City, April 9, 1941)

Two patrolmen were in attendance when Francisco Páez opened up the sewer. Neighbours crowded the entrance to the house.

My parents had vanished.

Encouraged by Páez, the police and the reporter went to La Quebrada, my parents' store on Calle Guadalajara, but they were not there either.

SHE CHOPPED UP NEWBORNS

Don Francisco Páez is the still-youthful proprietor of the store La Imperial, located at 9 Cerrada Salamanca in Colonia Roma, directly beneath the apartment occupied by the clandestine midwife, Felícitas Sánchez.

"About a month ago the sewer pipes from this building to the street were blocked," Páez said, pointing to a spot covered by fresh-looking cement.

"They took out two little legs. We told the rent-collector about it. We complained because we couldn't stand the stench from the sewer or from the things wrapped in bloody cotton in the garbage."

In his article Ramón summed up the interviews he had done with the clerk at La Quebrada, with the maid that had replaced Isabel, with neighbours willing to talk, and with Francisco Páez, his wife, and the police.

When the patrolmen did not find Felícitas Sánchez at home, they learned she might be at a small store she owns on Calle Guadalajara, and arrived there a few minutes later.

The clerk, Señorita María González, told them the woman had left at six in the morning, but several others told investigators they had seen her fifteen minutes ago, which indicates she fled when she learned the police were on her tail.

It is thought, and rightly so, that Felícitas Sánchez saved the honour of a number of "society girls" in Colonia Roma, and of married women guilty of indiscretions. If her "science" did not result in a spontaneous abortion, she killed the newborns, then chopped them up and flushed the pieces into the stinking current that washed them into the Great Canal.

It is public knowledge that for some time the police have been finding foetuses or newborns at several spots around Colonia Roma. Given what we have put in writing, one might conclude that this woman is the one responsible.

As of last night the police had not been able to locate the "midwife" Felícitas Sánchez, who has caused veritable indignation among the neighbours on Cerrada de Salamanca and nearby streets, to the point that they have taken to calling her "The Fiend". However, we have learned from unofficial sources that a special team has been put in place to capture Sánchez as soon as she comes anywhere near her house or the store La Quebrada. The authorities are investigating where under the building she might have buried remains, as well as to locate the mothers who allowed their children to be chopped to pieces in such a gruesome manner, merely to hide their sins.

La Prensa (Mexico City, April 9, 1941)

THIRTEEN

Friday, September 6, 1985
10.14

Moving stiffly, his suit wrinkled from daily use, the personal secretary of Bernabé Castillo tells them again, "The judge cannot receive you, he has gone out to a meeting."

Humberto Franco, publisher of *Diario de Allende*, rises from the black leather chair where he has been waiting for half an hour alongside the deputy public prosecutor, Miguel Pereda, Franco's latest companion on his well-known adventures.

The Franco family owns a string of natural gas plants in the states of Querétaro and Guanajuato. Years ago Humberto Franco's late father sought political influence without getting into public life. Although the ruling Institutional Revolutionary Party offered him several chances to run for office, he refused right up to the end, saying he never wanted to be anybody's puppet; he wanted to be the one pulling the strings. He made that clear when he founded the newspaper and a radio station.

The family business made decisive contributions to many electoral campaigns over the decades. But the death of the old man complicated the Francos' romance with government. In an attempt to demonstrate his permanence on Olympus, Humberto installed a sign above the entrance to the newspaper, as if it were the Temple of Apollo: "Governments change, the written word remains."

Humberto was left in charge of that small provincial daily because his father did not trust him to run the other businesses, which were given to Humberto's more responsible and capable brothers. They send him a monthly dividend.

"No, young man, you cannot tell me that the judge is not in. You are forgetting who I am."

The secretary tugs at his tie and wipes the pearls of sweat dotting his brow.

"I saw him come in," Miguel Pereda insists.

"The judge is not here," the secretary says again, hugging to his chest a black leather folder that holds the day's urgent documents. A recent law school graduate, he is still uncertain what he is supposed to do.

At 187 centimetres and weighing more than a hundred kilos, Franco looms over the secretary, who measures barely 165. The younger man takes a step back, clears his throat, and says, "The judge instructed me to tell you he has already done what he could."

"Ssshhh!" Pereda, his height less imposing but his navy-blue suit fresh off the rack, manages to silence him. "Tell the judge that isn't good enough..."

Franco raises a hand. "You tell your boss we'll be back tomorrow at the same time and he'd better receive us."

The secretary retreats another step with every thrust of Franco's index finger into his sternum, until he is trapped between the door to the inner office and the newspaper publisher's bulk. He tries to turn the knob, but it's locked. Pereda tugs at Franco's arm and the two of them leave.

Outside the building, Franco cups the flame of his match and pulls hard to light the cigarette between his lips.

"It's all under control." Pereda takes a Marlboro Red from Franco's pack. "The visit to the judge was just to confirm we're on the same page. None of this is going anywhere. The investigation will pursue something else, no-one will link it to us. The prosecutor already called the judge and told him to take all the necessary precautions."

"Let's hope that's the way it'll be."

While the driver holds the door of his Grand Marquis, Franco straightens his tie and exhales a lungful of smoke. He and Pereda climb aboard and the car pulls out.

"I've worked out a way to get rid of the forensic pathologist. Esteban del Valle has a reputation for being persistent. We can't let him stick his nose into this," Pereda says, "though it's too bad because he's talented. Collateral damage."

"My name cannot come out." Franco lights another cigarette and lowers the window.

"We have the photographs that were in Ignacio Suárez's vehicle, plus the ones from the autopsy." Pereda takes them from the pocket of his suit coat and shows them to Franco.

"And what good is that going to do us?" Franco glances at the pictures and hands them back, disgust on his face.

"Oh, Humberto, I thought you had more imagination. We'll send them to newspapers all over the state. You'll publish them too." Pereda examines the photographs in his lap before returning them to his pocket.

"I don't understand. What will that accomplish?"

"We'll blame the writer for the murders and we'll say del Valle was the one who sent them to the papers. He wasn't happy when we blocked the autopsy. I know the guy, he obeyed the order, but he won't let it lie."

They fall silent, each lost in his own thoughts. The car stops in front of the newspaper office.

"Come inside with me. The driver can take you to work when we're done."

As they walk in, Pereda eyes the slogan above the entranceway. He thinks it's pretentious, and the offices look too fancy for the size of the paper. In the newsroom two reporters humbly greet their boss. Franco likes it when they act servile, although today he is afraid everything may come crashing down.

"Shit!" Franco says, pounding his desk. "How the fuck did those girls get themselves murdered? Do we have any idea who did it? We need to make sure our names are never mentioned. Nobody can know we were with them that night."

"For the moment the writer is the primary suspect."

"Stupid girls!"

The two men share a predilection for very young women.

Franco had phoned Pereda the day of the murders. "I'm taking my girl out to supper tonight with a little friend of hers who doesn't want to be a third wheel. Can you come?" Humberto had been seeing Leticia for several weeks.

The deputy public prosecutor hesitated. He had a dinner commitment with his wife, but it wouldn't be hard to cancel. "How old is your girl?"

"Seventeen."

"And the friend?" Pereda ran his fingers over his grey hair, slicked down with Wildroot cream.

"The same age, I think."

"Fine." Pereda felt a throb in his penis. After he hung up, he had to adjust his trousers.

To please Leticia, who wanted to go somewhere besides the bachelor apartment he kept for his trysts, Franco had agreed they would meet in a restaurant at the city limits. The girls arrived in a taxi. Looking at themselves in the restaurant window, they straightened their miniskirts and fluffed up their hair, piled high and held in place with Aqua Net spray. They had spent longer than usual dressing to look more adult, hoping that the make-up, hairdos, and clothes would add at least a couple of years. Before leaving home they took a few snapshots of themselves with Leticia's Polaroid, a birthday present from her father, which she brought along in her handbag.

"You know what? Let's not do this," Claudia said suddenly. The thought had crossed her mind in the taxi, but she had held her tongue, not wanting her friend to know she was afraid. She did not like Leticia's schemes, or her manipulative wheedling that if Claudia really was her friend she would go along.

"Don't be a nun," Leticia said as she strode into the restaurant.

Neither did Claudia like the date she ended up with — too dark, too perfumed, too grey, too smarmy, too old. "Lovely", "precious", "tender", and "baby" were only a few of his endearments as he edged ever closer. He touched her thigh, her cheek, put his arm around her shoulders. "Have another tequila, beautiful, it's the expensive kind, we aren't going to waste a drop."

Claudia tried to bat away his octopus hands, his vile breath. Both men were puffing on cigars. In the cloud of smoke she managed to whisper into her friend's ear, "Let's get out of here, please, let's go."

"Don't be a bore," Leticia countered. Caught between disgust at the man and fear of letting down her friend, Claudia sipped her drink.

Pereda kissed her on the neck and moved her hand onto his crotch. "Feel my prick."

Later they got into Franco's car and the driver took them to a motel on the highway to Hidalgo.

A knock on the office door interrupts the tense atmosphere.

"May I come in?" asks Leonardo Álvarez, Franco's pet reporter. The publisher knows how to read people and can tell this one has no scruples. He'll write whatever Franco wants, so long as it gets him ahead of the competition.

"Sure. You must know Attorney Pereda."

"Yes, I've seen him at several events." Álvarez holds out a sweaty hand. Pereda takes it reluctantly, then makes a show of wiping his palm on his trouser leg.

Franco, leaning on his desk, points to a chair. "Sit down." Álvarez eases into it, while Pereda paces the office, stroking his black moustache. The tinted wax he uses each morning darkens his fingertips.

"The Attorney came to tell me about several photographs that turned up in Ignacio Suárez's car and others of the autopsy," Franco says. "It seems the pathologist sent them around. I don't know if we ought to publish them, out of respect for the victims' families. What do you think?"

The young man rubs his hands nervously, drums his fingers, sweeps one hand over his curly hair, heavy with gel. "I think if the other papers are publishing them, we'd better not get left behind."

"You think we ought to publish them?" Franco asks. "It would be an utter insult."

Pereda shows Álvarez the photographs. The reporter takes his time examining them and says, "When the writer turned up dead it reminded me of one of his novels — I can't remember the title right now. Did you read it? The murderer left his victims positioned just the way those girls were, leaning against the wall of a funeral home. It was based on real crimes that occurred years ago."

"What else happens in the novel?" asks Franco.

"They catch the murderer. I thought there'd be a sequel, but Suárez never wrote it. The killer in the real murders was never found."

"Suárez died the day after the murders, with the photographs in his possession. What are the chances that he was trying to escape?" Franco's question floats on the cigarette smoke he exhales.

"That's one of the hypotheses we're looking into," Pereda answers, and goes back to stroking his moustache.

"Instead of publishing the pictures," Franco says, "we could publish a story that we received them, but out of respect for the families we won't publish them. That should make people suspect the writer."

"Exactly," Álvarez agrees. "That's what will happen when the other papers publish them and say they were found in Suárez's vehicle."

"It would deflect attention," Pereda says, "and at the same time give the public the feeling that we're doing something to find the killer."

Miguel Pereda is thinking about the conversation he had in the state prosecutor's office after leaving the morgue the day the bodies were discovered. That morning two agents had come to his house to tell him about the crime. He was still drunk from the night before and had to hold his throbbing temples while his subordinates filled him in. At the morgue Esteban del Valle took him to see the body of the young girl with whom he had had sex only hours before. A sharper pain stabbed his brain when he laid eyes on her. He had to rush from the room and throw up on the washroom floor. "He may be the state prosecutor's nephew," one agent present commented, "but he sure doesn't have the stomach for the job."

"We cannot proceed with the investigation," Pereda told the state prosecutor that day. "Humberto Franco and I are involved."

"In the killings?"

"No, no. We were with the two girls that night and we left them in a motel room. We don't know what happened after that. If we proceed with the investigation, our connection with them will come out, and it will destroy our families, our careers."

"Jesus, this is a double murder. I can't just play dumb," the prosecutor said sharply. He went to the window and watched a woman getting into a car. "This is the sort of favour you pay for up front, Miguel. Your fixation with young girls is going to cost you a pretty penny."

Now Pereda wipes the sweat from his brow and says, "The writer has to be the guilty party and the only one. How the fuck can a dead man defend himself? But there's another problem. A Spaniard was with him in the car, the guy who owns Posada Alberto. Though he's in a coma."

"Will he come out of it?" Franco asks.

"It's an induced coma. The doctors don't know what shape his brain is in. For the moment, it's no big deal. If he wakes up, we'll deal with it then."

Franco pours himself a brandy from a crystal decanter. "Leo, write the piece we've been talking about and bring it to me as fast as you can."

Diario de Allende
September 7, 1985

FORENSIC PATHOLOGIST SUSPENDED

by Leonardo Álvarez

Photographs of the bodies of the young women murdered on Friday, August 30 were delivered to our office yesterday.

The publication of those images by other dailies has given rise to anger and indignation, since it violates the confidentiality of the investigation and desecrates the absolute respect the victims' families are due.

The photographs were discovered in the vehicle of Ignacio Suárez Cervantes, whose death we reported several days ago. The writer was in a motor vehicle accident along with one of the owners of Posada Alberto, José María León, a Spaniard who has lived in our city for some twenty years and who remains in a coma.

A police source revealed the current lines of the investigation regarding the murders. One leads to Suárez Cervantes, given that the young women were found in a position very similar to the victims in one of his novels, *The Saints*.

In related news, the Public Prosecutor's Office announced that, in accordance with its Policies and By-laws, forensic medical investigator Esteban del Valle will be removed from his post, presumably for divulging the images of the deceased girls.

Coincidentally, several days ago in China, the writer Liu Xan, author of several bestselling books in his country, was arrested on suspicion of murdering four people more than two decades ago, a crime he recounted in a novel published five years ago.

EIGHTH FRAGMENT

After nearly sixty pages I'm feeling intrigued. It's seductive to unearth all the fossilised memories I have inside, to dust them off with the curiosity and care of a paleontologist. I'm fascinated, even though writing about myself has caused me to fall behind in my novel, a new case for Detective José Acosta.

Reviewing what I've written to date, I am tempted to go back and correct the timid and fearful tone with which I began. I don't know if this unexpected euphoria will last, but I feel almost drunk.

I remember being happy. In spite of everything, I held on to a spark of joy, which on a few occasions brightened into a blaze of hope for a better life. Things did improve.

If Ramón were to hear me say things improved, he'd probably say that's a metaphor for life. Is that what you'd say, Ramón? Maybe this manuscript will reach your hands. I can almost see your long brown fingers turning the pages to find the things I never told you about. It's amazing that despite all that happened you still considered me a friend.

On the morning of April 9, 1941 the story about Felícitas was all people talked about in the corridors of the newspaper. Forget the bombing of Belgrade. Ramón was exultant. I had gone out very early, since I did not want to face either Isabel or Julián. I wanted the story to end right then and there.

But of course it snowballed, became an unstoppable avalanche that would crush us all.

Today I wonder, had I been aware of the consequences would I have still done it? I don't know the answer. Perhaps my parents would still be alive and my mother would have gone on killing children. How many did she kill? The newspaper talked about fifty, but we never knew the precise number.

Ramón intercepted me in the washroom. I had been avoiding him all morning.

"I want you to tell me everything you know."

I stood there for a few minutes, each of which seemed to last far longer than sixty seconds.

"Not here, let's go somewhere," I said.

Ramón strode down Calle Moneda with his hands in his coat pockets, his step firm, eager. He lit one cigarette after another.

"Please don't use my name," I begged.

We went to a cantina called El Nivel. Packed, it stank of cigarettes, sour sweat, shrimp soup, fried food — of life itself. The laughter and loud chatter of everyone elbow to elbow at the bar contrasted with my dark mood. We took a table across the room, Ramón waved his hand and asked the only waiter for two Coronas. The place provided me with distractions: a man got up from his bench and fell to the floor, only to get up and fall again; another dropped a glass which broke into sharp pieces just as my life would. These distractions were prophecies, warnings.

We clinked glasses and I drained my beer. It took a while to get around to my mother. Ramón was celebrating the success of his story. "We should continue the tale of the Ogress," he said finally. I was the one who had given her the name of the child-eating beast from "Sleeping Beauty".

So I began. "I worked as a servant for Felícitas and my uncle Carlos Conde." Claiming to be his nephew was a stupid idea that actually worked. I spoke nonstop for the next two hours. Then I repeated the story, when Detective Jesús Galindo interrogated Ramón and myself the following day.

I had still said nothing to Isabel or to Julián. Up to then they had not heard the news. Isabel never bought the newspaper, busy as she was with her work at the Flores household.

Answering the detective's questions I felt liberated and treacherous at the same time. I thought of Judas. Of all the apostles, he was the most important, although Peter might come close. Without a traitor there would have been no Crucifixion or Resurrection or Catholicism.

I am my parents' Judas.

It was Easter. What's more, it was Good Friday. Even if I didn't hang myself from a tree, I cannot deny part of me wanted to. I wanted to end it all. I was afraid, very afraid.

My parents were still on the run, but before long the police caught them at the house of a couple who helped them sell children.

I betrayed my parents and Ramón betrayed me. He used my name in the stories he wrote after Felícitas Sánchez and Carlos Conde were captured. He told me the editor wanted to give the story to another journalist with more experience, and his secret weapon, the ace up his sleeve, was his source and the source's relationship with the people involved.

- "Child-Chopper" arrested to answer for her awful crimes
- Beast of a woman assisted in her evil tasks by several "jackals" in human form
- Dante never dreamed of writing pages as dark as those wrought by this charlatan
- A vivid tale told by a sharp and outspoken boy

La Prensa (Mexico City, April 12, 1941)

These were the bullets Ramón used to hook his readers.

On Holy Saturday the newspaper featured the following stories: "German Forces Enter Belgrade, accept the city's surrender"; "Yugoslavia Crushed by German Forces"; "Priest Miguel Espinosa of Ixtapalapa Parish Calls Popular Passion Play 'Profane'"; and on page 23, the capture of the "Child-Chopper", featuring my name.

A BOY CONFESSES ALL

That's the way it was. I confessed everything.

Agents of the Federal District Police, among them Detective Jesús Galindo and his subordinates, José Acosta Suárez and Eduardo Gutiérrez Cortés, arrested the "Child-Chopper" Felícitas Sánchez when she emerged from a house on Calle Bélgica in Colonia Buenos Aires. She had been planning to slip the noose tightening around her and hide out in the port of Veracruz.

For at least fifteen years, Felícitas pretended to be a midwife, specialising in premature births, during which time she killed innumerable babies, sometimes by aborting them and other times by strangling newborns with her own hands. She cut the children to pieces and put them down the drain, which is how the sewer pipe of 9 Cerrada Salamanca got blocked, giving rise to the charges and later to her capture.

Felícitas Sánchez, the so-called "Child-Chopper", performed her operations in a dirty room with no hygiene to speak of. For years she maintained an astonishing ability to fool many husbands and fiancés.

The case came to light thanks to a 14-year-old boy, Manuel Conde Santos, who worked for a time as a servant for Felícitas Sánchez. He declared that he met her in 1939, when he was recruited to work for her by his uncle Carlos Conde.

"I know because I saw it happen," the boy said. "They'd take the foetuses or babies in a car to dispose of them far away."

Manuel Conde is your typical intelligent boy, as his features attest, and his declarations confirm all we have reported. He answers promptly and clearly, recounting in a lively fashion what he saw and heard during the time he worked for his uncle and his uncle's wife.

"I saw," he told us, "how the women would come in fat and go out skinny. At first I didn't realise what was going on, but that was striking. Bit by bit, I figured it out."

"Were a lot of the women rich?" we asked the boy.

"Many, but there were poor ones too."

Felícitas, a woman of evil instincts, all too apparent in her horribly protruding eyes and short, round, toad-like body, is the lynchpin of a drama that seems to have been plucked from hell.

To conclude our interview with Manuel Conde Santos we asked, "Did you know any of them — the fat women who left the home of Felícitas Sánchez looking skinny?"

The boy thought for a few seconds and said, "Yes, I knew Natalia, the wife of the shoemaker who has his workshop across from the store on Calle Guadalajara. She lives at Cozumel and Durango."

"And who else?"

"One who lives at Alixco and Juan de la Barrera. I don't remember the rest. There were lots and lots..."

Manuel Conde was detained to get him to "spill the beans" on all he knows. He was freed yesterday afternoon.

Felícitas Sánchez and Carlos Conde will be interrogated today.

La Prensa (Mexico City, April 12, 1941)

FOURTEEN

Saturday, September 7, 1985
09.46

An agitated Esteban del Valle leaves the office of the deputy public prosecutor and strides to his car. He is escorted by two policemen, who accompany him to the morgue in the basement of the General Hospital. At his desk they inform him that he cannot remove anything, as everything there is the property of the Public Prosecutor's Office.

"I'm only going to take my own things."

"Only your own, the rest is . . ."

"I know, I know, it's the property of . . . your fucking mother," he hisses.

"What did you say?"

"Nothing, I'm just taking what's mine."

He puts several photographs, a few notebooks, a thermos, and his pencils into a cardboard box.

"I didn't leak those photographs," he swore when he was accused of giving them to the press.

"Who else could have done it?" Miguel Pereda would not meet del Valle's gaze.

"I don't know."

"We cannot allow the rules to be broken . . ."

"The rules?" Esteban interrupted. "What rules are being followed when I'm ordered to stop examining a cadaver?"

"What?"

"You were there, you can't deny I wasn't allowed to finish examining the bodies of the teenagers after you left."

"You weren't allowed to finish?"

"And besides, I was overruled on the report."

"These are very serious accusations. Do you have witnesses?"

"Who could be my witness? You're the one who blocked the autopsy."

"How far are you planning to go with these accusations?"

"What I want is my job back. I'm innocent of what I'm being accused of."

"For the moment that is impossible, we cannot allow you to continue working for us. Those are the prosecutor's orders."

Esteban clenched his fists and jaw, and dug his fingernails into his palms. Wordlessly, he nodded and walked out.

Now he leaves the hospital as if someone were taking aim at his back. He sets the box on the trunk of his car to retrieve the keys from his trousers pocket, then puts his things inside. When he comes around to the driver's door he realises he is wearing a white lab coat with his name sewn above the pocket. Angrily, he unbuttons it. The last button resists and he yanks it from the fabric. The button falls and bounces away. "Go to hell," he says and throws the coat after it.

He gets into the car, backs out over the loose gravel, changes gears, steps on the accelerator. Then he slams on the brakes: a man is blocking his way. The man bangs on the hood with his fists, shouting something that Esteban cannot make out. The fellow bangs on the window too and Esteban lowers the glass. The man grabs Esteban by the collar.

"You bastard! Come out of there! Come on, get out!"

Esteban tries to break free and instinctively steps on the accelerator. The car jerks forward and the man falls to the ground.

"It was my daughter! My daughter!"

Then Esteban recognises him. It's Leticia Almeida's father. He puts the car in neutral and goes over to where the man is sobbing in the middle of the parking lot. He tries to help him get up, but the man refuses.

"You can't stay here, you'll get run over."

"It was my daughter, you bastard, not something you sell to a newspaper."

"It wasn't me."

The man remains on the ground. Esteban squats beside him. The sobbing eases and Leticia's father wipes his face and tries to get to his feet. Esteban walks him to the kerb. Several people are watching. "The show's over," del Valle tells the gawkers, most of whom work there. "Can I give you a lift?" he asks. Ricardo Almeida, who looks to have aged years in the past few minutes, shakes his head and points to his own car.

"Let me take you. You're in no shape to drive."

"No, no, I'm O.K. I'll do it. Who gave the pictures to the newspapers?"

"I think it was the Public Prosecutor's Office."

"No! Is that true?"

"I don't know for sure — I've been fired — but I'm going to try to find out."

"Do you think the writer killed them?"

"I'm certain it was not him. Have you asked your daughter's friends if they know anything? Would you be willing to help me investigate?" Esteban is surprised by his own words.

Leticia's father is slow to understand. "I'm no investigator."

"But together we could try to find things out. It's either that or expect an investigation from the people who are not going to do it."

"Yes, yes, I want to find the son of a bitch who killed my daughter." He chokes out the words with the little breath he can muster.

"Then I'll pick you up tomorrow."

FIFTEEN

Saturday, September 7, 1985

13.40

Standing before her, his fists on a peeling desktop, Agent Díaz has been firing questions at Elena for more than half an hour. "We are trying to clarify the death of Ignacio Suárez Cervantes. We need to be sure it was an accident, since he's a suspect in a murder, as you will have read in the newspapers. When his companion awakens from his coma, we will interrogate him."

"Neither Ignacio nor José María had anything to do with those murders."

"We do not know that to be the case and that's why you're here, Señorita Galván, to see what information you can provide us with."

Elena detests being called "señorita", a word that drips acid, reminding her that she could never have a child and will never be Ignacio's wife.

Two judicial police officers had arrived at Posada Alberto shortly before nine o'clock in the morning, asking for Elena. She was busy arranging flowers on the round cedar table in the lobby and barely looked up. "That's me." The white daisies trembled in her hands when she saw who it was.

"We need you to come with us," one said curtly.

"Why?" she said, turning back to her task to conceal her alarm.

"We want to ask you a few questions about the writer Ignacio

Suárez Cervantes and we understand you two had a relationship." The policeman took a step towards her.

"I can answer all your questions here."

"No, señorita, you have to come with us."

"You can't force me."

"Yes, we can. We have a warrant to bring you in. It's up to you whether you come quietly or you want all your guests to know." The man waved a paper at Elena, which she tried to read.

"We have to get going," the second policeman insisted, "and no scene."

Elena told no-one. She asked for a few minutes to get her purse and then got into the men's vehicle parked in a no-parking zone.

At the Public Prosecutor's Office the policemen shut her into the room where she now sits. On the walls, once white, black fingerprints stand out as the only decoration apart from a few dark stains. Elena imagines they're dried blood. There are curses scribbled on the melamine desk where Agent Díaz leans his fists. Some are in blue ink, some in black, some in red: "fucking cops", "faggot if you read this", "one, two, three, fuck the judge who fucked me."

The door opens and a strong odour of Sanborn's lotion announces Miguel Pereda. Díaz stands to attention and gives a nearly military salute. Pereda responds with a couple of nods, extends his right hand to introduce himself to Elena, and puts a thick blue folder on the desk. "Good morning, Señorita Galván, I hope everyone has treated you well. Agent Díaz, I will take over from here on."

"Yes, sir." Díaz leaves the room.

Pereda crosses his arms. "Did my men treat you properly? Did they offer you anything to drink? A coffee? Water? A Coca-Cola?"

"No, I don't want anything. All I want is to get out of here."

"In a moment."

"Am I under arrest?"

"No, of course not. You are here to answer a few questions that could help our investigation. As you know, it is our obligation to look into accidental deaths to discount the possibility of foul play. In addition we are investigating the deaths of Leticia Almeida and Claudia Cosío."

"I understand you want to blame that on Ignacio and José María."

"No, señorita, you are mistaken. It was irresponsible of the media to publish information on an investigation that is underway."

"An irresponsibility that tarnishes my family and Ignacio Suárez."

"I am sorry, señorita, but in this country we have freedom of expression."

"I can swear it wasn't Ignacio, I'll testify to it. He was with me that whole night."

"Where were you?"

"In my room."

"Is there anyone who can corroborate what you say?"

"Yes, my employees. They would have seen we were together from the afternoon until the following day. We had a glass of wine in my room."

"How much did you drink? Enough not to notice if Suárez went out of the room at some point?"

"No, señor, I don't tend to drink that much."

"How many bottles was it? Three? Four?" With his fingers Pereda indicated the count could go on.

"Two."

"Two bottles . . . that would be about four or five glasses apiece."

"I can assure you that I was in my right mind the entire time. What's more, the photographs they found in his car someone slid under the door."

"Someone slid them under the door? Do you know who? Do you realise how outlandish your claim sounds?"

"If I knew I would have told you already. But that's why Ignacio had them. He went out to find whoever did it. He said it was a message for him. You people should find whoever it was."

"Perhaps your mother's husband took the pictures and that's why they were together."

"No, José María was with my mother, he always is."

"Did you see it when they got slid under the door?"

"No, I was asleep."

"So you can't confirm they arrived that way. Maybe Ignacio Suárez lied to you and he took the photographs, or your stepfather did."

"No, no, that isn't what happened."

"Señorita Galván..."

Elena interrupts and gets to her feet. "I'm not under arrest, right? So I can leave whenever I want."

"If you are withholding information useful for this investigation, you could be accused of concealing evidence."

"What are you trying to insinuate?"

"I'm not insinuating anything."

"I have a lot of work at the hotel. We've got a full house. I have to go."

Pereda picks up the bulging folder. "We have proof," he says, and he bangs the folder on the desk.

"What proof?"

"Several years ago Suárez wrote a book about a murderer who had a *modus operandi* very similar to what occurred in this case."

"That doesn't make him guilty. Your proof is pretty dumb."

"His precise description could only have been written by someone who had seen a murder up close, or who had committed one."

"Well, I can assure you it wasn't him. I know him — I knew him well. And I can't waste any more of my time. Goodbye."

125

Elena walks to the door, fully expecting the man to intercept her. "We shall see each other again very soon, Señorita Galván."

Elena closes the door behind her and hurries out before they can stop her. When she reaches the street, she hails a taxi and gives the driver her address. The car pulls out and Elena cannot refrain from looking behind her.

NINTH FRAGMENT

The plumber, Salvador Martínez Nieves, Isabel's brother-in-law, turned up at the tenement on April 12, 1941. Children were celebrating Holy Saturday by dumping buckets of water on each other in the open courtyard. From his perch on the staircase, Julián was watching them getting soaked.

I got my own cold-water bath that morning when I read my name in the newspaper. I stayed in Isabel's room until I heard Ramón come in a few minutes before Salvador Martínez, and I went out to meet him.

He had one hand in his pocket, the other was holding a cigarette. I took him by surprise and punched him in the face. He fell backwards and hit his head on the ground. Several seconds passed before he realised what had occurred.

"What's with you, you bastard?"

"Asshole, you promised you wouldn't use my name!"

"I'm sorry, I had to do it. I had to make the story more credible."

"Thanks to you they're going to kill me when they get out of jail."

Ramón got up slowly, using the handkerchief he carried in his pocket to wipe the blood from his face.

Out of impotence, out of fear, I burst into tears.

We ended up sitting on the kerb outside the entranceway, Ramón stuffing the bloodstained handkerchief up his nostrils.

"I'm sorry, brother." He placed a hand on my shoulder. His apology was sincere, but the weight of his hand was like the weight of the guilt pressing down on me. I too was an accomplice to murder and ought to be arrested.

We helped each other stand up.

"You should get that looked at," I said.

"I'm not going to bleed to death, Kid Azteca. Maybe you should take up boxing."

That was when Salvador Martínez banged so hard on the door of Isabel's room that it loosened the old hinges. She opened in a hurry, still unaware of the news in *La Prensa* about her former employer. I hadn't noticed when the plumber entered the tenement, nor had I paid any attention to the banging on the door.

"Where are you hiding that stupid brat?"

He slapped her twice before she could answer.

"Where is the fucking bastard?"

He must have thrown her against the shelf where we kept plates and cups. We heard her scream and the noise of the china breaking. The dripping children had turned to statues, but now they raced to the room where Salvador Martínez was attacking his sister-in-law and swearing he wasn't going back to prison for anybody.

Julián and Jesús leapt at the plumber and punched him, but he swatted them away. He was twice their height and weight. The neighbour from room number four also tried to intervene, but he too was stopped with a punch that left him so bloodied his wife had to tend to him under the astonished gaze of his many children. By the time Ramón and I got there, someone had called the police.

"Fucking stoolie, you're going to die!"

The neighbour from number seven tried to hold the plumber back when he rushed at me. Salvador Martínez screamed, howled, shook off the arms pinioning him, and punched me in the stomach. I fell forward and he kicked me in the face. Several neighbours, Ramón among them, managed to pull him off before he could tear me to pieces.

The rest is hazy, up to the moment the doctor on shift examined me in the hospital. Isabel was on a cot a few metres away, unconscious. After the doctor finished with me, I went to look at her. Her left cheekbone was bleeding, her right eye was swollen shut, her lips were split open. She had to be operated on for internal bleeding.

Julián and I sat in the hallway, waiting for news of Isabel's condition. My face was swollen and bruised, and my mouth hurt. I had adhesive tape on my nose and plugs in my nostrils. Next to me a woman had fallen asleep while nursing her baby. From her nipple a few drops of milk fell on the child. I watched her breast until someone woke her up and told her to cover herself.

Julián brought his face close to mine, whispering so that neither Jesús nor his grandmother, a few steps away, would hear. He looked directly into my eyes, something he rarely did. "I heard you tell Ramón about our parents, and I warned them." My brother's face was transitioning from childhood to adolescence, and his voice was losing the flute-like off-key tones of his few utterances as a child. "I told them they'd be coming for them."

"Why?"

"Because I don't want them to go to prison. I want them dead."

While we were at the hospital, the police arrested Salvador Martínez Nieves. Ramón went to Public Prosecutor's Office No. 6 to hear him make his statement. The plumber loudly declared that he refused to work for my mother the first time they called him. He said that for more than three years tiny skulls, legs, arms, and innards were put down the sewers of the "criminal maternity ward". He accused Isabel of helping Felícitas kill children.

It was nearly ten at night when police detectives José Acosta and

Eduardo Gutiérrez turned up at the hospital to interrogate Isabel — yes, later on I borrowed Acosta's name for my fictional character. In the room were Isabel's mother, Jesús, Julián, and me. I was standing at the foot of her bed, not daring to speak to her or touch her. All I could do was stare at her reddish-purple eye swollen shut. She had stitches in her cheek, bruises all over her brown skin, and her upper lip was swollen and stained with dried blood. Isabel breathed with difficulty and moaned, despite the painkillers and sedatives.

"Maybe there are more things you didn't tell us about," Detective Gutiérrez said to me when he came into the room.

I shook my head. He was wearing the same beige suit, the same tie, the same brown felt hat as the last time. It was his police uniform. A year later, the two of them would capture Goyo Cárdenas, the Tacuba Strangler. In the pictures Ramón published in *La Prensa* they looked unchanged.

"What is your relationship to this woman?"

"We live with her," Julián broke in.

At this point Eugenia Flores, Isabel's employer, barged into the room, elbowing her way past the policemen to the bed. "The señora cannot answer any of your questions now, can't you see how sick she is?" She took Isabel's hand and lifted away the hair that had fallen across her face. Isabel's mother had telephoned her to let her know what happened and that we couldn't pay the bills.

Eugenia Flores cut quite a figure in her heels, her pastel red dress, her impeccable hairdo, and brightly painted nails. She told the policemen again that Isabel worked for her.

"Señora, with all due respect, we must verify what Salvador Martínez Nieves told us."

"For the moment that is inappropriate and an insult to the patient. Please leave. My husband is Congressman Ramiro Flores, a friend of President Ávila Camacho. I do not want to have to call him about this."

"Señora, we could arrest you as well, no matter whose wife you are," Gutiérrez threatened.

At that moment the doctor who had treated Isabel walked in and ordered everyone but family members out. Eugenia Flores, Julián, and I went into the hallway and remained there until we were sure the police had gone.

Then Eugenia Flores took me by the arm and walked me to the exit. I kept my eyes on my feet, not daring to look up until her fingers raised my chin. "Don't say anything about me, please. Don't ever let on that your mother treated me."

I shook my head.

"Promise me!"

"I promise," I whispered, in a voice that did not seem like mine.

"I'm going to have to trust you. As soon as they let Isabel out, I'm taking her to my house. No-one will bother her there."

Eugenia Flores went off in her chauffeured car. I watched from the kerb as rain began to fall. It continued all night long. I recall the rhythm of the water on a tin roof outside Isabel's room — tack, tack, tack — a sound I can hear to this day.

SIXTEEN

The Murder
Thursday, August 29, 1985
Hour unknown

They peed at the edge of the driveway, squatting, their minimal skirts pulled up to their waists and their lace panties, what was left of them, around their ankles. The puddle spread, reaching the high heels in which they could barely walk. They had sought someplace out of the way, shame even more powerful than drunkenness, and were in the dark shadows cast by a building. Claudia complained about the pain between her legs, the burning inside her vagina and around her labia. In the dimness she couldn't make out the red tint of the small river of urine running down the makeshift gutter, carrying off the memory of her virginity.

They had no idea where they were, lost from the moment they left the restaurant, climbed into the Grand Marquis, and heard Humberto Franco tell the driver to take them to Los Prados Motel. More than alcohol kept them from recognising the highway to Hidalgo. There was also the fondling and sloppy kissing from the men, who held them by the hair to have their way. After they pulled into the garage attached to the motel room, the driver drew the black curtain across the opening, concealing them from view. The men, each carrying a bottle of tequila, pulled the girls from the car and kept them on their feet.

There was only one bed in the room and it still smelled of the previous occupants.

Miguel Pereda poured tequila directly down their throats, counting to five while the liquor dribbled in. When his own turn came, he said, "The house gets double." Leticia and Humberto Franco counted from one to ten.

"Smile," Leticia said, raising the camera she pulled from her handbag. She pressed the shutter, capturing the other three on the bed with their eyes barely open, the men half-dressed. The newspaper publisher grabbed the camera.

"What's wrong with you? Are you retarded or what?"

"No!" she screamed when Franco moved to smash it on the floor. "Don't break it!"

Pocketing the photograph that slid out of the Polaroid, he ordered, "No pictures."

A relieved Leticia took back her camera. "No pictures," she echoed, her words slurred.

Pereda then threw himself at Claudia, who had collapsed onto the stained mattress. "I'm going to eat you alive, you little whore."

"Nope," Franco said. "We're trading sweeties. I've had this one lots and I feel like something new."

Leticia would have made a face, but her facial muscles were too numb to show her displeasure. Besides, Pereda was on her immediately, covering her lips and chin with his thick saliva.

Claudia's sedated brain scarcely registered the publisher's face inches away from her own or the pain in her vagina, a word she had never liked. It seemed harsh, offensive. She preferred "my little thing" or "down there". She tried to open her eyes, but her lids felt sewn shut. At one point she caught sight of Franco getting dressed and yelling for Leticia to get out of the bathroom. Then she saw Leticia holding on to the walls and furniture, as she zigzagged her way back to the bed. Claudia felt her friend curl up beside her, moaning, and she asked thickly, "Where are we?"

Leticia did not respond, and Claudia let herself float away on a tide that carried everything, mattress and all, to a pool guarded by monsters who would not let them escape.

The next thing they knew, a woman was rousing them and ordering them out. Claudia, still lost in an alcoholic fog, did not understand what she was being told. Even so, she made the enormous effort to get to her feet. Her panties were wrapped around her right ankle. Leticia, her brain less clouded, but evidently disconnected from the various parts of her anatomy, also managed to stand up. The room, reeking of alcohol and vomit, spun like a merry-go-round out of control.

Neither of them was aware of the man spying on them from another room. He had seen the Grand Marquis pull in and watched it leave with only the men. Fondling the keys to the car he had stolen a few hours earlier, he waited for the girls to emerge, saw them stumble and hold each other up. A chance encounter, or perhaps their fate was written on a motel-room wall.

That was when the girls squatted to pee some distance from the motel entrance.

Now they stood at the edge of the highway not knowing whether to go left or right.

"We'll ask someone for a ride," Leticia said. Claudia nodded.

Death pulled over, driving a two-door 1984 Nissan with plates from the State of Mexico. In the glove compartment was a woman's black shoe with a spike heel so narrow it looked like a nail.

SEVENTEEN

Saturday, September 7, 1985
18.20

The interrogation had exhausted her. When she got back to the hotel Elena spent a few hours working, but after wiping down tables in the dining room and taking inventory in the pantry she had to lie down. Now she rubs her gritty eyes. Since Ignacio's death she doesn't like waking up, not in the morning and not after a nap. It's hard to return from the amnesia of sleep and realise once again that Ignacio is dead. A spider on the ceiling distracts her. She watches it crawl forward, then abseil down an incredibly fine strand. She ignores where it lands, her mind caught up in images of Ignacio she does not intend to forget.

Two and a half years ago, on March 21, 1983, he returned to Posada Alberto. The city was bedecked in jacaranda blossoms, streets and sidewalks carpeted with violet bells that transformed everyone's mood into something more festive.

"You came back," Elena said, as he got out of his grey Fairmont.

"I told you I would."

He handed her a box, one of many in his car. She came close to kiss him on the cheek.

"I'll be here six months. I'll speak to your mother about renting room number eight permanently. It's got style, and I like things that have style."

"Permanently?"

"Yes, I want to come every spring and leave every fall. It'll be my writing time."

Unable to repress her smile, she grabbed another box and led him exultantly to room number eight. Forty years old and I feel like a teenager, she thought.

Far from her mind were the months of darkness after her divorce, when depression had confined her to bed, hopelessness flapping about her head croaking, "Nevermore." Elena's plight reawakened the maternal feelings Soledad had lost when Alberto died. She spoon-fed her daughter and lay beside her, holding her head above the lapping waters. Little by little, she managed to coax Elena out of bed and help her feel secure on her own two feet. And Elena put love out of her mind, until the spring day Ignacio arrived along with the purple blossoms of the jacarandas.

"No, don't open that box." He stopped her. "Let me, I'll take care of unpacking."

She pulled away like a girl caught in some mischief. Ignacio sat on the bed and patted the mattress beside him. He stroked her cheek with the back of his left hand and she closed her eyes, losing herself in the sensation.

They had begun flirting the year before, during the three months of his first stay. She became his personal concierge, suggesting events he could attend, exhibits, walks, excursions, and offering to be his guide and companion.

"You must be bored with an old man," he once told her, while they strolled through the gardens of the central plaza.

"No." She pulled off a piece of the cotton candy she was holding. "I'm not a kid either." On that sunny day Ignacio had told her his life story, without mentioning his two sons or the real reason he was in San Miguel. She had seen one of the movies he wrote, "Blood Game", but she had never had any interest in crime novels. She liked fiction, historical novels especially. And she read articles on archeology and books about painting and restoration.

On one of those afternoons she was at a table on the terrace, trying to repair a broken cuckoo clock. She had acquired a taste for mending things as a child in this very house, where she lived with her grandparents. Her grandmother was a hoarder, and even had two rooms built at the back of the garden, next to the stables, to store whatever she could not bring herself to throw away, plus all the useless things she kept buying. "Garbage," her grandfather called it. For Elena they were treasures to be rescued and restored. From her grandmother she also inherited the urge to accumulate, and the rooms at the back are still full.

Ignacio crept up on her. "That cuckoo is never going to sing," he said, startling her.

"Cuckoos don't sing." A little alarmed, she removed her glasses and the face shield she wore against dust and mould.

"Tell me the story of the clock."

She felt his breath on her neck and could not keep herself from responding to the call of his chemistry. "You'll have to make it up, I'm no good at fiction. All I can tell you is that it's from the Black Forest, it's in the Bahnhäusle style, and it dates from about 1900. Some of the carving is missing, it's got bits of glue on the roof, and the cuckoo has a broken wing. But the wings and beak still move. Plus it's missing a few numbers."

"Maybe it's because you like things from the past that you like being with me."

Elena let out a nervous giggle and the pliers fell from her hand. She bent down to pick them up, giving herself time to recover. "You insist on making me feel like a little girl. I'm not."

"Do you suppose you could restore an old writer?"

"Maybe. I'd have to take a look at the machinery to see just how damaged it is."

Ignacio smiled at her nervousness and she could see how attractive he found her. Or perhaps it was just the luminous afternoon, bathed in a light that does not exist in Mexico City. Or maybe it was the scent of jasmine or the tracery of the vines on the arbour above their heads filtering the sun.

In time he would confess how relaxed he felt when he was with her. He would speak of his surprise at finding himself engrossed in after-dinner conversations with her, when previously long discussions gave him a sharp pain in the gut. "You have no idea of the darkness inside me," he said one evening, averting his gaze.

But on that golden afternoon the cuckoo bore witness to the beginning or perhaps the confirmation of a new feeling. Elena looked up and spied her mother watching them from behind the curtains of her bedroom, and saw the disapproving look on her face.

"I'm a terrible partner, Elena. I'm addicted to falling in love. I get bored and I have to look for someone new," he said the morning after they first slept together, a few weeks into his second stay at the hotel. "I like my freedom. I won't be good for you. Go on with your life and don't tie it to mine." Ignacio was trying to pick up the thread of the speech he made whenever he ended one relationship or started another. He plagiarised himself every time.

"We're all addicted to something," she said, thinking of her addiction to wanting a child. "Psychologists should talk about addictions, not pathologies." Elena was leaning back against the bedhead, her hair tousled. "Maybe you're addicted to getting women to fall in love with you, addicted to seducing. After all, that's what writers do, they seduce their readers."

Ignacio considered. "Maybe I am. I also have darker addictions, which perhaps I'll never tell you about."

Elena snuggled up to him. "Maybe the world is a big rehab centre. Maybe life is all about overcoming addictions or learning to live with them."

TENTH FRAGMENT

According to the other inmates in the group cell, she screamed and yelled about a girl she had to pick up at school. None of them would go near her or speak to her. They wanted nothing to do with Felícitas Sánchez, who lay on the floor talking to herself and shouting to be let out.

The exception was a homeless woman charged with robbery, who was driven by the acute need of a cigarette. She stank. Her mouth was a toothless cavity. "Got a smoke?"

That pulled Felícitas out of her delirium. She eyed the woman's dirty clothing, the toenails that reminded her of an animal's. Layers of rags conveyed a certain heft, but the woman's bony face and fingers like dry twigs gave away the truth.

"Child-killer, don't you like my feet?"

Felícitas scrutinised her fiercely. "No."

"People say you like to eat children."

The midwife went back to screaming and a guard banged a nightstick on the bars. "I'm going to shut you up good."

Felícitas crawled to a corner and leaned against the wall, her legs outstretched. She spread her fingers across her obese belly. The tramp moved off and tried to bum a cigarette from someone else.

Ramón, from the other end of the cell, witnessed the scene and snapped a photograph of my mother in the corner. He took notes and said nothing. A policeman whom he paid monthly to keep him abreast of things had let him in.

"She won't eat," he told me. "She swears they're trying to poison her. She has convulsions and they don't know if she's faking it or what. They had to take her to the infirmary."

I made as if I did not care. "I hope she dies." I spat out the words.

As days went by, I grew more afraid that Julián and I would be charged as accomplices and locked away too.

Julián had retreated into mutism, a hard shell I could not crack. His silence was angry, aggressive, a wall I banged up against over and over, like a moth at a lightbulb. I got burned, I got hurt. He punished me with his silence.

Ramón went on writing the story of my mother without consulting me. Felícitas' story was now a prison tale and he let it fly with his imagination to keep his readers hooked. He heightened the tone of my mother's statements and exaggerated his descriptions of her. "I don't lie," he told me, "I give people what they want to read." He saw her in an isolation cell and he even got into the women's infirmary to hear her give her statement.

> It's true, I often took care of the women who turned up at my door. I stopped their haemorrhages, which were serious, some because they had been beaten, but most because of the things they had ingested in order to abort. I took care of people who needed my services, and once the obstetric work was done I put the foetuses down the sewer through the toilet. The hundreds of infanticides I am accused of are but fantasy.
>
> *La Prensa* (Mexico City, April 17, 1941)

The dead do not go away. The dead remain. People speak of their dead as if they belonged to them. What dead belong to us? The ones who die on their own, or the ones we kill? I made my dead; my mother made hers. "Foetuses and infants," she said in her statement, as if she cared, when in reality she called them "that", as in "Throw *that* away", "Get rid of *that*", "Bury *that*", "Burn *that* ..."

They were a business. They were money.

"All I did was help those women. I saved their lives," my mother kept repeating to the judge when he demanded the names of her clients.

"They are as guilty as the midwife," the judge insisted, "murderers of their own children."

> We were face to face with the Hyena-Woman, whose criminal acts have jangled the nerves of everyone who has read the astounding story of Felícitas Sánchez Aguillón, better known as the Child-Chopper because she would cut newborns to pieces and flush them down the toilet.
>
> Judging by what Felícitas declared "from her lips out", as the expression has it, señoritas were turning up at her rudimentary clinic, girls from all social classes, most of them office workers.
>
> On the horizon lies a scandal of formidable proportions. It will break when a few of these unnatural mothers are apprehended, mothers who did not mind risking their own lives so long as they destroyed the fruit of their transgressions.
>
> The police now have the names of many of these vain girls ...
>
> *La Prensa* (Mexico City, April 17, 1941)

My mother was always aware of the value of her silence. The women she treated knew it too.

The only pictures I have of my parents are the ones that appeared in the newspaper at that time. Once, early on, we did take a family photograph in a studio. It was a Sunday and we wore our school uniforms, maybe because they were the best clothes we had. She put on a dress and high heels, and she got her hair done. He wore a tan suit and a felt hat, and topped it off with a handkerchief in his coat pocket. I remember the colour of the suit because before he put it on he laid it out and I was curious to see how it felt. I put one finger on the trousers and he slapped me.

"Cut it out, you brat, you'll get it dirty!" I imagined some speck of dirt sliding off the tip of my index finger.

"Are we going to school?" Julián asked, when we were in the street.

"No, we're going to get our picture taken." My mother reached out to take my brother's hand so she could walk along as if we were a normal family.

I dropped behind, in step with my father. I couldn't take his hand because he was holding a cigarette, and I didn't know what to do.

A feeling spread through me, a sort of sudden exhalation that took a while to dissipate, like your breath on a windowpane. I felt happy and hopeful. Undefined hope. That we would become a family? That she would love us? At that point we were not yet emptying buckets or burying remains. If I had known what was coming I would not have smiled for the photographer, or felt practically hugged when he told us to stand closer together and my body ended up firmly pressed against hers. I felt her warmth.

"You can see this kid is happy," the photographer said, pointing at me before he pressed the shutter.

I don't know what happened to that picture. They never framed it or hung it up, and in time I forgot about it — until today.

Right now I'm looking at the photograph of my mother sitting on the floor of the cell, the one Ramón took. Her legs spread apart, one hand on her fat belly, the other holding her head.

In another photograph she is pressing her right hand against her forehead, as if she were denying what had been said about her. Her left hand holds her purse.

Felícitas liked shoes and handbags. She used to say that to be a woman with class you had to have a good pair of shoes and a purse that matched.

In a third picture she is reading her statement.

There are two other photographs that provoke in me a morbid fascination. I'm not sure if "fascination" is the right word. Maybe "distress". In the first she is on the floor, as if she were throwing a tantrum. I look at her in the midst of all that filth. Two police officers are on either side, but you can only see their shoes. She looks defenceless, harmless.

The second image, another of Ramón's, has her sleeping on one of the cots in the jail. It was published as the picture of her cadaver. She looks tranquil, her face is relaxed, placid. What I find most disturbing about that photograph is that despite everything the Ogre slept peacefully.

Photographs are a mechanism for stopping time. As long as the image exists, the action portrayed goes on. *Ad infinitum* my mother will read her statement, or lie on the floor convulsing, or sleep on that cot, and I will smile at the camera, hoping for a better life.

I don't know where she's buried.

I don't know if she was buried or cremated.

Did the worms enjoy eating her? Did she taste like the foetuses we buried?

Perhaps our individuality lies not in our fingerprints, our physiognomy, or our D.N.A., but in our way of dying. Perhaps the reason we are here is to find our particular route for escaping this world.

EIGHTEEN

Sunday, September 8, 1985
10.00

Lucina Ramírez Campos listens to the heartbeat in the womb of the woman lying on the table. Contractions began last night and her waters broke early this morning.

Lucina has never liked Sunday births. She tries not to stay up late on Saturday nights, but most of the hospital staff come in bleary-eyed, either hung over or obviously still drunk.

She has always been prudent and stable. That is, except for the years she and her mother and brother spent living like nomads, hiding from Lucina's father. By the time she turned nineteen she had lived in eighteen different cities. She could not hang on to friendships. Dozens of faces flow over one another in her memory, and she cannot recall precisely where she met any of them.

"Your child's heartbeat is strong. There's no sign of stress," she tells the woman who has not stopped crying since she arrived at the hospital.

"Will he live?"

Lucina runs a hand over the woman's sweaty brow. "We'll do all we can, but I can't promise you anything." And to a nurse, "We're going to operate, get the O.R. ready."

The husband of the pregnant woman enters the cubicle and hugs his wife. She stops crying while he consoles her, saying repeatedly that everything will be alright. "Will it, doctor?" she asks Lucina, whose presence has been somewhat eclipsed by the husband's.

Lucina has brought many babies into this city that has the feel of a small town. In San Miguel there is only one other gynaecologist, a man, and his patients are mostly foreigners fully into menopause and not at all like women from here, where shame is a way of life and rare is the woman willing to undress in front of a man other than her husband, no matter how much of a gynaecologist he may be.

None of her patients, seeing her so sure of herself, so professional, so capable, would imagine that Lucina spent most of her childhood flitting from town to town. Whenever she mentions that time in her life, she says, "It was hit and run, like in baseball." By the time she was twelve, they were living in poverty, in a hot, dry, dusty town of barely two hundred inhabitants near the U.S. border. She angrily confronted her mother, demanding to know who it was they were running from.

"You want to know who?" Her mother grabbed her and shook her. "From your father and his brother, that's who."

The answer took her by surprise. As far as she knew her father was dead, since that's what her mother had insisted every time she asked. Suddenly he wasn't.

"My father is alive? Why are we hiding from him?"

"Because."

She kept pestering for an answer until her mother slapped her, knocking out a loose molar. Although her mother hugged her afterwards and begged forgiveness, something more than a loose tooth was lost between them. Lucina caught her mother's fear of the faceless father, all the while remaining enormously curious about him.

Lucina slices through the layers of skin and fat, separates the abdominal muscles, and gently pulls away the peritoneum to reveal the uterus. With infinite care, she reaches into the mother's womb and extracts a barely defined shape.

"It's a boy."

"Can I see him?" The mother's voice is heavy with emotion and anaesthetic.

"In a moment."

Lucina cuts the umbilical cord and hands the baby to a nurse, then removes the placenta and prepares to suture the uterus.

"Doctor," one of the nurses calls out.

Lucina leaves off stitching and goes to the baby, who seems to want to leave this world before discovering it. She takes the newborn in her hands and massages his chest while whispering to him, "Don't even think about it."

"What's wrong?" the mother asks, her voice thick.

Without answering, Lucina presses on the tiny chest still covered in blood and custard. She gets the stethoscope in place, such an outsized instrument on the diminutive body lying on the bloodstained sheet. She asks for silence.

"We have a pulse," she says, her own pulse racing. Every time she saves the life of a child or a mother, she feels her own heart skip a beat and she can barely breathe.

The nurses wrap the resuscitated newborn and whisk him away. Lucina returns to stitching. "The pediatrician will have a look at him," she tells the mother and orders more sedation.

After she finishes, she finds the husband and explains, unable to assure him the child will survive. "The first few hours are essential. The paediatrician is in charge now," she says.

Doctor Lucina Ramírez says goodbye to the new father, who heads for the nursery. She walks to the washroom, unable to hold back her tears. The only time she allows herself to cry is after saving a life.

Ten minutes later, in the parking lot, she climbs into her white Datsun, her tears still close to the surface, her nerves still raw. She attaches her seatbelt and looks at herself in the rearview mirror, wipes her eyes with her fingers, smooths her eyebrows.

"Christ," she says rubbing her cheeks. Glancing at the passenger seat, she sees the white folder lying where she left it. "Ignacio Suárez Cervantes" is written in black pen on the cover. She has read its contents several times in the last three days, since her father died. She runs her finger over the name and says again aloud, "Christ."

Her father delivered this folder on the very day he died. His grandson had opened the door, the grandson Ignacio had seen less than a dozen times in three years. Lucina was very careful about that. Giving herself the opportunity to get to know the man who claimed to be her father was one thing; allowing him to have a relationship with her son was something else entirely.

"It's the call of the blood," she had said, persuading herself to meet him the first time. She was terrified, she admits, terrified of the man she had spent half her life fleeing from. And she certainly did not want to put her son at risk. She never told her son that Ignacio was his grandfather, and she insisted he call him "señor".

In fact she told no-one that a man claiming to be her father had appeared. She did not even come clean when her husband, now ex, confronted her with the rumour that she was having an affair.

"You're going out with an old man," he accused her. Only later did Lucina realise that that was the moment when their marriage began to unravel. It came to a close without her ever explaining who Ignacio was.

After three years, she was still wary. "What are you doing here?" she asked, after her son shouted that Señor Ignacio was at the door.

"I've come to give you these papers."

She interrupted him. "I asked you to never come to my house."

"I know, I know, forgive me. But you should have this. If anything happens to me, I want you to read it." His words tumbled out nervously. "Promise me that if something happens you will read this," he repeated, gripping her arms.

"Alright, I promise."

He kissed her forehead, then ran to his car and was gone before she could recover from her surprise.

Lucina picks up the folder, rereads a few pages, and her eyes alight on a word. "Midwife," she says out loud. Her memory conjures up a scene from when she was fourteen years old in a town named Corea, where she lived with her mother for a time, a tiny place in the centre of Mexico that shared the name of a country thousands of miles away. On a bus, Lucina watched her mother go to a woman who was screaming and holding her belly. Her mother had the woman lie down on her shawl between the rows of seats. Then she helped her bring a baby girl into the world. Fifteen passengers and a caged chicken witnessed the birth.

"I worked for a midwife for many years," was the only explanation her mother gave. She did not see Lucina's staggered and proud expression. And she could not know that in that moment Lucina decided on her life's work.

Now she slams the folder shut, gets out of the car, and strides back into the clinic.

"Doctor, I thought you'd left," says the nurse at Reception. "Are you alright? You look upset."

"I'm fine. It's just that I don't like Sunday births. I need to make a call."

"Here's the telephone."

Lucina pulls a notebook from her bag and looks up the number of Esteban del Valle, the only friend of her father's she ever met. Ignacio introduced him one day as his great buddy. She and Esteban were already acquainted, nothing unusual in a small city, especially among doctors. She found it strange that Esteban would befriend her father, given their age difference. But she liked Esteban, even if the gossip among doctors had him preferring the company of the dead to that of the living.

Now she needs to tell him about the manuscript. She first read it in one fell swoop, and at the end she was surprised to find herself trembling, so much so that she had to take a tranquilliser to face her next patient. Today, during the Caesarean, she could not get it out of her mind. "Maybe that's why the baby nearly died," she thinks, "thanks to my family's accursed past."

"Esteban? This is Lucina Ramírez."

Lucina detects a wariness in Esteban's silence.

"I'm so sorry," he says after a few seconds. "I thought of going to see you, but so many things have happened. I'm so sorry about your father's death."

"I have to see you. I need to see you and Elena. Could you arrange a meeting for the three of us?"

NINETEEN

Sunday, September 8, 1985
13.30

Patricia gets up from the park bench across from the church. Since the death of her friends Leticia and Claudia, she attends Mass every day. She has not been back to school, cannot stomach the idea of walking into a classroom bereft of them. They were a trio. Claudia and she shared the burden of excessively religious parents, and both were attracted to Leticia's carefree personality. Other classmates, fearing another murder, will not so much as set foot outside their homes.

"Patty." Leticia's father approaches.

"Señor Almeida." Tall and blond, she was born in San Miguel to an American couple. Now that the murders have disturbed the peace they found here, the family is talking about going back to Colorado.

They greet each other with a quick kiss on the cheek. He holds her shoulders, looks into her eyes, and then pulls her into a tight embrace. It's as if he is trying to reach some part of his daughter. The bright sun offers a warm hand on their backs.

"I'm sorry, I'm so sorry," she says, teary with emotion.

"It's alright."

From the churchyard a few steps away, under one of the Indian laurel trees pruned in the shape of a cube, Esteban del Valle observes the scene. It is near noon and the place is full of children running and playing before Mass. Several women carrying bags of fruit and vegetables are chatting, vendors are selling balloons, tamales, and homemade crafts. In their sorrow, Señor Almeida and Patricia seem far removed from the hubbub around them.

Esteban walks over and Almeida introduces him. "Patty, I wanted to see you about Leticia and Claudia. We need to find out who killed them. The police aren't going to lift a finger and a murderer is still at large."

Patricia feels a chill go up her spine. She drops back onto the bench, the tips of her fingers on her cheek. "What do you want me to do? I don't have anything to tell you."

"Do you know who they went out with? Who they might have been with on that day?"

Her fingers go to her straight blond hair. "I think she told Claudia things. But she never shared her secrets with me."

"You must have heard something, you were always together."

"She broke up with her boyfriend."

"Yes, and I keep turning that over in my mind. I think if she hadn't left him, she'd still be alive."

"She was seeing a married man, a rich guy. That's all I know. I heard them talking about it one day, but when I asked they wouldn't tell me who it was."

"A married man? Who?"

"I don't know. It's the truth, I don't know."

"Yes, you do." Almeida grabs her arm. "Who is it? Who? You have to tell me!"

"Stop," Esteban breaks in. "Stop it, easy now."

Almeida lets go of Patricia and covers his face. "I'm sorry, I'm so sorry. Did I hurt you?"

Patricia shakes her head. "I've got to go. I'll ask around and see if anyone knows anything. I'm sorry, Señor Almeida. I'll see you later."

Patricia waves, then runs across the street and around the corner.

Ricardo Almeida again brings his hands to his face. "I know nothing about my daughter. I don't know who her friends were . . . who she went out with . . . How can I expect other people to know anything when her own father didn't know her?"

ELEVENTH FRAGMENT

Julián and I went back to the tenement alone, while Isabel spent another night at the hospital. The neighbours all wanted to know how she was. My brother said nothing and went straight to the room. I tried to keep my account brief. I swore I didn't know why Salvador Martínez had attacked her. A woman offered to bring us some hot food.

Before going in I sat on the stairs to smoke a cigarette, hoping Ramón would come in so I could get the latest on my parents. I heard the quick-stepping heels of Lupita, the prostitute, whose too-tight skirt was moulded to her body. Her make-up and elaborate hairdos, meant to disguise her age, reminded me of Carmen Miranda. She must have had a voluptuous body in her youth, but from so much misuse it had taken on the doughy shape of something worked and kneaded.

"Kid, have you got a smoke?" She leaned her hip against the wall, her hair slipping free of its pins and revealing various shades of a tint badly applied. Like her body, her hair seemed to be battling her attempts to subjugate it.

I held out the pack, struck a match. She came close and the flame lit up her face. "Can I sit down? How is Isabel?"

I shrugged. "Last I saw her she was asleep."

"She's a good woman, the only one who talks to me without giving me the once-over."

I nodded and took a long drag.

"Her brother-in-law beat her because of what you said, I heard him say so when he came in."

I blew the smoke out slowly.

"Poor kid, you've had it hard."

She put a hand on my knee, gave it a couple of pats, and left it there. We finished our smokes in silence.

"I didn't want her to get beat up," I said.

"Things almost never turn out the way we want. I know the midwife. She took care of me..."

"You're one of those women!" I kicked my leg away from her hand. She pulled it back.

"And you are her son. Julián and you, you're Felícitas' children. When I went to your house, you opened the door. I could hardly walk then, I'd taken... I'd tried to end the pregnancy. I could barely stand and you helped me get to the room where your mother was. She was busy with another woman. You called to her, softly and then more loudly. 'Another señora is here,' you said. She turned and shouted at you not to interrupt her... I was afraid. The dirty room, your mother's shouting, it all terrified me. Then I fainted. By the time I woke up, it was all over."

I had forgotten her face. I'd force myself to forget the faces of the women who came to my mother.

"I recognised you when I read the story in the paper. Now when I look at you, I can see the features of the boy who helped me."

She stroked my cheek, took my face in her hands, looked at me with her tired eyes. I saw my own eyes in hers: many years younger, but just as weary. She brought her face close and put her mouth on mine. I shut my eyes, inhaled her rancid breath and thought mine must smell as bad — of exhaustion. An infinite weariness took hold of my body. She hugged me and we cried together. We rose from the staircase, arms still around each other. She took me to her room and without a word took off my shoes and put me to bed as if I were a little boy. Then she slipped off her heels, squirmed out of her skirt. In her underwear she lay down beside me and hugged me tight.

I fell instantly asleep.

TWENTY

Tuesday, September 10, 1985
09.15

Esteban del Valle had asked her to meet him in a café on the central plaza. How long has it been since she last went out for coffee? She cannot remember. Alone at the table, holding the mug close to her lips, Elena feels the steam enter her nostrils and awaken the ghost of another life, before the death of Ignacio, before meeting him even.

A blue ball bounces towards her, chased by a sweaty, red-faced boy. Elena sets down her mug and catches it. She tosses it to the boy, who runs off shouting that it's his turn to play goal. She takes a sip and watches the children kick the ball and run after it.

"I can't have children," she told Ignacio one day, nearly a year after they had been together and four years after her divorce. During her marriage she had tried every possible way to get pregnant. They made love on her fertile days, or when the temperature of her body was perfect, or the moon was full or new, or after drinking herbal concoctions friends recommended.

She never imagined that having a child would become an obsession or that the lack of one would make her feel incomplete.

A psychologist suggested her true yearning was not to become a mother, but to restore her mother's lost child. Soledad still set a place for her dead son at the table. Many times Elena heard her conversing with Alberto's spirit in his bedroom, which she kept exactly as it had been when he was alive, as if she hoped he might at any moment return. Elena had stalked out of the psychologist's office, slamming the door so hard it sent the university degree tumbling from the wall. "He's an idiot," she said, when explaining to her husband why she would not go back. "People become psychologists to try to solve their own problems. I don't need to restore anything to anybody."

The ball bounces close again, drawing her out of her musings about life before Ignacio.

"Elena," she hears her name as if she were under water, feels a hand on her shoulder that makes her jump and spill her coffee.

Esteban hastily helps her mop the table and her clothing. A waiter comes over. Elena excuses herself and hurries to the washroom to sponge off her white trousers. Despite her usual habit of wearing dark colours, she had promised herself she would not dress in mourning for Ignacio. She did not want to look like anyone's widow. Indeed, she did not know what to call herself. To avoid the blacks, greys, and navy blues that filled her closet, she was obliged to wear the same white trousers several days in a row.

She dampens a paper towel and tackles the brown stain shaped like Australia on her right thigh.

"Idiot," she says to herself, as she rubs the fabric to little effect. "Stupid, stupid." The tap is on and water splashes beyond the sink. She takes another paper towel and catches sight of her face in the mirror, the thick black tears running down her cheeks. She must have started crying again. She washes her face until the trails of mascara are gone. The cool water calms her.

Resigned to her messy trousers, wishing she could just go home and not have to speak with Esteban, determined to excuse herself and ask to meet another day, she leaves the washroom. Sitting with Esteban is a woman who looks familiar, but at a distance Elena cannot place her.

"Elena . . ." Esteban says, getting to his feet. "Are you alright? Did you get scalded?"

"Look, let's meet up another day."

"This is Lucina, Ignacio's daughter."

"Doctor Ramírez?" Elena says, floored.

"Hi, Elena."

"Ignacio's . . . what?" She tries to formulate a question, but cannot.

Lucina nods. Elena thinks of the last time she saw her, when she made a scene not unlike that at the psychologist's, screaming in front of the astonished patients waiting their turns, "You are utterly incompetent, a horrible doctor!" A moment earlier Lucina had told her, "Elena, we've done everything we can. Sometimes nature does not want to cooperate. You can't have children."

Esteban, accustomed as he was to working with the human body, seeking out differences and measuring changes, takes note of Elena's pallor, her trembling hands, her agitated breathing. What he can't know are Ignacio's words now bouncing around Elena's brain: "I can't have children either." She knew that his two sons were adopted, and he had never mentioned a daughter.

Elena sinks into her seat. "Ignacio never . . . Ignacio couldn't have children," she says. She feels faint.

"I know he didn't tell you about me. I asked him not to. Christ, I didn't want you or anyone else to know. Esteban is the only one who knew. There is a lot in my father's past you don't know about."

"What? Esteban? You knew and you didn't tell me?" Elena pushes a lock of hair behind her ear.

"I was at the burial," Lucina says. "You didn't see me?"

Elena shakes her head, half-closes her eyes, tries to bring to mind the scene at the cemetery. But all she can recall is the sound of the earth falling on the casket. She practically hears it happening now.

"I didn't want my father's family to see me. They may not know about me."

"Why did you ask him not to tell me?"

"Because my mother and I spent years hiding from him. She was afraid of him and I thought he was a monster."

"Why?"

"My mother was afraid he'd take me away from her, or do something worse . . . She never gave me a coherent explanation. Her fear seemed irrational, but I got swept up in it. When I finally met him, I tried to get him to tell me what happened between them, but he lied to me. He told me my mother made it all up, that he had spent his life looking for me. He made it sound as if it was my mother who had kidnapped me. Only now I've learned the truth . . . in fact my mother isn't even my mother . . ."

Elena tries to guess Lucina's age. She's short and wears her dark hair cut short too.

"Esteban, we've seen each other so many times and you never said a thing, why?" Elena can't articulate or even grasp what she feels.

"I couldn't tell you, I promised Lucina and I promised Ignacio."

Elena gets to her feet and picks up her bag. "I think I'd better go. This is the last thing I need to hear today. I don't need to know Ignacio had a daughter. I really don't. I've got a lot on my mind."

"No, please, wait. Christ, wait a minute."

"Sorry, but I don't want to hear another word."

"I have something important to show you." Lucina pulls the folder from her briefcase and lays it on the table. Esteban and Elena glance from the folder to each other. "The day my father died he brought me this."

"The manuscript of a novel?" Esteban asks.

"No. It's the story of his life."

Elena picks up the folder and weighs it in her hands. "Not many pages for an autobiography."

"It's the story of my family, and the worst of it is that there might not be anybody who can tell me if it's true or not."

"How's that?" Esteban takes the manuscript from Elena and flips through it, stopping on a page.

"I made a copy for each of you," Lucina says, pulling two identical documents from her briefcase. "I want you to read it, we could read it together, we have to figure it out . . ." Lucina hesitates, then reminds herself that these are the only two people with whom she can share the questions plaguing her since reading these pages. "I thought I knew who I was, where I'm from . . . If what he says here is true, Ignacio has destroyed everything I believed. I have to find out."

"I don't get it."

"You will, Esteban, once you've read it."

Lucina's pager interrupts them, she glances at it. "I've got to go. Births don't wait." Visibly distressed, she picks up her purse and briefcase, puts away her folder. "You should read it right away. We can see each other when you finish. It's incomplete." Lucina opens Esteban's copy to the final page. "See? It ends in the middle of a sentence, or maybe there were other pages he didn't give me. We'll never know for sure . . . Anyway, I have to run. My profession is the only part of my life I know is real."

"Lucina, wait." Saying goodbye to Elena, Esteban hurries after the daughter of Ignacio Suárez.

Elena is left standing beside the table. A waiter comes over to ask if she would like anything else. "Just the bill."

The blue ball bounces towards her again. She kicks it and watches the children enviously. If only her life were as simple as putting a ball between two posts.

TWENTY-ONE

Tuesday, September 10, 1985
15.20

As in every other city the Spaniards built in Mexico, the streets of San Miguel are narrow. The town lies on the route between the capital city and the mining centres to the north, and originally served as a way-station for travellers.

The settlement was founded in 1542 by a monk, Juan de San Miguel, at a place the indigenous Chichimecas called Itzcuinapan. He dedicated it to his patron saint, the Archangel Miguel. The Chichimecas, none too pleased, waged a violent campaign against the settlers, obliging them to move a few kilometres to the northwest, where they founded San Miguel el Grande in 1555, at which point Viceroy Don Luis Velasco offered livestock and land to Spaniards willing to move there. And to calm the Chichimecas, he exempted them from paying tribute and allowed them to be ruled by their own chiefs.

In colonial times, the home of Elena's grandparents, which later became Posada Alberto, was where the monks put up visiting priests and travellers passing through. On the walls of the courtyard they painted illustrations of Bible stories from the Old and New Testaments, and used them in catechism classes for Chichimecas who had abandoned their gods and adopted the beliefs of the strangers who did not look like them and did not speak their language.

When Elena was a girl, her mother tried on several occasions to have the pictures painted over, much to Elena's dismay. Fortunately, neither Elena's grandparents nor Consuelo nor Soledad's husband would allow it. One of the first things Elena did when she took over the hotel was to have them restored to their original beauty.

A rendering of the crucifixion of Christ sits above the door to room number eight, where several judicial police officers are rummaging through Ignacio Suárez Cervantes's possessions, the few, that is, which remained after Elena and the writer's children had their turns.

"What's that?" one of the policemen asks, not knowing what to call the statuette of Moloch staring at them from a shelf. The figure has the head of a bull and the body of a man with arms extended in expectation of an offering.

Elena shrugs and says nothing. She can hear Ignacio's voice telling her with a passion she could not fathom all about the bull god venerated by the Phoenicians, Canaanites, and Carthaginians. "In the temples the ceremony began with priests playing trumpets, drums, and cymbals. The statues were hollow and a fire was kept burning inside. The high priest would climb up on the altar and place a newborn in the statue's arms."

Elena remembers how shocked she felt. "I don't want to know any more," she said. Ignacio's response was to take her by the arm and draw her closer to Moloch. "The priest," he continued, oblivious of her attempts to break away, "then pulled chains that made the arms rise until the infant tumbled into Moloch's mouth and onto the flames below."

"Señorita?" one of the men asks.

"Yes?"

"We need you to explain why Ignacio Suárez had these statues."

"I don't know."

Leonardo Álvarez crosses the threshold, a camera hanging from his neck. "Sorry to be late."

"And you are . . . ?" Elena asks.

"Leonardo Álvarez." The young man raises his Nikon and looks through the eyepiece before snapping his first shot. "I'm a reporter for *Diario de Allende*." He extends his hand, which she disregards.

"No photographs inside the hotel. Please do me the favour of leaving."

Now the reporter ignores her and asks the men, "What have you found?"

"Didn't you hear me? I'm going to call the guard and have you thrown out."

"Negative, señorita, this young man has every right to do his job," one of the policemen says.

"He does not. And neither do you. This is a violation, an injustice . . . a . . . a crime coming onto my property like this."

"Negative again, señorita. We have a warrant, we are investigating a possible crime."

"Good afternoon," a man interrupts from the door, his voice so commanding that everyone looks up.

"Attorney Pereda," one of the agents says.

"Gentlemen." He raises his hand in a salute.

"Attorney," the policeman continues, "the señorita here wants to prevent us from carrying out your orders."

"What are you doing here?" Elena asks. She feels a chill run down her spine. This is the second time she has laid eyes on this man and he still scares her. Maybe it's because she feels so vulnerable since Ignacio died.

"Good afternoon, Señorita Galván." He offers his hand, she does not take it. "We have a warrant to search this hotel. For the moment we will only go through Suárez's room. I cannot give you any further explanation. But if you do not allow us to carry out our work, we will be obliged to charge you with obstruction."

A man and a woman, hotel guests, pause to observe the scene from the courtyard, then scurry away.

Elena glances at the walls and furniture, tries to remember if there is anything else besides the devil figurines, anything that might cast suspicion on Ignacio. She wonders whether she ought to leave, or stay to make sure the police don't plant false evidence. "Now I'm thinking like a crime writer," she reflects as she closes the door to keep other guests from looking in.

"I'll stay right here while you do your work. What about him?" She points at the reporter.

"He can do his job too," Pereda says.

"Have you got any other suspects besides a dead man who can't defend himself?"

"Your stepfather, as I already told you."

"One dead and the other in a coma. Those are your suspects? It's easy to blame people who can't defend themselves."

"Señorita Galván, you have no reason to doubt us."

Elena puts a chair beside the door and sits. She crosses her legs and recalls the manuscript Lucina gave her. She hasn't begun to read it because she is furious that Ignacio never told her he had a daughter, who to cap it all was her own gynaecologist. He forgot to pass on that detail? Unforgivable. So, why is she protecting him? She ought to tell Attorney Pereda she knows Ignacio killed the girls. That would ruin his reputation for good, as well as his daughter's — and with it her own, since she was his lover for three years. "That's why I won't say a thing," she thinks. "Not for you, Ignacio, you liar. For her, and for me." She nearly says it aloud. "For my sake, I'm going to keep them from blaming you. I'm not going down as the girlfriend of a murderer."

The reporter finishes his roll of film, rewinds, and reloads the camera, distracting Elena from her thoughts. The deputy public prosecutor picks up the figure of Moloch, scrutinising it. He reads out the inscription on the bottom. "'And you shall not deliver any of your own descendants to Moloch, nor shall you profane the name of your God: I am Yahwe.' Do you know what this is about?" he asks Elena.

"No." Her answer is a near-whisper and her eyebrows are arched. "I've never seen that statue before."

TWELFTH FRAGMENT

"They're going to let the midwife out," Ramón said. He looked awful, defeated, nothing like his relentlessly optimistic self.

That was on April 27, 1941. My mother had been imprisoned for less than a month.

"You told me she would never be freed."

"This is how the justice system works in this country."

I shrugged, pretended it didn't matter, and wandered off to empty the rest of the wastebaskets. We were at the newspaper, him with his newly won popularity, me trying to keep a low profile, hoping to make myself invisible.

Two of her patients had intervened after Felícitas threatened to reveal the identities of the ones who were married to rich and influential men. She kept a blacklist she could pull names from, like numbers at a bingo game. The first was Eugenia Flores, who my mother knew had hired Isabel and had helped me and Julián. Felícitas got the clerk from La Quebrada to deliver the message. The second was the wife of an executive at Pemex, the state oil company.

My mother's counterattack was so precise, so effective, that her impending release was announced on the front page of the paper, displacing news of the fall of Greece to Germany. Her scheme reached right into the courtroom, and the judge only sentenced my parents for breaking the burial law.

The finding by Attorney Clemente Castellanos, Third Judge of the First Circuit Criminal Court, is inexplicable, and leaves their offences, including abortion, criminal association, medical and technical culpability, shrouded in mystery. Equally unexamined is the question of collusion between the judge and the defence team. Let us hope the curtain will be pulled back somehow, since the public demands punishment for crimes of such enormity.

La Prensa (Mexico City, April 27, 1941)

"They'll go free as soon as they pay the fine. I'm sorry," Ramón said, as if he were responsible for how things turned out. His words landed on me like a death sentence. I knew my head would roll.

Using his only weapon, my friend wrote another article, raising doubts about the honesty of the judge. All that achieved was a letter from the magistrate rejecting all insinuations of a deal with the defence, and indicating he would speak to the public prosecutor about investigating *La Prensa*.

Ramón's article did delay my mother's release, and it obliged the judge to raise the fine from a thousand to five thousand pesos. But that was it. Ramón went back to the prison to interview Felícitas one last time. She assured him she was incapable of killing a chicken, but she would cut me to pieces for bringing such misfortune on her, and then they'd be right to call her the Child-Chopper. "I'm going to eat that kid alive," she said.

Ramón did not include my mother's threat in his article.

"She's your mother, I know. I suspected it from the beginning, but I wasn't sure. I couldn't ask you. If I made you tell the truth, you'd stop talking to me about her and I'd lose the story." He said this with a hand on my shoulder. "I'm sorry, brother, I'm truly sorry."

Maybe friendship is only an illusion, an act of convenience, one of the many inventions we humans come up with to make life a little less insufferable.

Diario de Allende
September 11, 1985

WRITER HELD BLACK MASSES

by Leonardo Álvarez

An operation led by the Public Prosecutor's Office brought to light several objects used in Satanic cults.

Yesterday, pursuing one of the lines of investigation into the murders of Leticia Almeida and Claudia Cosío, a search warrant was executed at Posada Alberto, a hotel in our fair city.

The writer Ignacio Suárez Cervantes lived for long periods in room number eight of that establishment. Among the evidence collected were statuettes that police speculate were used in Black Masses.

Scattered about the room, some on a desk, others on a table or a shelf, were images and representations of Lucifer, Satan, Leviathan, and Amon, plus other presumed inhabitants of hell whose identity could not be ascertained. That is, except for the largest of them: Moloch. The name was written on the base, along with an inscription that left no doubt as to its use.

Adoration of Moloch included the ritual sacrifice of newborns.

The agents conducting the operation are convinced the search helped clarify certain aspects of the investigation underway.

TWENTY-TWO

Wednesday, September 11, 1985
11.11

Evangelina de Franco likes taking her husband's clothes to the dry cleaners. Actually, she doesn't like it, she has to do it. She could send one of the maids, but her husband Humberto will not allow anyone but his wife to handle his clothing. He finds creases and other problems that no-one else can see. The clothes hanging in his closet have to be arranged by colour, each hanger separated by a finger's width and each suit in a clearly marked garment bag. Ties, shirts, socks also by colour, from darkest to lightest. The shoes, same story. Before building the house near the lake, Franco had the architect draw up special plans for the closet in the master bedroom, and he made the carpenter re-do it until he was satisfied.

For not keeping her husband's garments to his liking, on occasion Evangelina has ended up with numerous "cardinals", which is what her mother calls bruises. He also insists she keep her nails perfect, no nicks, and her hairdo and make-up impeccable. They take shopping trips once or twice a year to Europe or the United States to acquire the latest fashions, which spark much gossip and set the tone for the stratum of San Miguel society in which Franco likes to rub elbows.

More than once Evangelina has confided to her sister that she wants to divorce him. He has been unfaithful on dozens of occasions, another well-discussed topic in town. There was a time when the gossip filled her with such fury that it got her up in the morning determined to look perfect and hide her age, although there was no way she could compete with the young girls her husband preferred. Then her anger ebbed, giving way to an impenetrable shame for having allowed things to reach this point, a shame she clung to with the strength of Atlas.

She feels especially mortified under the gaze of her only child, Beatriz. She wishes she could teach her teenage daughter to become a very different sort of woman: better, full of self-respect, not submissive, not fearful, not tame, not stupid. But she has trouble rebuking Beatriz. "What right have I to scold her?" she tells herself.

Divorce is not really an option. She belongs to that generation in which women who leave their husbands have no place in society. They are scorned and rarely befriended. She herself has shunned them. Her husband puts it bluntly: "You cannot be seen with So-and-so or So-and-so because she is divorced, and you cannot invite her to our house." He insists that Beatriz not have friends whose parents are divorced. "Because," he says, "they have other values."

"Better betrayed than divorced," she said to her sister a few days ago. "We idiots are better off than the brave ones."

For days Humberto has been in the foulest mood she has ever known. But instead of adjusting to the climate and walking on eggshells, she has taken to asking him, "What's wrong?" "What's going on?" "What happened?" Every variation of the same question she can imagine. He grunts in response or ignores her entirely.

Franco has spent more time than usual at home, holed up in his study, surrounded by bound copies of the newspaper from every year since its founding. He keeps them because his father kept them. They are part of his inheritance, in addition to the dividend which his brothers deposit each month. The room, redolent with his cigars, is off-limits to other members of the family. At Humberto's insistence, Evangelina enters it only to supervise the cleaning.

Yesterday, however, she was intent on picking up Beatriz from school — her daughter has suffered dizzy spells and anxiety attacks since the murder of her classmates — and she told the maid to clean the study on her own. "But be careful, don't move a thing, just vacuum and leave." Her tone was threatening.

The maid, jittery at finding herself alone in that holy of holies, yanked on the cord of the vacuum cleaner and managed to knock over the liquor decanter on the table next to the easy chair. Franco surprised the girl anxiously trying to clean the rug. "What did you do? Where is the señora?" The servant blanched and could not utter a word. Dropping the shards of glass she had collected, she began to sob. Right then Evangelina arrived, her daughter in tow.

"How many times have I told you?" he screamed at his wife, providing the servant with enough of a distraction to escape to the kitchen.

"What happened?" Evangelina was hanging her purse on a hook next to the door.

"What do you mean, 'What happened'?" he shouted, hauling her towards him. "How is my study supposed to be cleaned?"

"I . . . I had . . . Beatriz . . ." Before she could explain, he threw her down on the shards of glass dropped by the maid, who would flee the following day, taking with her all the money in the señora's handbag hanging on the hook. Evangelina did not feel the wounds in her hands, or notice the blood dripping from her fingers onto the rug reeking of expensive cognac.

"Clean up the mess your whore of a servant made."

"Humberto, don't get cross. I had to go pick up Beatriz." She spoke from the floor and could say no more, because Franco gave her a shove and kicked her in the stomach. Evangelina brought her hands to her belly and curled into the foetal position at her husband's feet.

"Papá!" Beatriz screamed from the doorway. "Leave her alone!"

Humberto Franco paused, suddenly aware of his intense desire to kill his wife. He wanted to destroy the woman in the bloodstained blouse moaning on his floor. He could never have killed Leticia Almeida. She was the friend of his daughter, who was now kneeling to help her mother sit up. But he could certainly kill his wife. A sharp and bitter liquid rose from his stomach into his throat.

"Stupid whore," he spat out, before turning on his heel and slamming the door.

At the dry cleaners, Evangelina now looks at her hands, the perfect red polish, the white bandages covering her wounds. Her daughter had gone with her to the hospital. She had a bruised rib, but no internal bleeding, no stitches were needed. The doctor suggested she spend the night so they could monitor her, but she refused. She did, however, ask him to bandage her hands, since the gauze and tape covering the cuts would not be enough to cause Humberto any remorse. The doctor also bound her abdomen and prescribed complete rest for at least two full days.

Thanks to painkillers, plus her Prozac, she feels only a mild discomfort in her ribs, obliging her to stand up straight. She hands her husband's clothing to the clerk, who goes through it and returns the contents of her husband's trouser pockets. Because of the bandages she does not look closely, sees only that it's a few coins and a photograph. She takes out her wallet and discovers it is empty.

"I'm sure I had money," she says, surprised.

"Don't worry, señora, you can pay when you pick it up."

Evangelina returns to her car, a white LeBaron, too large and cumbersome for San Miguel. Waiting for her there is her driver, Juventino, who has received a few insults for having parked in front of the dry cleaners, blocking the narrow cobblestone street.

"I had money. What could I have done with it?"

"What was that, señora? I didn't hear you."

"Nothing, Juve, nothing, I was talking to myself."

Distracted, she turns over the Polaroid the clerk had handed her.

Squinting to bring the photograph into focus, she stops asking herself where she spent the money. Even without the glasses the eye doctor recommended, she can make out Humberto with his trousers undone (the very pair she just gave to the dry cleaner), his shirt unbuttoned, his face wearing that dumb expression he gets when he's drunk. Next to him is her husband's new friend Miguel Pereda, smiling stupidly. His trousers are down, his light blue shirt hanging open and his chest visible. Between the two men, her eyes nearly closed, sits Claudia Cosío. It is her. The place she does not recognise. She moves the image closer, then farther away, to bring every detail into focus.

"It's Claudia, I'm certain of it," she says out loud.

"Excuse me, señora, I didn't hear."

"It was them," she says, speaking up.

"Who?"

"My husband and his friend. They were with them."

Evangelina brings a bandaged hand to her lips. Her eyes are very wide. She feels a twinge where her husband kicked her and she shifts her position to ease it. The photograph causes her no pain or fear. Unlike every other time she discovered some infidelity, she does not feel like a victim.

She closes her eyes to tune in to her emotions and finds a sensation similar to what she felt the day she gave birth to her daughter, or when she won the speech contest in grammar school. It is not unlike when she wins at canasta and hides her pleasure, since no doubt one of her women friends will say, "Lucky at cards, unlucky at love," and she will have to pretend to giggle because they all know how unlucky she is at love.

For years she has bought a lottery ticket every month, hoping to win enough to run away with her daughter, away from her husband and from the friends who mock her.

She looks again at the photograph, observes the absurd expression on her husband's face.

She has the winning ticket in her hand, the jackpot.

"Juve, take me to my sister's house."

THIRTEENTH FRAGMENT

If I could, I would place some of my memories into an extractor and spin them until they are as dry as a bone. Other recollections I would put in mothballs, so I could dust them off every so often. One that I would preserve is the image of my mother dead, her body on the floor, her eyes bulging out of their sockets, her dark face flushed violet.

Julián was standing next to her, that is, next to her body. My mother's gaze was fixed on the face of her son. If there were a way to examine the eyes of the dead to detect their last vision, deep in the dark pit of her pupils would be my brother.

He did it at night, a week after we returned to 9 Cerrada de Salamanca, a week during which my mother, to my great surprise, said nothing and did nothing to punish me.

I'm astonished to recall how meek we were when they came to get us. Maybe it was because we knew our place was not Isabel's room. We knew we had begun to lose everything the day I told Ramón about a woman who killed children.

Carlos Conde and Felícitas Sánchez turned up at the tenement a few days after their release. My brother and I were with Jesús and his grandmother, as Eugenia Flores had taken Isabel into her home to convalesce. Isabel's mother had done her best to keep the ship afloat, but thanks to us two it was clearly sinking. Exhausted, drained, I followed my parents without protest, while the neighbours watched out of the corners of their eyes, murmuring amongst themselves. "Murderer!" shouted Señora Ramírez, two of her children clinging to her skirts. My mother seemed to want to answer back, but my father tugged on her arm and she continued walking, glaring at Señora Ramírez as she went. The señora had to look away and the murmurs grew louder. We hurried our steps and I did not dare look back. Then and there we abandoned our last hope of becoming something other than what we are today.

Julián was staring at her, rivulets of sweat running down his forehead, cheeks, and neck, panting as if he were suffering an asthma attack.

My brother had surprised her at the kitchen table, where she was writing to the lawyer who got her out of prison and who was manoeuvring to take control of her store.

Julián had crept down the staircase, snuck up behind her, and clubbed her on the head with an iron pipe. Felícitas, stunned but semi-conscious, fell to the floor and tried to say something. Into her open mouth Julián then poured a spurt of nembutal, which my mother kept in the room where she had attended to the women. He held her lips shut until she had swallowed the poison. She convulsed and in her spasms she kicked over a chair.

Julián climbed on top of her. He was tall and thin, some mischievous gene having turned him into a giant compared to the rest of us. He put his knee on his mother's sternum. When I walked in, she was fighting and foaming at the mouth like a rabid dog. Julián glanced up at me before pressing his left hand harder over my mother's mouth and nose. He put his right hand on top of his left to hold her fast against the floor.

She stopped fighting.

She neither closed her eyes, nor looked away from her son.

I stood facing the two of them, feeling absolutely calm. And I did nothing.

Shocked. Euphoric.

After a while, he uncovered her mouth and got to his feet.

Stepping closer, I looked at her and then at him, as he panted and wiped the sweat from his brow with the back of his hand.

We left her sprawled on the floor, the bottle of nembutal at her side.

We climbed the stairs to our room, undressed, and went to bed without making a sound. We said nothing. I lay for a long while with my eyes open, scrutinising the darkness, attentive to Julián's breathing, which slowed as he lapsed into sleep. The tranquil rhythm of his breathing in and breathing out lulled me into unconsciousness and I slept deeply for the rest of the night.

When we went down in the morning, my father was squatting next to her, holding a small mirror in his hand. "I've checked. She's dead," he said without looking up, his voice trembling. Then he let out a long sigh and sat on the floor next to the woman who had been his wife. Never will I know what he was feeling, but his face showed something akin to the overwhelming sadness one must feel at the loss of a loved one.

I had never imagined the dimensions of Julián's hatred for our mother, a hatred incubated in the shadows of his silence, fed by the daily mistreatment, the pain, the trauma, the rancour. Perhaps not even he knew how much space it occupied in his soul. Yet nothing surprised me as much as my own indifference. I am certain I felt something very close to hatred for my parents, but that morning, after having watched Julián murder her the night before, I simply felt empty.

"We should carry her to her bed," Julián said, "the floor is really cold." Between the three of us, we picked her up.

The story Ramón wrote to conclude the tale of the Ogress of the Colonia Roma said she had committed suicide.

Infamous Chopper Felícitas Sánchez, Tortured by Remorse, Commits Suicide

The woman who thwarted the birth of many human beings, and who threw human embryos down the drain, could not in the end withstand the load weighing on her conscience and took her own life.

The little angels she kept from being born welcomed her! They surrounded her bed, flapping their wings, visibly pleased. For what pleasure is there being born into a life that is nothing but tears and bitterness, disappointment and pain?

Yesterday the authorities found her dead in her bed, lying on her back, her mottled face a bit pale, her protruding eyes a bit sunken. She said goodbye to the world, leaving two visibly nervous letters at her side.

In the twenty-five years of her professional life, Felícitas Sánchez, better known as the "Child-Chopper", may have thwarted thousands of births. She preached birth control — no matter that Mexico is practically depopulated — killed many children, and secretly buried them.

La Prensa (Mexico City, June 17, 1941)

The police asked us a few questions, not enough to clarify the cause of death. It was obvious they had no desire to investigate any further.

Julián and I never spoke about what happened. We never used the far-too-sophisticated term "matricide". The few times I have mentioned the death of my mother I say she committed suicide and offer no details.

TWENTY-THREE

Wednesday, September 11, 1985
16.33

Elena parks her car beside the lake, near the dam. She hopes contact with nature will help clear her mind. Before leaving the hotel, she delegated a few pending tasks: checking out guests, supervising the cleaning, laying out the lunchtime buffet. Yesterday's adventure with the judicial police had left her too exhausted to read the manuscript Lucina gave her, and instead she went to bed early.

Even as a girl she had been fond of this place. It's her spot for reflection, for letting go of her worries and forgetting herself.

She would have liked to study ornithology and spend her days observing the birds that live here. She catches sight of Maximiliano, the American white pelican that a few years ago hurt its wing and had to remain in these murky waters. Maximiliano used to arrive at the beginning of November and depart the following April. Most white pelicans venture farther south, to the states of Michoacán and Jalisco, but a few stop right here.

With the windows down, she can feel the cool breeze off the water.

She remembers the day she brought Ignacio here for the first time and showed him the pelican. "I first spotted him in May, after all the others had migrated north. All except Maximiliano," she said. They were sitting on the hood of the car facing the lake.

"Maximiliano?" Ignacio said, amused.

Elena's broad, frank smile lit up her face and crinkled her eyes, making her look almost like a child. "I had a dog when I was five, named Maximiliano. He didn't live long. He drank an emetic my grandfather made for the cows and died. I thought of him when I first saw the pelican." She started to smile again, then hunched her shoulders and pursed her lips. A boat had startled the pelican and it took flight. "I think I'll feel sad and disappointed the day that he migrates . . . like you," she said, laying her head on his shoulder. "You ought to stay here for good, like Maximiliano."

Ignacio took Elena's face in his hands, brought it close, and gave her a quick kiss on the lips. "Maybe someday," he whispered, and he hugged her tight.

A knock on the car makes Elena jump and pulls her out of her daydream. The pelican has landed on the hood and is now observing her, his head at a tilt.

"You're going to dent the car."

The bird hops closer to the windscreen, shakes its head from side to side.

"Looking for Ignacio? He isn't here. He'll never come back. He migrated to the other world. To hell, that's where a liar like him must be."

A giggle escapes her, then a full-throated laugh. Her body needs to let off steam, and she feels ridiculous talking to a pelican.

"I'm going nuts," she says out loud.

Her cheeks are wet with sudden tears and the car rocks unsteadily. The pelican opens its beak as if about to laugh too or say goodbye. Then it spreads its wings and takes off. Elena waves her hand to wish it well. She wipes her face, looks in the mirror, leans back in her seat. She picks up the manuscript, caresses the cover, and begins to read.

Once upon a time, there was a woman the press called the Hyena-Woman. Infant Annihilator. Witch. Child-Chopper. Butcher of Little Angels. Monster. The Ogress of the Colonia Roma.

Julián and I called her mother.

Her name was Felícitas Sánchez Aguillón.

Your grandmother.

I'm not sure what motivates me to tell you the story of my mother: our story. No-one recalls her life except in fragments, nothing but snippets of the play in which we were obliged to act.

TWENTY-FOUR

Wednesday, September 11, 1985
16.40

After visiting her sister, Evangelina de Franco crosses the threshold of her house and hurries to her bedroom.

"Mamá?" she hears her daughter ask.

"I'll be right out," she says as she locks the door.

She goes to her walk-in closet and shuts herself in. Taking the photograph from her handbag, but not knowing where to hide it, she spins around like a planet out of orbit. Then she puts it back and hides the entire bag under a pile of sweaters on one of the shelves. She thinks of the times her husband has rummaged around among her things, claiming he has the right to do so because he pays for them.

To catch her breath, she sits on the bench next to the full-length mirror. Carefully, she removes the big bandages on her hands, leaving the gauze; no need anymore to make Humberto feel bad and oblige him to beg forgiveness. He will not hit her ever again. In the bathroom she washes the tips of her fingers, taking care not to wet the gauze. She sniffs her blouse and decides to change; she stinks of sweat and nerves.

Awkwardly, due to the pain in her ribs, she changes into a white shirt with a double row of red flowers alongside the buttons. She opens her bottle of Opium and dabs perfume behind her ears and on her wrists. Once she has disguised her odour and her apprehension, she goes into the dining room to look for Beatriz.

"Sorry to keep you waiting," she says, and soon they are chatting about school. The girl is more pleasant and attentive than usual. She can't stop glancing at the gauze on her mother's hands, and neither does she miss her grimaces when she moves.

"Does it hurt a lot?"

"No . . . well . . . a bit. He won't touch me again."

"Mamá . . ." She takes her mother's hand. "Leave him, he'll end up killing you. Let's go off together."

Beatriz does not understand why her mother won't leave him. She detests the answers she usually gets: "Because I can't"; "Because it's not so easy"; "Because people will talk"; "Because you need a family"; "Because we wouldn't have any way to support ourselves."

She expects something similar, but her mother announces, "It's going to be over soon."

"What's going to be over?"

"Everything, you'll see. You can relax." And she kisses the back of her daughter's hand.

"What are you going to do?"

"I need you to go to your aunt's house and sleep there tonight. I'll join you tomorrow when you get back from school. I need to speak with your father."

"He's going to hit you again, I can't leave you alone."

"Don't worry, I promise you I won't let him touch me. Not anymore."

"No, Mamá. I can't go and leave you here."

Evangelina hugs her tight, kisses the crown of her head, breathes in the aroma of her hair, a comforting smell that reminds her of when Beatriz was small. She looks her daughter in the eyes and says, "I promise, everything will be alright."

An hour later, Evangelina climbs into the back seat of the LeBaron. She doesn't know what she is going to say, or how she's going to put it, but she has to do this. Mónica de Almeida has been her friend since grammar school, one of the very few friends she has.

The day Leticia was buried, she tried to stay by her friend's side. She has called her nearly every day since.

What she is going to tell her will put an end to their friendship, she knows. It's inevitable.

She inhales deeply, holds her breath, then lets out an awful sigh. "I have no choice," she thinks, "because Mónica is my friend and Leticia was like a second daughter." She forces herself to focus on Leticia the girl, not the young woman who went with her husband to that place, who knows where it was.

Dropping her face into her hands, she feels the weight of the task at hand. She is going to tell the Almeidas that Leticia was with Humberto and his friend, and that they may have killed her.

"I have to show you something," she had said as soon as she got to her sister's house that morning. "Your husband and children aren't home, right?"

Her sister shook her head. "What happened to you?" she asked, alarmed by the bandages.

"Nothing, nothing at all. It doesn't matter anymore." Evangelina led her by the hand into the first-floor bathroom, and closed and locked the door behind them. "I don't want the servants to hear," she said. She took the photograph from her purse.

"What is it?"

"Look at it carefully," Evangelina urged her.

Her sister focused her eyes on the snapshot. "That's Humberto," she exclaimed, pointing.

Evangelina nodded, anxious for her sister to understand. "That's Claudia Cosío." She pointed her out.

"Who's Claudia Cosío?"

"The girl who got murdered, our daughter's friend."

"It can't be."

"It is, it's her. That other one is somebody named Pereda from the Public Prosecutor's Office. The picture was taken the day they were killed. Humberto was wearing those trousers that day."

"You think they . . . ?"

"I don't know. I haven't stopped shaking since I found it." She held out her trembling hands.

"Where was it?"

"I found it when I took his clothes to the cleaners. Can you believe it? The idiot left it in his pocket."

"What are you going to do?"

"What should we do?"

"Go to the police?"

"To the police? Didn't I just tell you my husband's buddy is a big shot at the Public Prosecutor's Office? Besides, Humberto has friends everywhere."

Evangelina sat on the lid of the toilet. "Yesterday I had to pick Beatriz up early at school and I left the maid alone in Humberto's study. The silly girl broke a decanter. Then when I got home, Humberto threw me down on the broken glass and kicked me." She held up her bandaged hands.

Her sister eyed the bandages without a word. "Your husband is a jerk. Let's go see your friend."

"Which friend?"

"The one who owns *Observador de Allende*. We'll tell him to publish the picture and then everyone will know." Her sister tapped the corner of the Polaroid on her lower lip as she talked.

"You're going to get it dirty," Evangelina scolded her, snatching it back.

"Let's go to the newspaper."

"I don't know, I don't think that's a good idea."

"You say we can't go to the police."

Evangelina sighed, shrugged her shoulders. "Alright, let's go."

The driver stops the car. Emerging from her thoughts is like climbing out of water. Evangelina pulls a little mirror from her purse and reapplies her lipstick, as if having her mouth perfectly painted would somehow blunt the effect of what she is going to say.

She clears her throat and slowly climbs out of the vehicle.

She rings the bell. She should have called first, but she was in too much of a hurry. Adrenaline courses through her veins, an electric current from head to toe. She brings her nose to her right underarm, sniffs, and makes a face.

"It's Evangelina de Franco," she tells the voice on the intercom. "Evangelina Montero," she corrects herself, thinking she won't use her husband's name anymore. "I've come to see the señora."

After a pause, she hears the same voice. "The señora isn't home. We don't know when she'll be back."

Over the telephone Mónica has told her many times, "I don't want to see anyone. I don't want to get dressed or get out of bed. Nothing."

Evangelina is about to give up and return to the car, when the maid opens the door and asks her in.

FOURTEENTH FRAGMENT

He picked her out at random from the list in my mother's notebook, the only thing of my mother's he cared about. Her name was Estela García. Felícitas was meticulous about keeping track of each patient and the procedures carried out, a medical record of sorts. Maybe she learned that from the doctor who trained her in La Huasteca. Or maybe she intuited that the information would someday be a life-saver — and indeed it almost was.

After my mother died, the three of us stayed on in the house. We never talked about the incident, never reached a common understanding. I continued working at the newspaper, while Julián sometimes worked at my parents' store, La Quebrada, and at other places I don't know about. I have no idea what my father did. He had always been his wife's helper, a man whose strength of will, the youthful ambition he displayed in the oilfields, was crippled even before his withered arm prevented him from getting a good job. The arm itself grew more deformed over time, like a broken wing that kept him at her side. She was his only source of income, so he egged her on.

The three of us were housemates, nothing more. My father charged us rent, and each of us went his own way. Sometimes we crossed paths in one of the rooms, but the abiding tenant was silence, a silence that expanded or contracted like a heartbeat, a presence.

Until the day Julián fractured the silence with a phrase: "Come with me."

Shortly after midnight on June 6, 1944, three years after the death of my mother, twelve hundred Douglas C-47 Dakota planes took off from England, carrying more than 18,000 paratroopers to Normandy. The tide of war was turning. By then I was writing small news stories for the paper. After being the office boy and working in layout and with the typesetters, I got the chance to become the overnight reporter covering what would become my specialty, the crime beat.

It was cool and clear when D-Day dawned. Julián and I were hiding in a doorway across from a house in Colonia Polanco. At about six a man came out, followed half an hour later by a woman. Julián made a sign and we followed her for a couple of blocks. She was wearing high heels and a white dress with purple flowers. Her hair was pulled back, not a strand out of place. She was good-looking, elegant — she had style, as my father liked to say. She turned a corner and stopped beside a black Chevrolet. The driver did not get out to open the door for her; we saw only his hat. She got in quickly and the vehicle pulled away.

"Who is she?"

I had not spoken until that moment, so accustomed was I to my brother's silence that it had not even occurred to me to ask why we were following the woman. I had made a few conjectures along the way, even wondering if he was in love with her. Nothing could have been farther from the truth.

"Estela García," he answered and said no more. We went home without another word.

At ten o'clock that night, Julián turned up at the newspaper: "Come with me."

I insisted I had to stick around in case there was news.

"Come with me," he insisted.

We went home, straight to the room at the back of the yard, where my mother had attended to her patients.

"What's going on?"

My brother opened the door, turned on the light, and I saw a woman curled up underneath my mother's work table. Her hands and feet were bound, and she had a gag across her mouth.

The room stank of mould, of rot; we had not opened it since my mother died.

"What did you do?"

Julián squatted with some effort due to his bad leg. He tried to drag her out; she defended herself and managed to squirm farther under the table, as if she would be safe there. I could smell her nervous sweat. Her eyeliner had run and smudged her cheeks. The perfect hairdo of the morning was a mess. Screams, wails were trapped in the fibres of the cloth that gagged her.

I squatted down. Unthinking, I pulled off the gag.

"Please! Please!"

She was a frightened, cornered animal. She raised her head a little. Then let it fall against the floor.

"Please! I couldn't have it! I told him why!"

She screamed. She begged. She moaned.

My brother pulled the gag back over her mouth. She resisted, but he grabbed her by the hair and banged her head on the floor. The woman went limp.

"Don't touch her!" Julián shouted when I moved my hand towards her. I don't know if I wanted to caress her, release her, wipe her face, or just touch her. It was terrible and it was beautiful. I stood and took a step back.

"She's one of them," he said cuttingly.

There was no need to explain. She was one of the women my

mother helped. Maybe she had an abortion, maybe she had a child and left it behind. I wanted to ask him what her sin had been, but I couldn't find the words, and in any case it didn't matter. She was one of "the women that fed us", as my father referred to them. "We should thank these old whores," he said one day, when three or four of them were in what my mother pompously called "the waiting room". I don't know if my father said it to me, to himself, or to no-one. At that stage I did not understand, yet his words nestled into some corner of my brain and spread like a virus, transforming the women my mother called "clients" or "patients" into the ones responsible for my mother being an abortionist and a child-killer. Responsible for making us bury foetuses, flush them down the toilet, hide them in garbage cans and empty lots. I never imagined the virus would hit Julián so hard. That it would awaken my parents' accursed genes and turn him into a freak.

"Help me hold her up," he said.

I shook my head.

I could not take my eyes off the woman. I was hypnotised.

He kicked her in the stomach and knocked the wind out of her. The woman coughed, unable to catch her breath. Then he turned Estela García face up and put a knee on her chest, just as he had with my mother, and wrapped his hands around her neck.

I watched her fight for her life. Her wrists and ankles were bleeding. Her body convulsed from lack of oxygen. My body, meanwhile, did not seem to react, besides holding my breath. I recognised the approach of death and witnessed its arrival.

Now, trying to describe the details of her death, I think perhaps she is still dying. Maybe the dead only really die when everyone who recalls them disappears. Dying is a continuum.

I don't know when she stopped breathing. Julián shouted something I didn't understand. I remained immobile, converted into a passive assassin. An accomplice.

He got up from the floor, wiped his brow with his forearm, and lit a cigarette. He held the pack out to me and we smoked without speaking. Then, from one of the shelves, he picked up an unexpected object: one of my mother's high-heeled shoes. I recognised it immediately, black, nearly new, because she rarely wore them. They gave her blisters, so she kept them in their shoebox like treasure. Julián raised it high and brought the heel down right in the middle of Estela's forehead, as if making a third eye. He had modified the shoe with a sharp metal heel, something I suppose he learned when he worked with the shoemaker. That would be his mark.

Later on, in the small hours of the morning, when we thought there would be no witnesses, we took her in my father's car to Chapultepec Park. Julián had every detail planned since who knows when. He had washed his face, combed his hair. We left her leaning against a tree, her legs spread, her hands on her belly. Julián had brought along a pillow that he put under her dress, so that from a distance she looked pregnant and about to give birth. The same way my mother appeared in one of the pictures in the paper.

"Here you go," he said. "You've got your story." And he left.

I went back to the office and asked a photographer to accompany me, saying I'd got a tip about a woman's body in Chapultepec Park. I told the police that an anonymous call had come in, and that was that.

The story appeared on page one. My first front-page story. I wrote about the discovery of the body, the conjectures of the police, the identification of the victim, and the notification to the family. After the maid revealed that the señora had a lover, the prime suspect was the husband. I wrote another story about the near certainty of a crime of passion and the detectives' speculations about the strange position of the body. Accusations bounced like ping-pong balls between the husband and the lover. I kept writing in order to take the story as far as possible from Julián and myself. It was almost fun.

Two years before, Ramón had covered the story of Goyo Cárdenas, the Tacuba Strangler, who raped and murdered four women and buried them behind his house. In one of my interviews I asked the police if this could be a Cárdenas copycat. The police did not discount the idea, neither did they embrace it. But it helped lead the story farther afield.

Reflecting on my own behaviour, I have to admit that what I felt more than anything else was fascination. I was as much my mother's son as my brother was, another freak. But I was more like my father, who participated and profited without actually killing. I wonder if remorse kept my father awake at night. Did some internal alarm wail, urging him to confess, even though that would have meant years in prison?

How much did Julián enjoy killing? Did he suffer through it or was he fascinated by the transformation of a human being into a dead body? Did deciding whether someone lives or dies make him feel powerful?

When the story began to be swamped by all the other crimes that happen every day, I wished — and that is the right word — that my brother would kill again.

Then I met Clara. Clarita. Clara who smiled at me from behind a desk. At me. "I like your stories, I like how you write." And suddenly I noticed her face, her hair, her gestures. Then at the movies: her hand, her lips. Touches. Kisses. Caresses. Excitement. Erection. The park. The cafeteria. The street. Her room. The game of love.

How great it feels to have someone waiting for you at the door of a cinema or a cafeteria, in a park, between the sheets. To my surprise, in her bed I shed the hard shell that had kept my inner temperature so cold. Clara had come from Guanajuato to the capital two years before. She lived in a rented room downtown and dreamed of having a family. Before I knew it, I was caught up in her dreams and I too began to long for a life as warm as her skin, soft like her pubic hair, a life without shocks. Boring. Ordinary.

Meanwhile, Julián picked out a second woman, three months after the first. He found her address and followed her for a few days. Lower middle class, a waitress at Café Tacuba. He spied on her, watched her in her uniform serving table after table as if it were a dance. I suspect he liked her tiny figure. She was thinner than the other waitresses, short. She smiled. She kept a smile on her lips the whole day long, as I later learned, even on her breaks when she went into the street for a smoke. As if she were in love.

Here is what I think happened. For three days in a row, he turned up at the café and ordered the same thing. He made sure she was the one to take his order. On the fourth day, he waited for her to ask, "The usual?"

"How can you remember what people want?"

Julián saw her blush. She asked him again if he wanted the usual.

"The usual is coming here to see you."

She altered her smile and tried to get things back on track. Julián ate the usual, smoked a cigarette, then another. He paid and left, forgetting his hat.

She went out after him. "Señor!" she called a couple of times.

Julián waited before turning, he had the scene well rehearsed. "My hat, I'm always forgetting it. Thank you, Señorita..."

"Pilar, my name is Pilar Ruíz."

Then he asked her out: lunch, or supper, or for a cup of coffee. She answered that she couldn't go out with a customer, and he promised never to eat there again.

The following day he took her for ice cream and a stroll through the old part of downtown. Two days in a row he went out with her. On the third, he took her to the house at 9 Cerrada de Salamanca. She would not go in.

"What's wrong?"

"Here..."

He forced her inside, just as he had Estela García, and then he knocked her out with chloroform.

She awoke on the very table where the midwife had attended to her. It took her a few minutes to realise where she was and recollect the last few hours. A bare bulb hanging from the ceiling illuminated the place where she had given birth. She was alone.

Julián left me a note at the newspaper, where I was on the nightshift, saying the body was in Chapultepec Park near the lake. It wasn't easy to find. The same position, leaning against a tree. The hole in the forehead. Her face swollen and purplish, her eyes bloodshot. I made an anonymous call to the police and again pretended the newspaper received one too.

"I've got nothing to do with it," I repeated to Detective José Acosta Suárez when he interrogated me. He knew who I was, my relationship to the woman he had arrested three years before, the Butcher of Little Angels. He insinuated that I might be the murderer. The detectives threatened to use more effective methods to get at the truth.

I wrote up the story and indicated that the police were trying to incriminate me, because they had no idea who could be the murderer of "the Saints", which is what I baptised the victims after someone in the newsroom said that women who die while giving birth are saints and go straight to heaven.

The second victim, found in the same position, as if she had died while giving birth like a saint, answered in life to the name Pilar Ruiz. She was twenty-five years old, a metre fifty tall, hollow-cheeked, and with her entire life ahead of her.

Years later I used the name for a book I wrote, *The Saints*.

My brother developed a routine: he would kill and then disappear for two or three days, to pacify the beast that had taken hold of him. Dr Jekyll and Mr Hyde.

Late one night, I was drinking a cup of coffee and smoking a cigarette, having just returned home after the night shift. Julián came in and sat across from me, picked up the pack of cigarettes, and lit one. I looked at him without speaking.

"You have a girlfriend. She's pretty."

I didn't answer. I didn't nod. I felt something akin to the terror I felt as a child: blind fear that he would do something to her.

"Do you love her?" Julián finished his cigarette.

I was suddenly aware of how exhausted I was. I'd been up for three days waiting for my brother to appear. I looked at his grimy clothes, his greasy hair in disarray, his filthy hands, the blackened fingernails. "Where have you been?" I said.

Ever since Ramón called my mother an ogress, I've felt a perverted fascination with monsters and their stories. Years later I edited a series for the publishing house Novarro. Each story captured the same feeling of terror that seized me that night facing Julián. He was the monster who killed and I was the monster who told the story. Neither of us was interested in hunting down the beast and putting an end to the killing.

"Do you love her?" he repeated.

"I don't know. We monsters don't know how to love." I have to admit, I was terrified of imagining her dead, murdered by my own brother. Was I afraid for her, or afraid of being alone again?

"Pilar Ruiz was pretty too," Julián said after lighting another cigarette. "If she hadn't been one of those women, I might have liked her. She didn't scream, didn't resist. She had a weak heart, like a bird's. I told her about the baby she left with our mother and how he died.

She cried for him and said she hoped eternity would be long enough for him to forgive her."

He finished his cigarette and I caught a hint of disappointment in his expression. Then, as he smoked one cigarette after another, the details poured out. His habitual silence contrasted dramatically with the scrupulous narrations he would make of his murders.

"I'm going to bed," he said, after he put out the last cigarette.

He slept for two full days.

TWENTY-FIVE

Wednesday, September 11, 1985
19.17

Elena was born premature. Her mother was nineteen years old. Soledad had the physical strength and her twin sister Consuelo the brains, at least that's what their father said, and from hearing it so often, the sisters fell in line. Soledad grew to be sturdier and more coordinated than Consuelo. She ran faster, and rode bicycles and horses like a boy.

That is, until she met Elena's father, who disrupted her rough and tumble ways. The entire family was surprised by Soledad's suddenly feminine behaviour, which she exaggerated to convince her future husband she could become a good señora. Love so transformed her that at the end of her pregnancy she could not stand the pain of the contractions or the opening of her pelvis.

Soledad gave birth to a healthy girl, but succumbed to an infection that for a week had her life hanging by a thread. A wet nurse was found, and Consuelo was put in charge of the newborn, who cried nonstop for nearly six months. Fourteen years went by before Soledad got pregnant again, and once Alberto was born she only had eyes for her sickly son. Teenage Elena felt displaced, abandoned, and above all betrayed, very much as she feels now.

Returning from the lake at dusk with Ignacio's manuscript under her arm, Elena meets Consuelo at the front door.

"I'm going to the hospital to see José María," her aunt says, but Elena walks on without replying.

"Elena, where were you all afternoon?"

"Out and about."

Consuelo grips her arm. "Elena, I get it that not much time has passed since Ignacio died. I understand you're in mourning. But I can't take care of your mother and the hotel and José María all by myself."

"Yes, yes. Auntie, I promise I'll put more effort into the hotel. I just need two or three days, that's all. I have to sort out a few things about Ignacio, and then I'll take charge of the place the way I used to. Just a couple of days."

"Are you alright?"

"I'm fine. Sad and angry. The usual."

Consuelo strokes her cheek, the way she did when Elena was a newborn, running the tip of her finger across her face to calm her sobbing, make her sleep.

"I know, but you'll get over it. Time heals all wounds, you'll see."

"Some wounds can't be healed."

"How's that?"

"Don't mind me. I'll tell you about it later. Give my love to José María."

"Do I have to worry about you too?"

"No, auntie, no. I'm fine, really."

Elena kisses Consuelo on the forehead and walks to her office, where she dials Lucina's number.

"Can you come to the hotel?"

"Now?"

"I just read it."

"I'm finishing up with a patient. Let's hope I don't have to run and catch a baby."

"Someone's looking for you, señora," one of the staff says.

"Esteban?"

"Sorry for dropping in like this."

"I was going to call you. Lucina's on her way over. We need to talk about what Lucina gave us to read. Sit down."

Esteban takes the chair across from Elena. Her copy of the typescript lies on the desk.

"Ignacio was Manuel?" she says.

"Who knows? It looks to me like notes for the sort of novel he used to write."

"Notes he left unfinished." Elena shakes her head, as if she were denying it, her eyes fixed on the ceiling. "How can we know if it's true? It mentions his children, his marriage, Lucina. What about the murders? Do you think he could have killed..."

"Leticia and Claudia? As far as I got in my examination of the bodies that seems unlikely, although it's true I didn't have time to finish. I don't want to jump to any conclusions. Besides, I've been doing some investigating with Leticia Almeida's father. On Sunday we met up with a friend of hers and she told us Leticia was going out with an older man. We couldn't get more out of her because she was really scared."

"You went with Leticia's father?"

"He came to see me when the photographs were published. I was planning to tell you and Lucina, but I didn't get a chance."

"Do you think that older man is... was Ignacio?"

"I don't think so."

"But you read what he wrote."

"Yes, he wrote that his brother was a murderer."

"And he was his accomplice."

"Elena, we can't take everything he wrote there at face value. He wrote fiction, it could all be made up."

"Why would he give it to Lucina if it weren't the truth?"

"Maybe it's the manuscript of his last novel and he gave it to her so that it wouldn't get lost."

"I'd like to think it's a novel. Really, I would. If it's not, then I've spent three years with a murderer. Can you imagine? I can't believe it. How could I not have seen it? Or at least suspected it? Suppose he is the murderer, what's going to happen to this hotel? To my life? To my family? I don't want to think about all the things people will say."

"Elena, take it easy. Don't be so hard on yourself."

A couple of knocks on the door interrupt them, and Lucina opens it timidly. "The receptionist told me you were here."

"Are you feeling any better?" Esteban asks, taking her hand and staring into her eyes, not giving her the chance to look away.

"Yes, better," she nods.

The day before, after Lucina gave them the copies, Esteban had caught up with her in the street. She was muttering that she should have listened to her mother, that she was an idiot, a jerk for having believed Ignacio. Suddenly she yelled, "Godammit, Esteban. He was a bastard, a murderer!"

The pathologist had tried to calm her, but living people were not his forte.

"And on top of everything else, she wasn't my mother. Isabel was not my mother."

Esteban listened, although he could not understand.

"It was a lie, Esteban. A lie." Lucina's voice was so loud that passersby turned to stare. Esteban awkwardly wrapped his arms around her.

Now Lucina sinks into one of Elena's office chairs. "I spoke with my brother Jesús, Isabel's son, and he confirmed part of what's in the memoir. My mother — Isabel, asked him not to tell me the truth. He couldn't live with us because we were fleeing all the time. That was the reason. And it was all because of me, it was my fault."

"Running away was Isabel's decision," Elena says. "Don't blame yourself."

"We have to find out what's true and what's not. And I've got more to tell you," Esteban says, taking a pack of Viceroys from his shirt pocket. Elena reaches for one. "I thought you didn't smoke," he says. "And besides, there's no smoking in the hotel." He strikes a match and lights her cigarette, then his own.

"I quit five years ago," Elena says, spreading her hands. "One of the things I did to get pregnant, right?" She points at Lucina, who shrugs. "This is the moment to start again." She inhales the smoke, feeling a little dizzy and at the same time captivated by the nearly forgotten pleasure of the first drag.

"Leticia's father and I went to places where his daughter hung out," Esteban says. "We talked with her friends."

"Wait, wait," Lucina interrupts him. "You went with whom? Why? Slow down."

"Sorry." Esteban recounts how he met up with Señor Almeida and told him he didn't think the police would investigate the murders.

"What do you mean, they won't investigate?" Lucina says.

"From the beginning they wouldn't let me finish the autopsies and they rewrote my reports."

"They brought me in for an interrogation and showed me a folder full of documents," Elena says. "I think there is an investigation, but it's focused on Ignacio and José María, because the pictures were in Ignacio's car and José María was with him."

"They were just trying to scare you," Esteban says confidently.

"How do you know that?"

"Because I know the system, I've spent years working inside it. What did they ask you?"

"They wanted to know what Ignacio did that night. I felt like they were forcing me to make a statement against him. They wanted me to say I got so drunk I lost track of him."

Esteban says, "They like to use a file full of documents to make it seem like they have proof. It's one of their tactics, the most innocuous."

"Did you and Señor Almeida find out anything?" Elena wants to know. She's on the edge of her seat.

"We looked up their girlfriends, asked them the questions nobody else had asked. We took it one step at a time. The authorities are probably betting on people's short memories and desire to just get on with life. We Mexicans don't like digging around in our wounds. We always hope they'll heal, even when we know the flesh is rotting underneath."

"But what did you find out?" Elena insists.

"Sorry. I get carried away. Leticia's old boyfriend was first on Señor Almeida's list. The kid didn't want to talk to us, but his mother invited us in for coffee and tried to tell us how sorry she was. The boy opened up a little. He swore he broke off with her because she was fooling around with someone who bought her expensive gifts. Almeida didn't know anything about it."

"Poor fellow."

"The boy suspected it was an older guy, nobody his age could afford presents like that. He gave us the names of other friends and their numbers."

"Do you think that older guy is the murderer?" Elena asks.

"I have no way of knowing."

"Honestly, it's terrible to say, but right now I don't care who killed the girls," Lucina says. "I need to learn the truth about me. Who was that man who claimed to be my father? Manuel? Or Ignacio?"

"I understand," Esteban says.

"I remember the day he walked into my office unannounced. 'You're a gynaecologist,' he said. 'You look like your mother.' I shook my head. I told him he was mixing me up with somebody else. 'I'm your father,' he said. Just like that."

Lucina gets up from her chair and steps to the window looking onto the courtyard. She buries her face in her hands and heaves a deep sigh. Elena and Esteban watch, not daring to speak. Then Lucina crosses her arms.

"I asked him to leave. 'Isabel can corroborate that I am your father,' he said. Again I asked him to leave, I even thought of calling my husband. 'Wait, please,' he pleaded with me, 'I've been looking for you for years.' He told me he had hired private investigators, but whenever they got close to us, we disappeared. Isabel must have had a sixth sense. 'Allow me to convince you I am your father,' he said. My mother's words kept going through my head: 'Your father wants to kill you. Your father wants to kill you.' But my curiosity was greater than my fear. I agreed to meet him again, even though my knees were shaking. So I saw him again, but always in public places with lots of people around, and always near the exit. Little by little, I lowered my guard, I let him into my life . . . Was I ever stupid! Now I'm thinking I should go see Julián in prison. He's the only one who could tell me the truth, though I don't know if he would. Still, I ought to try."

"I've got friends in the Public Prosecutor's Office who could get you in."

"Yes, Esteban, please. I need to know the truth."

"I'll go with you, Lucy. I promise." Esteban goes to her and rests his hand on her shoulder.

"What astounded me, reading the memoir," Elena says, "is the lack of feeling."

Esteban sits back down. "What do you mean?"

"Didn't you see? Ignacio was like a spectator to everything, an observer who witnesses the most atrocious acts but never feels a thing. He doesn't get upset, he doesn't get frightened, he doesn't run away or try to steer clear, and he certainly doesn't try to stop any of it."

"I did notice that," Esteban says. "It's why I thought maybe it was the draft of a novel."

"I need to show you something else," Elena says. "Come with me."

Esteban and Lucina follow her along the side of the pool, drawing curious glances from the guests.

"How could I have been with him for so long and see not a hint? I'm blind and stupid." Elena shakes her head as she walks.

"He was a charmer," Esteban suggests.

"A charmer. That's the word," Lucina agrees. "The first day we met I was impressed with his manners, his way of dressing, his grey hair combed straight back. That ascot he wore was so out of fashion, but it looked good on him. His hands were big and manly, yet manicured like a woman's. He took such care with his appearance, I assumed he was gay. Later I figured it was his need for control. He couldn't allow even a hair out of place."

At the door to her room, Elena says, "Ignacio wouldn't let me touch his things. He'd lock his room and wouldn't let anyone clean it unless he was there. The day he died, he told me to hide all his belongings, so that his children wouldn't find them."

Once inside, Elena opens a box and shows them the contents. Lucina brings one hand to her mouth to stifle a scream. Esteban reaches in and picks up a woman's shoe, one of a number in the box.

"Why would he have . . . ? Why would he keep . . . ? Are these the shoes of the women his brother murdered? Or maybe he was . . . ?"

Elena puts her hands on her cheeks. "I don't know."

Esteban turns the shoe over, then puts it back in the box. "I'm thinking these are trophies, like souvenirs, good-luck charms, a fetish of some sort. But I don't want to get carried away." He picks up another shoe. They are all singles, unmatched. "Now I know what the murderer used to leave his mark on one of those girls: a shoe. Just like Julián would do. Stiletto heels, two millimetres wide . . . I had been thinking it was a pistol, a Kolibri."

"What's a Kolibri?"

"A pistol as small as a hummingbird. Ignacio gave me one. Very few were ever made. I have to confess that after I read Ignacio's memoir I thought he might have been the one who killed them, especially given the hole in Claudia Cosío's forehead. It's so much like something that happens in one of his novels. Could it have been done with her own shoe? To find the murderer we need to find the pair, like in Cinderella."

"My God!" Lucina says. "This box makes Ignacio a murder suspect."

Esteban puts the shoe back and closes the box. "I'm going to take this with me, Elena. Let's not guess at it or jump to conclusions, let's investigate."

TWENTY-SIX

Thursday, September 12, 1985
10.00

The stone chapel built by Juan de San Miguel in 1542 today sits in the community of San Miguel el Viejo, a few kilometres outside the city. Adolfo Martínez spends some days keeping the old chapel clean, and other days fishing for carp and bass in the nearby lake that formed when the Laja River was dammed.

Every day he rises before dawn to feed his animals: seven hens, a rooster, a cow, a pig, and his horse. Adolfo is a man of few words, most of them directed at his horse. With his wife, single syllables and grunts somehow suffice. Their house is made of stone and adobe, windows without panes, a thatch roof, and dirt floor, much like the others in this village of rocks and dust, where days are long and most of the inhabitants are related. Adolfo knows the names of all of his neighbours, yet he never says hello when he sees them. He offers a nod from high on his horse, maybe a touch of the finger to the brim of his hat, and that's all.

Today he is racing into the village at a gallop, slapping the sides of his mount. He loses his hat to the branch of a mesquite. He doesn't know who to go to. One of his many compadres happens to cross his path. "A dead woman," he manages to say nearly breathless. Those three words are the only ones he has spoken to his compadre all year. Adolfo gets off his horse as quickly as his seventy years allow. "A dead woman," he says again.

Most days, after the fog lifts, ducks and herons make the reflection of the dawn sky ripple across the lake's surface. Adolfo often imagines his boat is navigating the heavens and the fish are flying through the clouds. This morning he was hauling his boat to the water's edge when he found her, face down in the mud, up against the trunk of a fallen tree.

The lake has swallowed the young and the old, women and men, to feed the hungry branches that line its depths. He turned the woman face up and out of her mouth came a thick black vomit of dirt and liquid. Her blue eyes were discoloured by the water, or so it looked. They reminded him of his blind grandfather's, a gaze that has always haunted him. Had he been a reader he would have thought of the old man's eye in the Edgar Allen Poe story. Her hands were balled into fists and her chestnut-coloured hair snaked like eel grass. Her blouse, once white, had taken on an uncertain tinge somewhere between tan and green, against which the double row of red flowers stood out like lotuses.

The news spread fast, and people gathered at one end of the dam, where the lake's waters empty into what's left of the Laja River. Shock had kept Adolfo from recognising the woman, but soon someone does and Evangelina's name travels all the way to the Montero home, where the family is still asleep. Insistent knocking gets the old man out of bed. It's one of the maids, her face sweaty and flushed after running the five kilometres from the lake. Her tongue is so dry words stick to the roof of her mouth as she tries to explain what Evangelina's father has trouble comprehending: he has to go to the lake, because his daughter has drowned.

Señor Montero slips on his brown shoes and hurries out, still wearing his striped pyjamas. At the lake no-one can stop him from elbowing aside an officer and kneeling beside the body of his daughter. Calling her name without pause, he hugs her to his breast.

"Señor . . ." one of the officers says to the nearly eighty-year-old, "You can't be here." He ignores them. He hears nothing but his own voice repeating Evangelina's name. He doesn't even hear the shouts of his son, who followed him out of the house. The officers insist on separating father and daughter so they can examine the scene. The son tells them he will reason with his father, but when he sees his sister's drowned eyes he too falls to his knees.

Now Evangelina's sister raises her voice above the rest, drawing everyone's attention. "It was Franco! It was Franco!" she screams at her father, at her brother, at Miguel Pereda who has just arrived. She is standing in the mud, not daring to go any closer. She does not want to see her sister dead. "He always beat her. He killed her."

Driven by the same protective impulse he felt when his sisters were small, her brother leaps to his feet to go and find his brother-in-law. The officers take hold of him and decide they had better detain him all morning.

At ten o'clock an ambulance takes Evangelina's body to the morgue. The Montero family follows close behind.

In his study, the publisher of *Diario de Allende* endures Miguel Pereda's reproaches and takes a swig from the bottle of Bacardi in his hand. Bottles of various brands litter the carpet, as do books, pens, picture frames, paperweights, bits of glass, and several objects not easily identified, each of which had its place before falling victim to Humberto Franco's rage.

"Humberto, listen to me, you have to tell me what happened. What did you do to your wife?"

Franco, his face half-hidden behind the bottle, observes Pereda with eyes shot full of alcohol, blood, and hatred. "Do you know what that dimwit did?"

Pereda shakes his head.

"She took the picture to Antonio Gómez. The fucking bitch who never should have been born took the photograph to him."

"What photograph? What are you talking about?"

"The picture that kid took of us that night. Don't you remember?"

"No."

Franco smacks his forehead in despair and takes another swig. Pereda snatches the Bacardi from him. "I need you sober for what's coming next. You're going to have to make a statement."

"A statement? No way . . ." And hiccupping, he goes on, "I'm not going to say an-y-thing. No-thing. Gómez brought me the picture, he's not going to publish it. Take a look, I've got it here."

Franco walks unsteadily amid the debris, bits of which get crushed under his weight. Trying to reach the desk, he trips and cracks his head on the corner.

"Ah, fuck," he shouts. Blood pours from the wound. He brings both hands to his forehead. "Fucking mother!" He rises slowly with help from Pereda, who looks tiny beside his stout companion. Franco manages to get himself to the bathroom, examines the cut on his forehead, and is about to punch the mirror when Pereda grabs him from behind.

"Enough, calm down," he orders. He picks up a towel and soaks it under the tap to clean the wound. "This won't do the trick, you might need stitches."

Humberto Franco stares at himself in the mirror, bends over the sink, and splashes water on his face. Fat drops of blood fall onto the white ceramic. "Fucking whore of a mother!" he mutters as he dries himself.

The deputy public prosecutor goes to the desk. He hears the crunch of glass breaking under his shoes, unaware that it's the framed photograph of Franco's father holding a copy of the newspaper. Humberto himself took the picture when he was twelve and has kept it on his desk since the patriarch died.

Pereda picks up the colour photocopy lying beside an overflowing ashtray. His eyes widen. "Where did this come from?" He studies his own drunken face in the picture. "I look like such an imbecile," he thinks. He stares at Claudia Cosío and something he has not felt in a very long time awakens within him, something close to compassion, but it is only a spark and it quickly burns out, giving way to fear.

Franco comes out of the bathroom, his shirt soaked and bloody, holding the towel to his forehead. More lucid than he was, he avoids the jumble on the floor and collapses in a leather loveseat that by some miracle has come through the massacre unscathed. "Leticia took it that night."

"When? I don't remember."

"After we got to the motel."

"How did your wife get it?"

"Because I'm an idiot. I forgot it was in my trouser pocket. I remembered when Gómez gave me the copy. My wife kept the original."

"Why the hell did your wife give it to Gómez?"

"To fuck with me. She thought he'd publish it. She told him she had the story of the year for him. A long time ago Gómez and I had a disagreement, and we aren't friends. He's a competitor, but he never became an adversary. Last night he came here with the copy and gave it to me. He doesn't want trouble with me or with you."

Franco does not divulge that the disagreement was over Evangelina, who had gone out with Gómez a couple of times before she became Franco's fiancée. Small town, big hell. When Antonio Gómez started up his paper, *El Observador de Allende*, he wanted it to be a counterweight to the stridently pro-government *Diario de Allende*. It wasn't long before he learned that he too had to find allies and win the government's favour, so much so that Franco called him a bootlicker.

"What happened to your wife?"

Franco sighs, shrugs, and ponders what part of the scene from the previous evening he had better not reveal, though in truth he hasn't been able to remember it all. He won't tell Pereda that he was waiting behind the door when she came home, or that he grabbed her and hauled her into his study. Neither will he tell him how he shoved her against one of the side tables, shouting, "What were you going to do with that photograph?" She was begging him not to hit her. "Where have you got the original?" he insisted. "Give it to me!" Probably she never imagined Gómez would betray her. She looked like a little girl caught doing something she shouldn't.

"My wife walked out yesterday when she saw that I had a copy of the picture." Franco presses the towel against his bleeding wound. "She hasn't come back."

"What about the original?"

"I don't know. We'll find out when Evangelina turns up."

"She's dead. Don't you know? A man found her this morning at the edge of the lake, not far from here."

"What?"

"Humberto . . . don't try to fool me. Tell me the truth. What happened?"

"I am telling you the truth. We had a fierce argument and she stalked off."

"Are you sure?"

"Shit, Miguel, of course I'm sure."

Pereda looks him over from top to bottom. The deputy public prosecutor is shaking, his career could be in ruins. "We think it was an accident, Humberto. She tripped in the dark and hit her head on a rock. She fell face down and in the mud she couldn't breathe. They've taken the body to the morgue, but we still don't have a forensic pathologist approved by the state prosecutor. Things are getting very complicated."

Franco can hear his wife's screams. Like images from a movie viewed long ago, his memory projects the scene of Evangelina running ahead of him. It was dark and all he could see was a stumbling shadow. The wind carried her screams away from him, over the surface of the water. When he caught up to her, he put his hands around her neck and squeezed.

"Let's go, let's go. I have to take you in for questioning."

The big man allows Pereda to take hold of his arm, while his brain replays the moment he threw Evangelina down. He hears the crack of her skull when it hit the rock.

The door bursts open.

"Señor!" one of the maids shouts. Behind her is a man who pulls a pistol from his jacket pocket and points it at Franco and then at Pereda. As soon as she spies the weapon, the maid runs out and the man closes the door behind him.

Franco strides towards him. "What the fuck . . . ?"

"Hold it right there!"

Pereda yanks on Franco's arm. "Easy." He puts his hands up and speaks to the intruder. "Easy."

"Ricardo?" Franco says, recognising Ricardo Almeida.

"Who was it? Which of you killed my daughter?" Almeida points at one, then the other. "Which one?" His voice is unravelling.

"Easy," Pereda says again.

"Ricardo . . . no . . . neither of us."

"You were with her that night! You were with her!"

"Yes, I was with Leticia. I don't deny it . . . Look, Ricardo. I don't know how . . . how your daughter . . ."

"Shut up, asshole! Don't you dare talk about my daughter. Shut up!"

Franco brings his hand to the wound in his forehead, which is bleeding again. A red rivulet runs into his right eye.

Almeida raises his pistol. "If you aren't going to tell me, I'll have to kill you both."

"We didn't kill her," Pereda tries to explain, keeping his hands in the air. "We don't know who did."

"You were the ones who took them away."

The previous evening, Evangelina de Franco had gone to the Almeidas' house. But it was not the Evangelina who had been there so many times before. This was a wounded animal, a rabid animal, itching to bite and spread the infection. She had not come to talk, to make amends, or even to try to excuse what her husband had done. No. The Evangelina who crossed their threshold wanted blood.

Mónica de Almeida, in the pyjamas that had become her daily attire since her daughter's death, had thrown on a dressing gown more out of habit than to make herself presentable. "Eva, only because it's you. Really, I don't want to see anyone."

"Moni..."

"Eva, I didn't want to be rude to you. You've been so good to us since it happened."

"Moni, I need to speak with you about Lety's death. I don't know how to do it... I have to show you something."

Mónica de Almeida watched Evangelina take the Polaroid out of her purse and give it a glance, then in what seemed like slow motion, hand it to her. Mónica looked at the photograph, then pulled her glasses from a pocket of her dressing gown. The image came into focus and she recognised her friend's husband and Claudia Cosío, but not the other man. She studied the photograph for what to Evangelina seemed like an hour.

Since Leticia's death, Mónica has been unaware of the passing days. Now time stopped for the two of them, time as they had known it. Mónica felt an electric tremor run up her spine, press both sides of her brain, and seize her heart. She went to one of the living-room chairs and fell into it. The chair creaked under the weight of all she suddenly understood. Her daughter had taken the picture, using the Polaroid camera her father had given her.

Evangelina had no idea what to say. She had gone to the Almeidas' home driven by hatred, anger, frustration, the urge for vengeance, bearing a throbbing pain in her ribs and a dull ache where her husband had hit her.

"Ricardo! Ricardo!" Mónica wailed from the chair where she had collapsed.

Her husband came running down the stairs.

"What's wrong?" So intent was he on his devastated wife that he did not bother to acknowledge Evangelina, who had taken two steps back and was gripping her purse as if it were a lifejacket that could save her from the tempest she had aroused.

Mónica handed him the Polaroid.

"Leticia was with them," Mónica explained, when her husband said nothing.

He turned to Evangelina. "Do you know what happened?"

She shook her head. At some point, amid all the questions Leticia's father threw at her, she asked if she could sit down. She told them the same few facts she had shared with Antonio Gómez, although in that conversation her sister did most of the talking. On the way home, her sister had suggested she go to the Almeidas. "They should know the truth before the news comes out." Now the couple were discussing whether to call Claudia Cosío's parents. Evangelina excused herself.

"I have to go home."

If she had stayed, she would have been privy to the conversation between the Almeidas and the Cosíos about what to do.

She would have heard Mario Cosío — a man she did not like because he mistreated his wife — insist that no good would come from confronting the police. His mind was set on leaving things as they were, because nothing would bring his daughter back.

She also would have heard Martha de Cosío call her husband a coward.

She would have seen Ricardo Almeida step between the two of them. But above all, she would have seen Martha point her finger at her husband and declare, "No, Mario, you aren't going to hit me anymore."

Neither did she see Mario Cosío storm out and slam the door behind him. Or the two women embrace.

Had she witnessed the scene, she might still be alive.

Martha and Mónica decided to consult a lawyer, and through him get to a judge and the state prosecutor. They made a list of their acquaintances in government, the ones they imagined were less corrupt. Ricardo agreed, disagreed, voiced his opinion, but in his mind an image was gaining strength: his Smith & Wesson .38 special, which he liked to take to the shooting range once or twice a month.

"The only way I'll find some peace is when those swines are in prison or dead," he told Mónica hours later, when he finally climbed into bed hoping to get some sleep. He got none.

In the morning he went out, promising to be back in time for the meeting with the lawyer. Outside Humberto Franco's house, he learned of the uproar caused by Evangelina's death, and he sat in his vehicle until he was sure only Franco and Pereda were there.

Mónica waited all morning for him to return. Then, guessing his intentions, she looked where he kept the gun and, seeing it gone, raced to Franco's house.

Now Mónica de Almeida throws open the door to Franco's study. "No, Ricardo!" she screams.

Taking advantage of the distraction, Franco dives at Almeida.

Leticia's father pulls the trigger.

The scene freezes, then Franco falls to the floor amid the clatter and crash of things breaking.

FIFTEENTH FRAGMENT

After my mother died, my father no longer cared about his appearance. His beard, untrimmed and uncombed, was a patchy mix of dense, sparse, and non-existent. His facial hairs seemed to be avoiding each other, the way we three murderers shared the same space, but never touched. As I said, all we did was split the rent.

He stopped wearing his suits. If shoes were my mother's prized possessions, my father's were his tailor-made suits. He spent the money his wife earned on hats, jackets, shirts, ties.

There ought to be a taxonomy for different types of accomplices to murder. A simple accomplice participates in a crime without being its direct author, while someone who consciously and voluntarily collaborates, fulfilling an essential role, is more like a co-author.

My father was both. His specialty was selling children. Maybe that's why he enjoyed dressing up like a door-to-door salesman hawking encyclopedias or vacuum cleaners: "Ladies, I have the latest thing in children for your home." But he was also the brains behind the operation, the one making the decisions. The creation of the Ogress was his inspiration.

Bereft of my mother, his life lost meaning. When the dog died, so did the rabies, as well as his merchandise and his complicity. One day he sold La Quebrada and vanished, leaving his suits hanging in the closet. Since he often slept elsewhere, I did not take note of his absence until he had been gone a week. I asked Julián and he merely shrugged.

A few days later, I explored the unknown terrain of my parents' bedroom. Stepping into that forbidden chamber felt like a heinous crime. The closet still held my mother's clothing and her scent, an aroma so repellent that I recoiled and found myself on the floor, the wind knocked out of me. From there I observed the clothes on their hangers, suspended in time. Fibres of the past clinging to the present. I got up, pulled them off their perches, and piled them on the floor, building a mountain of the geological layers of my mother's life — and my own. The memories made me dizzy.

Her clothes, shoes, and purses shared the fate of the foetus remains. I put them in burlap bags and abandoned them in empty lots and distant garbage cans. I wanted those remnants far, far away from me. Today perhaps the Ogress' clothing adorns a beggar or a garbage-picker, their body odours mingling, the wearer oblivious to the fact that the weave, like my genes, holds the evil beating heart of Felícitas.

I left my father's things untouched in case he returned, although one thought kept churning through my neurons: maybe my brother was behind his disappearance. I did not find out then, and I do not know now. I'll never know. The reason I never asked, I confess, was that deep down I wanted him to have done it.

Eventually I got rid of my father's things too.

A few years ago I wrote a short novel that sold well and has been through several printings. I wrote it to exorcise a recurring, obsessive fantasy about meeting someone wearing my parents' clothes. It had got so bad I went around examining beggars' attire. The novel tells the story of a man who sees a woman wearing a dress of his mother's that he had given to a charity shop. He trails the woman to a house in a middle-class neighbourhood, not far from where he lives. He introduces himself and in time they become friends. The woman, who works at the same charity shop, admits that the employees often keep the best items for themselves. The first and only time they make love, he asks her to put on the dress. He hugs her, kisses her, sniffs her all over, desperately seeking some trace of his mother. At one point he thinks he detects her scent, and he thrusts into her, clinging to the fabric, which tears as he climaxes, shouting ecstatically, "Mamá!"

TWENTY-SEVEN

Friday, September 13, 1985
11.45

The march is about to begin. It will set out at noon from the central plaza. The sky is leaden, like the spirits of the people gathering. All of them are dressed in white. The idea originated with a woman named Tierry Smith, a neighbour of the Cosíos, who at seven this morning sent out word, inviting everyone to protest the authorities' apparent unwillingness to solve the murders of Leticia Almeida and Claudia Cosío.

Martha de Cosío had stayed so late at the Almeidas' house discussing what to do about the photograph, she spent the night on their sofa-bed. Returning home in the pre-dawn darkness, she was relieved to find the house was empty. Although she had lived there for the past twenty years, Martha felt as if she were entering her house for the first time. The floors, the walls, even the paintings which she herself had hung, seemed alien, as if the house belonged to someone with different taste. She noticed the smell, something she had not even been aware of before, and did not like it. A foreigner in her own home.

She ran her hand along the kitchen counter piled high with dirty dishes left there by her children and her husband. The few times she got around to washing and cleaning after Claudia died, it was only to keep from thinking. She no longer cared.

In the shower, the water felt like a baptism, rinsing tears and dead skin into a whirlpool at her feet. While she dressed she considered making the bed and tidying up a bit. Instead, she stared at the photograph Mónica de Almeida had given her. It was the last picture of Claudia and she brought it to her breast. Guilt was eating away at her. She was the one who had given Claudia permission to go out. She was well aware that her daughter might sin, but at least she would be safe from her violent father. Anything I do in penance will never be enough to find forgiveness, she thought.

An image of the Virgin sat on a shelf above the prie-dieu where Martha knelt daily, praying to the god who had allowed two demons to abuse and kill her girl. With one swipe of her hand, she sent the porcelain figure flying. Mary landed on the floor tiles, decapitated. Crucifixes scattered across the floor too, along with rosaries and medallions, the shards of twenty years of marriage.

As she and Mónica had agreed, at six-thirty she knocked on her neighbour's door. Tierry Smith, the wife of a lieutenant colonel who had fought in Vietnam, had moved to San Miguel a few years before. Martha told her the story and said no-one in the city dared confront Franco or the Public Prosecutor's Office. "Maybe no Mexican would dare," Tierry told her, "but we Americans aren't afraid. We live here too, and we aren't about to let an atrocity like this go unpunished."

News of the march spread like wildfire and by mid-morning dozens of Americans had agreed to take the lead. Copies of the photograph were handed out and the face of Claudia Cosío, perched precariously on the motel bed, became their standard.

The first drops of rain begin to fall as the marchers set out. The sky rumbles a few times. Unintimidated, they stride resolutely over the cobblestones towards their destination, City Hall.

Taking short nervous steps, Miguel Pereda paces the mayor's office. With him are three others: criminal court judge Bernabé Castillo; the public prosecutor for the state of Guanajuato; and the mayor himself. "Judge Castillo, you wouldn't see us when we went to your office," Pereda repeats for the third time. The judge looks out of the window, hoping it will pour hard enough to scatter the demonstrators.

"I didn't want to see Franco. I can't stand that arrogant bozo."

"Things got complicated," Pereda says. "We tried to contain the story. We even found a culprit. It only got out of hand thanks to the idiot Franco."

"Miguel, buddy, you've got to resign or we'll have to fire you," the prosecutor says. "There's no way around it."

"If I'm going down, everyone's going down: Franco, Judge Castillo, you."

"Don't threaten me, asshole. You two are the only ones in that photograph. The Americans are all riled up and neither the governor nor I can allow that. Be a good guy and resign. Later on, we'll see, maybe you'll be able to come back."

"What about Franco?"

"Miguel, you worry about yourself," the mayor intervenes. "The two of you are the main suspects in the murders. Besides, it certainly looks like Franco murdered his wife."

"Franco's wife is another story, but I can assure you we did not kill those bitches."

"You don't have the credibility to assure us of anything," Judge Castillo says.

"For the moment we've given del Valle back his job; he can take charge of the autopsy of Evangelina Montero," the state prosecutor says. "Miguel, I'll expect your letter of resignation. It's your best option. You can say you're leaving because you're innocent and you don't want to taint the investigation, plus you're eager to cooperate. We have no idea what will happen after the march."

The demonstrators advance slowly, their signs in Spanish and English rising and falling with each step. The rain pours down on the marchers and the sizable crowd of spectators, but it does not drown out the chants of "No Impunity", "Punish the Murderers".

The shouts echo off the walls of the General Hospital, where Esteban del Valle is unearthing the secrets held inside Evangelina Montero's body. He observes her face, now washed clean of mud.

"What happened?" he says. He is not able to reconstruct the entire scene from the body of this woman still beautiful in death. He can imagine the moment she fell and the blow she received at the base of her brain. He doesn't know that she ran out into the dark to get away from her husband, convinced she was running for her life. Neither does he know that Franco threw her to the ground or that her skull hit a rock and her body rolled to the water's edge, face down.

None of that will be in del Valle's report. However, he will write that she had other wounds, older ones, sprained ribs, internal bruising. He can imagine Humberto Franco hitting her. "He was a bastard, wasn't he?" he says, as he wipes the side of her body with gauze.

The rain lets up, defeated by the marchers' resistance. The chanting lets up too and now what echoes off the walls and tile roofs, the narrow streets and low kerbs, is silence.

Virginia Aldama holds a closed umbrella in her hand. Despite the downpour she never opened it. Leopoldo López had come over early to tell her and her husband about the march. Since the murders, the two funeral home owners have renewed their friendship. Virginia, however, marches alone; her husband refused. "A murdered girl is not like any of the other dead bodies that come here," she told him.

His only response was to raise an eyebrow. Virginia pats her sopping hair in an effort to repair the irreparable. She feels very close to Leticia Almeida, as if finding her in the intimacy of death had made her part of the family.

The wave of white reaches the offices of *Diario de Allende*, where it pauses briefly. Cries of "Coward", "Murderer", "Abuser", "Rapist", reach the newsroom, where minutes before the editor and reporters were debating whether to publish a notice of Evangelina de Franco's death, and whether to cover the march. Leonardo Álvarez closes the windows to block the shouting.

In the hospital, three floors above the morgue, the widower Humberto Franco asks a nurse for more painkillers. With him are his daughter, his driver, and his lawyer. Outside the room stands a police officer. Officially, Franco is detained, a murder suspect, but the envelope full of money his lawyer delivered ensures no-one says so publicly and the guard is just for show.

"Papá, tell me what happened. Did you kill her?" His daughter is at his side because his driver, at Franco's behest, has blocked the door.

"You've got your plane ticket, you leave tonight," the lawyer talks over Beatriz. "You've got to get out right away. We'll take you by helicopter to the airport in Mexico City. Everything is ready, the specialist in Houston will be waiting for you."

"Houston? You're going to Houston? Papá, tell me the truth, did you kill Mamá?"

"Of course I'm going. Here, they want to amputate my leg and lock me up for a crime I didn't commit. And you're coming with me."

"I'm not going anywhere with you. Besides, we have to bury..."

"Your aunt and your grandparents will take care of the funeral."

"No! I can't leave. I don't want to go! You're crazy!" Her voice breaks into a sob.

The night before, at her aunt's house, she and her cousin had snuck a bottle of tequila from the dining-room cabinet and taken it into the bedroom. Her cousin told her she had to forget her troubles; she shouldn't have to deal with her parents or their squabbles, or be her mother's protector. For all those reasons, they kept toasting each other straight from the bottle, and soon laughter took the edge off their worries. Her aunt let them both sleep in. Not until mid-morning, and only after Esteban del Valle called to say the autopsy would take some time, did she break the news to her niece.

"Your mother is dead," she said, sitting on the edge of the bed where the two cousins were struggling with their hangovers. She intended to leave it at that, but her own frustration and anger took over. "I think your father killed her." Her words came out in a strangled voice and she had to lie back on the bed to catch her breath while her daughter hugged Beatriz.

"You can't all be in here at once," a nurse says sternly when she and a doctor walk in.

"Humberto, if you leave," says the doctor, "there is no guarantee they'll save your leg. You might get blood poisoning and gangrene."

"It doesn't matter. I can't stay."

He fears for his leg, but what really terrifies him is the rest of what may happen. And he cannot wipe from his mind the sound of his wife's skull cracking against the rock.

Hundreds are now marching towards City Hall and the photograph Leticia took is everywhere.

Three floors down, Evangelina's sister waits outside the morgue. She blames her brother-in-law, even started shouting his name and calling him "murderer", until the hospital staff made her stop. Sitting in the same chair where days before Mónica de Almeida had waited for the body of her daughter, she holds a perfumed handkerchief over her nose. She has not cried for her sister. She refuses to allow tears to dilute her furious desire for vengeance.

The march passes by Posada Alberto. Several American guests watch from the entranceway. "What happened?" a girl asks her father.

Consuelo answers from behind them. "Somebody murdered two girls a few days ago. They're marching to insist the government catch the murderer."

Consuelo recognises many of the marchers, greets them with a wave or a nod.

"Chelo, come with us," a woman calls out.

"I can't. We've got a lot of work."

"This is more important. You aren't going to have any work at all if crime keeps the tourists away."

"I know, but I can't," she says firmly. She asks one of the employees about Elena and learns she went out some time ago. "I'd better hire another nurse for Soledad," Consuelo thinks, "until Elena can do her part."

Down the hall from Humberto Franco's hospital room, Elena Galván observes José María's uneasy breathing, his diminished state. "Josema," she says in a low voice. She feels silly, but everyone says people in a coma can hear what's said to them. "You have to wake up and tell me about the accident with Ignacio. Why were you together? I just found out that Ignacio wasn't Ignacio, he was Manuel. He was the son of a child-killer and he changed his name. His brother's in prison for murdering four women, including his mother. I won't read you what he wrote; it's brutal and callous. I don't know if you can hear me. Maybe I'm saying things I shouldn't. He kept a box of women's shoes. Oh, and he had a daughter. That's why he came to San Miguel and that's why he stayed. I spent three years in a relationship with a stranger. Well, in reality, it was only a year and a half. I don't know if I'm in mourning or if I'm angry or astonished or what."

Elena takes a deep breath and everything she hasn't said, all her doubts and accumulated exhaustion, are expelled in one long sigh. She strokes his forehead and kisses him between the eyebrows. "I'll be back soon," she says, and leaves the room.

In the corridor she hears someone shout, "I won't go with you!" She turns and finds herself face-to-face with Beatriz Franco walking beside her father, who is laid out on a gurney pushed by an orderly and a nurse.

"I'm not asking, stupid girl."

"Try to make me."

"Sebastián, make her," he orders his driver.

"No, Humberto. Leave your daughter alone. Everything's in the car. We've got to go right now, before they stop you."

Beatriz slips by Elena and pounds down the stairs, while the men disappear behind the elevator doors.

The sun peeks out from behind a cloud nearly as white as the attire of most of the marchers. They are a little more than a kilometre from their goal.

Uncertain of herself, Lucina steps into the street. One of her patients pats her on the back and congratulates her. "I wouldn't miss it," Lucina says. "Leticia Almeida was my patient."

The woman's husband speaks up. "You did right to come, doctor. Those imbeciles in government have to stop screwing around and find who did it." His white shirt gleams above his jeans.

"You had better get going," the state prosecutor tells Miguel Pereda. "The gringos' march will be here soon and I don't want them to see us together. You have to resign, Miguel. It's for the greater good."

"I'll think about it," he says, picking up his coat.

"It's an order."

Pereda opens the office door and the shouts of the marchers reach them.

"One more thing, Pereda," Judge Castillo stops him. "Let Ricardo Almeida go. We have nothing on him. The shot was Franco's fault, you know that."

"He went there to kill us."

"He didn't kill you. Too bad. Release him immediately."

The mayor edges to the window, straightens his tie, and brushes off the shoulders of his suit. In the distance he spies a rainbow and under its arc come the first marchers in white.

TWENTY-EIGHT

Friday, September 13, 1985
21.00

Consuelo sits down to take off her dark stockings. Since José María's accident, she has moved into Soledad's bedroom to keep her company. She knows her sister is uneasy, anxious about her husband. The twins have had that intuitive bond since birth.

Soledad's eyes follow Consuelo as she moves to the bathroom, the closet, the chest of drawers. The pyjamas Consuelo puts on are identical to her sister's; she still enjoys dressing like her twin, if only for sleeping. The vanilla scent of her skin cream fills the room.

"We've got no vacancies," she says, rubbing cream into her sister's arms. "This'll keep you hydrated and you'll smell nice instead of like bed." She turns her sister on her side. "It feels great, right?"

She straightens Soledad's pyjamas and smooths the sheets, fluffs the pillows, brings her a glass of water with a straw. "Today a pipe broke. You can't imagine the chaos. Room seven was flooded and the plumber was late because of the demon — Ah, of course, you don't know..."

Consuelo busies herself folding her clothes and putting them in the closet to distract her sister from what nearly slipped out. She has told her nothing about the murders or about José María's accident. Concentrating on the hangers, she counts them in her mind, a strategy she has employed since she was a girl whenever she doesn't want her sister to read her thoughts. If her sister manages to get into her head, all she'll find are numbers.

On more than one occasion she has gone to Soledad with a pillow in her hands, tempted to put an end to this life that is no life. Seeing her sister like this has put her through every emotion: anger, fury, frustration, sadness, denial, compassion, pity.

"One, two, three, four, five . . ." She slides the hangers along the rod. She already knows there are fifty-three, but she concentrates as if she didn't. "Seven, eight, nine . . ."

"Josema?" she hears suddenly. Poking her head out from the closet, she says, "Are you getting inside my head?"

It has been so long since she last heard Soledad's voice, husky like her own from years of nearly two packs a day. Consuelo stopped smoking soon after Soledad came home from the hospital transformed, as she says behind her back, into "my sister the piece of furniture". Consuelo smoked her last cigarette while loudly declaring she was quitting because they did not taste the same without Soledad. "We started smoking together and together we'll quit," she swore, and she stubbed it out so her sister could see.

"Josema," she hears again.

"Chole? Did you say something?"

She goes to her and sees that her mouth is open as if to speak, but nothing more issues from her lips. Consuelo wipes the saliva from her sister's chin and stares at her. "Since Soledad's stroke we've lost our connection," she'll explain to anyone willing to listen, and then she'll mention the day they first menstruated. They were sleeping in the same bed. They were in grade four, but there was no way to persuade them to sleep apart. Consuelo was the first to wake up when she felt the seepage between her legs. Half-asleep, she went down the hall to the bathroom and sat on the toilet, eyes closed. She opened them to reach for the toilet paper and she saw the blood in her panties and in the toilet. Before she could scream, her sister joined her in the bathroom.

"I'm dying," Soledad said. "I've got blood on my legs and there's blood on the mattress."

"Me too," Consuelo said. "Something broke inside me. Look at my underwear. We're both going to die."

Alerted by her daughters' wails, their mother found them hugging each other. "We're dying," they told her, and she brought a box out of its hiding place among the towels, and gave them each a little white napkin folded over three times.

"This happens to all of us women. You're going to bleed every month." The following day their mother got rid of the double bed and brought in two singles. "Since you're not girls anymore, you'd better sleep like adults."

Now with her face very close, Consuelo can smell her sister's rancid breath. "Chole?" She gently closes her mouth, again wipes her chin, caresses her cheeks. They are no longer identical. Since her stroke Soledad seems to have aged ten years.

Consuelo turns Soledad onto her side, slips between the sheets, and presses her body against her sister's. Even after their mother separated them, morning always found them together in one of the two beds. Consuelo puts her arm around Soledad. "José María will be back soon, I promise," she whispers in her ear, and she hugs her.

SIXTEENTH FRAGMENT

My children dropped by. That best defines what goes on between us: We drop by each other's lives, we don't stay. When their regret at having no relationship with their father becomes too intense, they try to ease their consciences. "Got to see the old man," they must tell themselves. They don't call ahead; they know I'm usually home. As soon as they walk in the door, they feel uncomfortable and are ready to hurry away. They don't know it, but the ghosts of dead children are climbing up their backs, whispering in their ears.

"Why do you like this house?" they ask.

"Because I grew up here." I ought to say, "I'm keeping the dead children company." Dialogue for a horror movie.

This time Andrés went over to my desk and rifled through a few pages of this manuscript without paying the least attention, a habit he picked up in childhood. Whenever he asked what I was writing, my response was always cold: "A book." He never liked that reply, so he would start fingering the pile of typewritten pages.

"Am I going to like it?" he would say.

"I don't know, but if you don't get lost no-one's going to like it." And I'd slap him. He'd run crying to his mother, who would give me a hard time for scaring him.

The other day Andrés asked his usual question and glanced at these pages. He wasn't expecting an answer. I wanted to tell him I was writing an autobiography of sorts, but before I had the chance to open my mouth he declared, "It doesn't matter, I won't read it."

None of my kids read my books. I don't lose any sleep over it, since I never expected them to. I've never written for them. Some writers write for their friends, their family, hoping they'll read it and continue loving them. Not me.

Whenever I'm asked why I write crime novels, I say the genre chose me. I thought I would be a reporter my whole life. No, I lie. I didn't think anything. I never imagined the future. I was a reporter, full stop.

In 1946 Ramón introduced me to the man who gave me a future, Antonio Helú. A son of Lebanese immigrants, he had just started a magazine for Mexican crime fiction, *Selecciones Policiacas y de Misterio*. By then Ramón was the paper's editor-in-chief and I was still writing stories for the crime pages, as well as features and interviews.

Antonio needed writers for his magazine. "Why don't you give it a whirl?" he said.

It took me weeks to come up with my first story. He rejected it, but said I had potential and appointed himself my mentor. He was the one who introduced me to Edgar Allen Poe, Arthur Conan Doyle, Agatha Christie, Raymond Chandler, Dashiell Hammett. It was love at first sight, from the very first page. On my third try he published a story of mine. Then he invited me to join his Morgue Street Club, where I met other writers of crime fiction and dreamed of becoming one myself.

Eventually, I wrote a few chapters of a book I called *The Adventures of Chucho Cárdenas*, featuring a reporter who worked at a newspaper identical to *La Prensa*. I started hiding behind a pseudonym. Soon I was writing for the theatre and the movies.

In between scripts, stories, reporting, and work for hire, I wrote my first novel, which was based on the never-solved murders of "the Saints". In it I resuscitated José Acosta, the detective who had arrested my brother and, before that, handled the case of my mother, the

Butcher of Little Angels. Of all the policemen I ever met, Acosta was the only anti-cop. He was honest, and he held himself to an admirable code of ethics. Investigating my mother, he always showed respect and empathy. Acosta died soon after I began the book, so I stole his name, his physical appearance, his mannerisms, and I ended up writing a series of novels with him as the protagonist.

It was also through Helú that I met Graciela, my wife, at an afternoon gathering he hosted. "My parents are Spaniards," Graciela told me. I replied that mine were likely from San Luis Potosí, but who knew? For some reason she thought that was delightful. A year later we were married.

Graciela learned that I could not have children a few days after the wedding. When I told her, I didn't explain why. The vasectomy I'd had a few years before was, perhaps, the only moral act I have ever performed. I wanted to put an end to my parents' evil genes.

We decided to adopt. Andrés and Antonio married good women, as Graciela likes to call them. I call them boring.

I always ask my sons about my grandchildren, but it's purely a formality. "Fine," they answer, in unison, their eyes on the clock. After they've listened to the ice cubes tinkling in their Coca-Colas for nearly half an hour, they depart. They are so unlike you, Lucina, blood of my blood.

My wife chose the boys' names, my ex-wife I mean. Forgetting the "ex" shifts the scene completely, taking me back to when we were a family: father, mother, and the two sons we imported from Spain. When my father-in-law learned I couldn't give him a descendent, he got in touch with some nuns in Madrid. I still remember the name of the one that delivered the children to us: Sister María Gómez Valbuena, a child-trafficker like my parents, but she had the blessing of the Church and could hide her crimes under her habit.

"We want white children, like ourselves," Graciela's father explained, when I asked him why go all the way to Spain. (I knew only too well how easy it was to find a child right here.) "We're Spaniards," he added pointedly, and it was obvious that his "we" did not include my dark skin. My sterility turned out to be a blessing for my father-in-law; his white family could remain unblemished.

Sister Stork brought us two newborns at the end of our four-month stay in Madrid, long enough to stifle any gossip about Graciela's claim to be the mother. I played along and made up a great story about her pregnancy. The two of them aren't even brothers. They were shown to my father-in-law so he could choose between them. He of course financed the whole thing, since the salary of a journalist and wannabe writer would never have covered the cost of two European children. He didn't know which one to pick, so he bought them both. "We saved them from General Franco and changed their lives," the proud grandfather said.

We never told anyone about the adoption. My ex consulted a few psychologists on whether to tell our children the truth, but my father-in-law forbade it and the topic was dropped. Andrés, Antonio, Graciela, and I were a family of four unknowns, a family with a dark spot in the rice that would in time unbalance the dish.

When my children come to this house, where my parents sold so many children, it makes me think that buying them was a restoration of the order of the universe.

TWENTY-NINE

Saturday, September 14, 1985

17.00

Leopoldo López carries a floral arrangement past one of Evangelina Montero's brothers and places it at the foot of the bier. The Montero brothers, all five of them, are standing guard around the coffin.

"I don't know what they're waiting for to lock up those bastards Franco and Pereda," Evangelina's sister repeats to everyone who offers their condolences.

"Franco fled to the United States," she hears people in the room murmuring. No-one dares say it outright to the family.

Beatriz stands alone beside the casket and won't let anyone approach her. In a whisper she begs her mother to forgive her for not protecting her from her father.

Humberto, knocked out by painkillers, had flown to Houston that morning. From the airport he was taken straight to the hospital, and as the visitation for his wife got underway so did the operation on his knee. Waking up from the anaesthesia, he felt for his calf. Still there. He went back to sleep, a smile on his lips.

Esteban telephoned. He needed to see them where they wouldn't be overheard, not the hotel or anywhere public. Lucina suggested her office after she finished with her last patient.

"I think the murderer is Julián, Ignacio's brother," he says setting his briefcase on the floor. Lucina points to a chair and he takes it, even though he would rather remain on his feet. It has been days since he could sit calmly.

Elena does not like Lucina's office and had suggested Esteban's house instead, but Lucina had insisted on what would be more convenient for her. Elena tries to recall how many times she has been here: five? six? "The bad news clinic," slips out of her mouth.

"What?" Lucina says.

"That's what I used to call your office: the bad news clinic."

"Elena, can we stick to what we came to talk about? Go on, Esteban."

In her mind Elena mimics her: "Can we stick to what we came to talk about?" She mouths the words.

Esteban regards them for a long moment, then says, "A colleague of mine works at the Federal Prosecutor's Office. I asked him for information on the inmate Julián Conde Sánchez at Santa Marta Acatitla prison. He told me Julián isn't there anymore. He completed his sentence."

Lucina says, "My brother remembers the day when Julián left me with Isabel and asked her to take me far away, because Manuel wanted to kill me."

"Wait," Elena interrupts. "Julián took you to Isabel? Ignacio wanted to kill you?"

"I asked Jesús twice: 'Are you sure it was Julián?' Both times he swore it was. My brother blames me for everything that went wrong in his life. When he was fourteen Isabel left him with a Señora Flores — maybe the same one Ignacio wrote about — so he could have a stable life and get an education. He didn't see much of his mother after that and he never forgave her for abandoning him."

Esteban interrupts. "Didn't you hear me? Julián is free. He finished his sentence."

Lucina leans back in her chair. "He got out? When?" Her eyes widen.

"Almost two months ago."

"Is that why you think he's the murderer?"

"Who else? Elena, in the photographs they put under your door somebody wrote, 'Look me up.' You said Ignacio went nuts and ran off to find whoever it was. He must have known it was Julián, since he'd killed the other women the same way."

"So you think Julián is here? In the city?"

"I don't know, Lucy. I really don't know."

"If it's true what my fa— Ignacio . . . Manuel . . . I don't even know what to call him anymore. But if what he wrote is true, then it was Julián who wanted to kill me . . . and maybe he wants to kill me now. Me and my son." Lucina gets to her feet. "I need to get my son and clear out. I don't know where to go. I don't have any other family. I can't go back to running from one place to another. I can't!"

"Take it easy, Lucy." Esteban puts his hands on her shoulders. "You're not alone, I'm with you." And he pulls her into a hug.

"My family has a house in Sierra Gorda," Elena says. "Maybe you could go there for a few days."

"It's not fair, I can't make my son live like I did."

"I have to take my suspicions to the prosecutor and the judge," Esteban says. "Miguel Pereda handed in his resignation this morning. I hear he's been arrested and he's being interrogated, or at least that's what they're saying to calm people down after the demonstration. Maybe you and your son could move in with me."

Lucina does not respond. She feels the way she did when she was a child: exposed, frightened, vulnerable. "I felt utterly lost when my mother died. I was twenty years old. But I stayed in school and my brother helped me out. I guess he thought that was what his mother would have wanted. Then I met my husband, and after we got married I wasn't so afraid. I thought he could protect me, though I never told him anything about my past. I'm like my father that way. Only I'm not good at making things up. As far as my ex knows, I'm an orphan with no relatives except for a brother I never see."

"I'm going to call the state prosecutor's office right now," Esteban says. "I have to ask for a meeting so I can tell him the whole story."

"Did you find out anything about the shoes?" Elena asks.

"I haven't had the chance."

"In the memoir it only mentions three women killed, and there were nine shoes, none of which match."

"I know. I'll have to send them to a lab for tests."

"And in the meantime, what do we do about Julián?" Lucina says. "We don't even know what he looks like."

"Yes, we do, Lucy. I've got a picture they faxed me from the prison."

Esteban pulls a folder from his briefcase and puts a sheet of paper on the desk.

"Is it recent?" Elena asks.

"They told me it was, but he looks awfully young."

Lucina stares at the face in the picture. "He doesn't look like a murderer, does he?"

"No." Elena tries to find some trace of Ignacio in the man with short dark hair, thick eyebrows and tiny eyes, broad lips and prominent cheekbones. "He doesn't look anything like Ignacio."

"Are you sure this is Julián?"

"Absolutely, they sent me his entire file." Esteban pulls out another folder. "It talks about Clara's death, which we read about. He was sentenced for murdering Clara."

"My God..."

"I have to hurry if I'm going to catch the prosecutor. We're safer going to the state level than dealing with the office here. I'll keep both of you posted. Lucy, are you going to be alright? You can come with me if you want."

Lucina thinks for a moment. "Can we go pick up my son? I'll wait in the car while you make whatever calls you have to. Alright?"

"Of course, that'll be fine."

In the street, watching them walk to Esteban's car, Elena cannot help looking right and left, hunting for a face like the one in the picture.

THIRTY

Monday, September 16, 1985
08.10

The story does not come out in *Diario de Allende*, which has not appeared since its publisher flew to Houston. After the demonstration provided plenty of exposure for the photograph showing Claudia Cosío sitting between Humberto Franco and Miguel Pereda, advertisers cancelled en masse. *El Observador de Allende* carries the story, including the picture that Antonio Gómez had at first refused to publish. The headline reads, "Ex-Public Prosecutor Miguel Pereda Aguilar Arrested."

The *Observador* story claims Franco's whereabouts are unknown and quotes authorities saying that Ricardo Almeida only fired when Franco attacked him. It also reports that Evangelina Montero was beaten before falling "accidentally" and fracturing her skull on a rock. A quote from the dead woman's sister alleges that Franco had abused Evangelina physically and psychologically for years. The story notes that Miguel Pereda is under arrest on suspicion of rape and having sex with a minor. Without saying as much, it implies his possible responsibility for the murders.

The owner of the paper wrote the story himself. Never before had Antonio Gómez dedicated so much time and care to an article, since he guessed most of his readers would be aware of his relationship with the dead woman. That's what he called her, "the dead woman". It was an attempt to distance himself from the guilt he felt and to dampen his wife's jealousy, since she certainly knew Evangelina was the love of his life. In the story he confessed that the photograph reached his desk first and that he had chosen not to publish it. On the society page he ran a nearly full-page photograph of Evangelina and a two-page obituary citing her leadership of the Montero family charity, which runs lending libraries of children's toys in poor communities.

The rancour that consumed Antonio Gómez as he wrote the story was nothing compared to the rage of Humberto's brothers, managers of the family's businesses. They closed ranks and refused to speak about the matter to anyone outside the family. And they suspended Humberto's monthly cheque as a way of pressuring him to come home and face the music.

A delivery boy on a bicycle, trying hard to perfect his aim, tosses *El Observador de Allende* into the Almeidas' garage. As on every other day, the dog brings in the paper, drooling saliva on the front page, where the photograph appears. In the kitchen, Mónica is watching the news on Channel 2. Host Guillermo Ochoa is talking about two unsolved murders that have San Miguel up in arms. He mentions the plot of Ignacio Suárez's book that seemed to implicate the late writer, and he points out that the story has been covered in the most important American papers, citing the potential impact on tourism, a mainstay of San Miguel's economy.

Mónica sips her coffee in silence, trying to absorb the words, hoping the caffeine will somehow attenuate the blow. She feels the liquid disappear into the yawning pit inside her, which she suspects will continue expanding until it consumes her too.

On Saturday they were again summoned to the Public Prosecutor's Office, and had to listen to the prosecuting attorney tell them their daughter and her friend were asking for trouble if they went out with married men. Thankfully, the lawyer they hired after Ricardo was detained for shooting Franco, spoke up: "You're blaming the victim and that's wrong, even if it is standard practice in this country." The prosecuting attorney went on to say that Ricardo ought to be under arrest for attempted murder, that he was only released due to widespread public anger, and he could be arrested again at any point. "So you had better be patient and not press for a quick resolution of the case." When they left the office, the Cosíos were awaiting their turn.

Martha de Cosío and Mónica de Almeida embraced. Ricardo shook Mario Cosío's outstretched hand, but Mónica barely acknowledged him. Mario was no longer living at home. Martha had cleaned out his things, then called the daycare centre where she had worked before her marriage and asked for her job back. Claudia's room remains closed up like a mausoleum. Every day Martha pauses outside, her hand on the knob, tempted to go in and lie on her bed, breathe in the smell of her pillow, maybe look at her childhood photographs or open the window to let in some air. She can't bring herself to box up her daughter's belongings because she cannot imagine what she would do with them. Give them away? Throw them out?

Martha now picks up today's *Observador* from the front step and thinks about the delivery boy's tossing skill. She opens it standing by the sink. It occurs to her to call Mónica, but the conversation might turn to her husband, a topic she is not yet ready to broach with anyone. She knows she might change her mind and she would look ridiculous if she tells Mónica she sent Mario packing, only to take him back. She stares at the photograph she knows so well, the drunken face of her daughter and the stupid faces of the men on either side, and with teary eyes she begins to read.

Diario de Allende reporter Leonardo Álvarez is in a café reading the same story. Under the newspaper lies a yellow folder with several copies of his C.V. He plans to hand them out once he finishes his coffee, starting with the manager of the café.

With the *Observador* under his arm, the Guanajuato state prosecutor steps into a meeting room at the department's San Miguel office. Awaiting him are Esteban del Valle and Judge Bernabé Castillo.

"Did you read the story by the owner of this lousy rag?" the prosecutor demands.

"And it's on the national news. We have to respond," the judge says, shaking the prosecutor's hand.

"Gentlemen." Esteban speaks up before the conversation gets off track. He clears his throat. "I did not invite the agents in charge of this case because, as you both know, Miguel Pereda and Humberto Franco wanted the investigation to point to Ignacio Suárez as the only possible culprit, so that their date with the murdered girls would not come to light."

"The investigation is still very active," the prosecutor says. "I was there when they interrogated Pereda yesterday, the fucking son of a bitch. Most people know the bastard got the job through me. The only thing we can accuse him of is not keeping his prick in his pants."

"We're talking about underage girls," Esteban says.

"Underage whores."

The judge interrupts them. "Let's not get caught up trying to place blame on anyone, we need a way forward. And it seems del Valle has found something." He raises an eyebrow and turns to the pathologist.

"They were so focused on making sure Franco and Pereda weren't implicated," Esteban says, "they restricted their investigation to Ignacio Suárez."

"You're repeating yourself, del Valle. We know about your friendship with the writer." The prosecutor gets up from his chair and smooths his suit, releasing vapours of Stefano lotion and tobacco.

A noise at the door diverts their attention and in walks Miguel Pereda's secretary, carrying cups of coffee on a tray. Pereda had hired her, he said, because he liked having a "good view" from his desk.

She needed the job and proceeded to dress to please her boss. No-one had asked her for coffee, but she thought she had better make an appearance in case they were talking about her future.

"Good morning." Under the gaze of the three men she sets down a cup in front of each, spilling a bit of Judge Castillo's when he stares at her cleavage. "Here is the cream and sugar."

"Thank you," Esteban says, anxious to continue. The secretary departs, feeling like she just signed her letter of resignation. A waft of her perfume obliges Esteban to bring his hand to his nose. While he can easily stand the stench of a cadaver, other aromas make him sneeze.

"Yes, Ignacio Suárez was my friend," Esteban says. "The supposed investigation was centred on crimes in a book of his that was based on something he covered as a reporter. Women were being murdered, they called the victims 'the Saints', and the culprit was never caught. Ignacio suspected a man who was arrested for the murder of a co-worker at *La Prensa*."

"Who is it? Drop the preambles and get to the point," the prosecutor says, unaware of Esteban's efforts to avoid mentioning Ignacio's memoir or his relationship with Julián and Lucina.

"A prisoner who just completed his sentence for murder at Santa Marta Acatitla. Ignacio covered the story, heard his statements, and interviewed him when he was in Lecumberri prison. The guy told Suárez he'd committed other crimes which the police had not uncovered."

"Suárez told you all that?" Judge Castillo says impatiently.

"He told me about it a few years ago."

"I hope this is the truth, del Valle, not some attempt to save your friend."

"There's no saving him. He's dead. Julián Conde Sánchez, however, is on the loose."

Esteban shows them the fax he received from the prison.

"Here it only talks about one murdered woman," the prosecutor observes.

"Ignacio interviewed him and he confessed to other crimes."

"Why didn't the writer tell the police?"

"The prisoner would not repeat his confession and the authorities decided to drop it. He was already locked up. In Ignacio's novel the killer is very much like the man he interviewed in prison, a man who is free today."

"We can't base an investigation on the plot of a novel," the prosecutor says, banging his fist on the table so hard the coffee cups jump.

Esteban counters, "Miguel Pereda and Humberto Franco used the plot to pin the blame on Ignacio. I don't see why it's no longer relevant. Besides, this guy is a murderer."

"I don't have time to waste on soap-opera conjectures. I thought this meeting was for something serious." The prosecutor storms out, leaving the door wide open. From her spot the secretary sees the disappointed faces of Esteban del Valle and Judge Castillo. Esteban sees her staring.

"I'll find out about Julián Conde," Castillo says. The pathologist nods and after shaking the judge's hand he leaves the room.

SEVENTEENTH FRAGMENT

This morning I took an expired aspirin. I noticed the date when I put away the bottle, so I ran to the bathroom and stuck my finger down my throat. I believe I managed to throw it all up. One of my obsessions is how I'm going to die. Having witnessed so much death makes me think a lot about my own. I'm not alone in this, I know. Although one day science may demonstrate the opposite, we humans seem to be the only species that worries about mortality. I'm surprised I had old aspirins on hand, since expiry dates are another of my obsessions.

I get so lonely in Mexico City. That's why I'm thinking about these things. Maybe I should move in with Elena. If I die here my body won't be found until it's stinking. There's a goal I haven't achieved: finding someone to take charge of my remains. I picked up that preoccupation from Lupita, the prostitute in the tenement. She was the only person I could talk to about my parents. With Ramón, every conversation turned into an interview.

Six months after my mother died, I went back to the tenement to see Lupita. I waited in the street, since I didn't have the courage to step inside.

"What brings you here, kid?" she said.

"Waiting for you."

"What do you want with me?"

"To talk."

During the daytime, Lupita did errands or slept or visited "friends in the profession", as she put it, who had got beaten so badly they were invalids and had to live off charity. She used to work in a brothel and share her room in the tenement with her mother. After her mother died and brothels were outlawed, she took up streetwalking. For a time she worked in a dance hall as a dime-a-dance girl. Later on, the madam she once worked for opened a restaurant as a cover for a bordello and she called Lupita when she had clients. "At one point I was somebody," she told me. "I worked in a first-class joint and earned 75 pesos a customer." Streetwalking, on the other hand, Lupita had to pay off the police, plus give a percentage to the hotel. But she got by. That is, until the day she was arrested. Streetwalking is a cutthroat business, and it was a competitor who turned her in. The fine was covered by a pimp, who made her pay it back three times over.

"How are you doing without a mother, kid? You probably won't believe it, but we girls, we miss her. She helped us out if we got pregnant. Only one of us ever died."

"Only?"

"We all knew the risks. Your mother was no doctor. Doctors are no help anyway. They charge the pearls of the Virgin, and still there's no guarantee you won't come out feet first."

It would be banal to confess I lost my virginity with her. I prefer to say I signed a contract promising to attend her funeral. Lupita wanted a nice funeral and a decent tomb, and she saved up for it. "A decent tomb, kid," she often told me. Every day she prayed to Saint Raymond Nonnatus, patron of pregnant women and unborn children, for the souls of the two children she never baptised. "I entrust them to you," she would say, and she'd kiss the medallion that now hangs around my neck.

Julián killed her on December 12, her saint's day, when normally she would go to the Shrine of the Virgin of Guadalupe to pray. The expiry date that so preoccupied Lupita fell on a Tuesday, three months after the death of Pilar Ruíz.

He came home carrying the medallion she always wore. He'd been away for days. Half my brain worried about him, while the other half wrote news stories on crimes of passion or robberies. I'd slip in a reference to "the Saints" every so often to keep the story alive, since I knew Julián would strike again.

"You bastard, you killed Lupita. Why?"

He didn't answer. It was the middle of the night. He had shaken me awake and when I opened my eyes the medallion was swinging in front of my face.

I knocked him to the floor and was about to punch him, when he raised a hand and asked, "Do you want to know where she is?" I held back my fist.

"She's leaning against the wall of a funeral home in Colonia Doctores. If you hurry you'll be the first." He gave me precise directions and it wasn't hard to find the spot.

I made an anonymous call to the police and arrived at the scene after they did. "You're late, ghoul," an officer said. "It's quite a coincidence, you always showing up."

"I don't show up. They send me."

He had left her just like the other two: seated in the same position, exactly like my mother in the prison photograph. I could not control my churning stomach. It was the first time one of Julián's murders made me throw up.

"What's the story? Lost your iron gut?" The cops patted me on the back and laughed. "Strangled, like the others," one said.

"She was a prostitute," said another, "but this wasn't her territory. She worked closer to downtown."

"The same wound in the forehead and she's missing a shoe," said a third.

"Where are the shoes?" I asked Julián when I got home, just as I had on the previous occasions. He shrugged and proceeded to sleep nonstop for three days.

I asked one of Lupita's friends, another prostitute, to claim her body and get the money for her burial from her room in the tenement, some of which I'm sure the friend kept. She also took Lupita's clothes, shoes, and jewelry. "It'll be of more use to me than to her."

I covered the rest of the expenses. I bought a coffin and wrote an epitaph for her gravestone. During the funeral I kept my distance, since I didn't want the people from the tenement to see me. I paid a priest to bless her voyage to the heaven of prostitutes. Out of her death I got three stories in which I made speculations, mentioned the previous murders, and prattled on about serial killers.

THIRTY-ONE

Tuesday, September 17, 1985
08.00

Elena folds a skirt and packs it in her suitcase. After spending the weekend mulling it over, she made up her mind to go to Mexico City. "I'll visit the house in Colonia Roma, I've never seen it," she explained to Esteban and Lucina on Monday. "Ignacio and I used to meet in an apartment he had in Polanco. I only learned about the Colonia Roma place when I read the manuscript. I found a key that's probably for the door, and I also found an address book with the number for his friend Ramón García Alcaraz. I'm not sure whether I'll call him, but if anyone can tell us something, it's him."

"Maybe I'll go with you," Lucina said. "It seems incredible that I'm in the same line of work as Felícitas. I bring children into the world all the time and I've done a few abortions. I don't consider myself a murderer, and neither do my patients. There are so many reasons why a woman might choose to abort. It's easy to criticise them, but no-one, absolutely no-one, knows the hearts of those women."

"I'm not so sure. You know how hard I worked to have a child . . ."

"If what Ignacio wrote is true, his mother also murdered babies," Esteban said. "You're no murderer."

"I haven't been able to stop thinking about the accursed genes he wrote about."

"Do you think you're capable of killing someone?" Elena asked.

"I don't think so. I don't know."

"You aren't like Felícitas' family. Don't torture yourself." Elena half-smiled without looking at Lucina. "You have other defects."

"I think I'll go with you to Mexico City."

Elena closes the suitcase, then opens it again and eyes her closet. She is nervous about meeting Ignacio's old friend and newspaper colleague, even though he seemed very warm on the telephone. When she first called Ramón, nobody answered. Maybe it's the wrong number, she thought. She made herself wait a half hour that seemed interminable, then she tried again. "Ramón?" she said, when someone picked up.

"Yes, that's me." A hoarse, masculine voice. In Elena's imagination he was the teenager in the manuscript, not a man nearing seventy.

"My name is Elena, Elena Galván. I'm . . ." She did not know how to introduce herself.

"Ignacio's girlfriend."

"Yes, Ignacio's girlfriend."

Ramón told her he had wanted to say hello when he saw her at the funeral, but he got distracted by several reporters he knew. By the time he got free of them, she had already left. Elena told him about the memoir and read him a few selections over the telephone. They agreed to meet the following afternoon at Ramón's home.

Early this morning, before packing her bag, Elena went to the hospital to see José María. She talked to him about her fears, about the hotel, about her mother. She still had a hard time believing that her mother and her stepfather were severed from life in the same way. "This has got to be the most melodramatic love story in the world," she told him. "It is utterly absurd that both of you seem to be asleep. What? Do you expect us to learn telepathy?"

A beep from one of the gadgets hooked up to him was his only answer.

"What should I do? Should I go see Ramón? I need to know the truth about Ignacio."

No sooner had she uttered the writer's name than José María's heart sped up, along with his breathing, and at that moment Consuelo and a nurse walked in. "What happened? What did you do?" Consuelo cried, leaving her purse on a chair.

"Nothing. I didn't do anything." Elena's eyes were wide and her heart was pounding harder than her stepfather's. The nurse examined the machine and the I.V. while Consuelo stroked his curly grey hair. The nurse injected a few millilitres of a solution to keep him sedated and in a few seconds his pulse and breathing eased.

Elena said goodbye and hurried out. When she reached her car, she realised she had left the keys in the room. She raced back up the stairs. The door was open and as she approached she spied her aunt kissing her mother's husband on the mouth. "I miss you so much," she heard her say.

Elena froze. Consuelo, seemingly unaware of Elena's presence, caressed her brother-in-law's face, which was now less swollen as his wounds healed, the skin around his right eye no longer greenish purple, but red.

Elena tiptoed a retreat, then came back. "Consuelo! I forgot my keys. I'm going now."

Her aunt jumped, dropping the hand she had been holding. "You're going to scare me to death," she muttered.

When Elena got home, she went straight to her mother's room and found her seated in an easy chair by the window.

"Good morning," said the nurse, who was feeding her breakfast.

Elena knelt in front of her mother and laid her head in her lap. She looked up into her mother's eyes, yearning for her to respond the way she used to when Elena was small.

"Oh, Mommy," she said, and kissed her hands. Then she put

Consuelo out of her mind. First she had to deal with Ignacio, then she could think about her aunt.

Elena returns the skirt to the closet. It has been raining for a while and she thinks it might be cold in the capital. She slips a pair of jeans off a hanger, then a blouse, takes a black sweater from a shelf, then hesitates. She doesn't want Ramón to think she's dressing in mourning for Ignacio. More than sad, she's angry and troubled, tired of the whole thing.

"That's why I have to see Ramón," she says out loud. "To find some peace. I need peace."

"Elena?"

A couple of knocks on the door. "It's me, Lucina."

There she is, in her white lab coat. "I'm still going with you to Mexico City, but I've got a birth to attend to. I'll have to meet you there tomorrow."

"Perfect. I've got a reservation for us at the Hotel Gillow. We can meet there."

"I woke up thinking about fate," Lucina says. "Do we have any control over our destiny or is that just something somebody made up? I'm coming to the conclusion that we don't control a thing. Too many decisions get made for us by genetics, circumstances, health, economics, politics, nature, chemistry . . . right? I had no choice about who my parents were or what traits I inherited or the circumstances that led me to this city. But maybe I can at least find out where I'm from and come to terms with who I am."

"That's it. We're going to find out who you are and who your father was."

"What do you think he was going to write on the page he left unfinished?"

"This is a novel!" Elena says, making quotation marks with her fingers. They both laugh and feel surprisingly relieved.

After Elena finishes packing, she runs into Consuelo in the hallway.

"Where are you headed?"

"Mexico City."

"Mexico City? What for?"

"To settle something. I'll see you in a few days."

"Girl, there's a lot of hotel work to be done."

Rather than respond, Elena quickens her pace.

EIGHTEENTH FRAGMENT

I am two people.

I have two names, the one I made up and the one I got from my parents.

I'm a writer and the son of the Ogress.

The real father of Lucina, and the fake father of Andrés and Antonio.

A crime reporter and the brother of a murderer.

I've often wondered which is the face and which is the mask. Am I a murderer masquerading as a writer, or vice versa? Which is the person and which is the character?

"Person" is derived from the Latin *persona*, which means both "person" and "mask". And it's related to *personare*, which also means "mask" and is the verb meaning "resound". That curious double meaning comes from the fact that in ancient Greece actors on stage wore masks that amplified their voices, like megaphones. Thus, people "resound" through their masks. Our characters come into being when we play the roles we have chosen to play.

I play two roles: a man who lives in Mexico City and another who lives in a hotel in the provinces. Hotel guests are forgotten once you change the sheets and towels. They are presences that vanish in a puff of air. By keeping my room in San Miguel rented all year, even when I'm not there, I make my presence more real.

I am the guest in room number eight.

The day the door of Lecumberri prison closed on Julián, I decided to change my name. I would sever all connections to the Ogress and the murderer of "the Saints", and become someone else. You might think a name change is a long process — I thought so — and it took me two years to make up my mind. Then I met a group of forgers who had a workshop on Calle Santo Domingo. In fact, I covered their arrest. They got out after a few months and, slick as a whistle, they changed my name to the pseudonym I used for *Selecciones Policiacas y de Misterio*, Ignacio Suárez Cervantes.

Ignacio was the name Clara wanted for our son. Suárez was Clara's maternal last name. Cervantes was the author of *Don Quixote*, a good omen for an aspiring writer. That was how I chose my new name, a little bit of whimsy.

The name felt right from the beginning. Uttering it aloud was a pleasure. I liked the feel of the words in my mouth. The change coincided with a story I wrote about an American soldier who underwent a sex change. That's how I felt about my new name: a change of identity.

Ramón insisted on calling me Manuel, but others at the newspaper adapted quickly. The high turnover helped, since for all the new employees I was Ignacio.

The editor was surprised. "You're just starting to get a name for yourself. People won't know who you are."

"You know it," I said. "That's enough."

After Julián killed Lupita I felt nothing but hatred for my brother. And I took refuge in Clara, in the comfort of her room. She liked to tell me vignettes from her past, each beginning with "I remember". I listened attentively, envying her childhood, appropriating any image that might help calm the bottomless anxiety in my head.

"I remember the first time I rode a bicycle, it was my cousin's. The women in my town weren't allowed to ride bikes."

"I remember when I was sent on an errand and I lost the money. My father chased me with a belt, but he didn't catch me. I learned I could run fast."

"I remember..."

I sought out Isabel. I wanted to beg her forgiveness, to introduce her to Clara, to share my new-found joy at having someone in my life. Clara and I visited her in the tenement, in the very room where we had lived. Isabel was afraid at first, but soon she hugged Clara and then me. "He's like a son to me," she explained, and she stroked my cheek.

Clara and I celebrated Christmas together. She wanted to go to her parents' house, so I could meet her family. I refused and her father did too. "No way can you bring a man here if you aren't married."

So we had Christmas dinner in her room. I had to give her landlady a little extra. "We don't allow men in here," she warned the first time she set eyes on me. Then she held out her hand and took the twenty pesos I offered. She also raised Clara's rent. One tenant does not cost the same as two. We ate chicken, exchanged gifts. She was happy and I wore a smiling mask to hide my apprehension, my worries about Julián, my rage at him. I thought we would have three months' peace before Julián killed again.

After Christmas I wrote several additional stories about Lupita. At that point it had not yet occurred to me to change my name. I was trying to become known and Julián's murders helped.

Towards the end of December, on the very day Clara told me she was pregnant, a streetcar ran over a child. A photographer and I went to cover the accident. The child was three years old and had slipped his mother's grasp while they were crossing the avenue. She was holding a baby and could not stop him.

The mother was on her knees sobbing, holding the baby in her arms. Someone was trying to get her to stand up, but she refused. The photographer pressed the shutter, refocused, shot again, thinking about camera angles, lighting, tomorrow's story. He paid no attention to the tragedy of it. The onlookers gazed right into the camera, smiling as if they were at a party. Gawkers emerge spontaneously. They come to witness death. Someone in first-century Greece said, "Death is terrible, but even more harrowing is the fear of it." Death and children should never mix. They're contradictory, antagonistic: antonyms.

"I have news for you," Clara told me when I got back to the paper. "But I'll tell you later." We were careful to keep our relationship a secret at work, since the editor did not want romances among his employees. In her room she said, "I'm going to have to move in with you, or maybe get an apartment for the two of us."

"Why?"

"I'm pregnant."

"A child got run over today," I said. "Children are fragile. I can't have children."

"It's your child."

"I can't have children," I repeated.

"Believe me, it's your child. I haven't been with anyone else. It's your child."

I was twenty-one years old. I loved your mother. I'd been clinging to her to keep from drowning. But that day I walked out. I didn't slam the door, didn't make a scene. I was afraid, in fact I was terrified. It wasn't a rational fear, but at the same time the most rational part of my brain was screaming that I should never bring into the world a human being carrying my accursed genes.

Lucina, daughter of mine, if at that moment I could have peered into the future and seen what a marvellous person you would become, I never would have told her to get an abortion. But I suddenly understood the fears of the women who sought out my mother. Maybe one of them, like me, imagined evil genes floating in her blood, ready to spread like a cancer. I could see things from their point of view.

Clara told me she would never do it. If she had to raise her child alone, she would find a way. I felt a renewed respect for her.

I told Ramón. We were outside, smoking. "I can't have a child. He might turn out like my family."

He knew what I meant. "Life is a flip of a coin," he said. "I think it depends how you raise him, the environment he grows up in. What would have happened if Dr Frankenstein had loved his creature?"

Clara and I rented a room together downtown, again in a tenement, this time on Calle Mesones.

Julián had not reappeared, but I did not want to bring Clara to live in the house in Colonia Roma, where she would have to breathe all that pain and death. I took my belongings, left everything else behind. At some point the landlady cleared the place out and no-one ever rented it again. Stories had got around about witchcraft and dead women and children. People said they heard moans and cries at night, and that the lights went on by themselves.

Ramón waited before he wrote a story about the haunted house on Cerrada de Salamanca. It was still empty when I bought it years later. Empty is a manner of speech. It actually became a refuge for homeless people who didn't care about the rumours so long as they had a place to sleep.

Months passed and Julián was still missing. I looked for him in the places he frequented. I walked many streets seeking him in the eyes of beggars or anyone who looked vaguely like him.

When Clara's pregnancy became obvious, she was fired. "We can't trust a pregnant woman," she was told. Without her wages we had to live on mine alone, and that made me feel grown up. Until then I had floated along on whatever came my way. Soon I would no longer be the son of the Ogress. I would be the father of a family.

You arrived a little early. On August 6, 1945, twenty minutes after "Little Boy" was dropped on Hiroshima killing more than 160,000 people, you came into the world, Lucina. Your cries went out into the universe, joining those of the unfortunate inhabitants of that city.

When Clara's contractions began, I took her to Juárez Hospital. The only person to visit was Isabel. She helped me pay the hospital bills, named herself your grandmother, and held you before I did. It was she who put you in my arms, as if I were a child who had never seen a baby. "Hold her," she said. "Nothing's going to happen to her." I was trembling. Impossible to describe my body's reaction. More than anything it was terror at all the things that might happen to you.

You were so small, so fragile. And you reminded me of the babies that came through our house. Clara gazed at you as if her whole life had been but a preamble to that moment.

On the morning of August 9, a second atom bomb, "Fat Man", was dropped on the city of Nagasaki. That was the day we returned to our room in the tenement. Clara and you went to bed and soon fell asleep. I went to the newsroom, my mind on the two of you as I worked, my senses full of you. You smelled so good, so you.

When I got back, Julián was beside the bed, out of breath, and you were wailing beside your dead mother. The entire room was a shambles. I stood for maybe a minute or two at the threshold, trying to decipher the scene, to translate the images into a language my brain could understand. Clara was spread-eagled amid the pillows and sheets, in a posture that made me think she was uncomfortable. I became aware of all the blood, her eyes out of orbit, her neck scratched and bruised.

I closed the door and walked to the bed, my gaze fixed on your mother and then on you. I don't know if Clara was asleep when he came in. She fought him, I'm sure. She wanted to protect you. My brother had teethmarks on one hand and scratches on his face, blood on his clothes and hands.

You were crying like a cat.

I leapt at my brother.

I can't recall the exact sequence of what happened next. We were on the floor fighting. A neighbour came in or several neighbours. I hadn't locked the door, just as I hadn't when I went out to the newspaper.

"I'm going to kill you," I was screaming. Someone tried to separate us. The police arrived. One of the patrolmen tried to hold Julián, but my brother pushed him aside, ran down the stairs, and disappeared into the street.

At some point in all the bedlam Isabel came in. She started to howl, but then brought her hand to her mouth and squatted by my side. "What happened?" She reached out to touch me, changed her mind, and went to you, Lucina. I again became aware of your cries.

"Everything will be alright," Isabel was saying, rocking you, trying to calm you down.

"Take her away. Please. Take her. Hide her from me and from Julián. That way I won't ever see her again, but he won't find either of you. I beg you. Take her away."

I heard the siren of the ambulance. Isabel wrapped you in a blanket, then slipped past the neighbours crowding around the door.

That was the last time I saw you, Lucina, daughter of mine, until I managed to find you more than thirty years later.

It took a week, but Julián was caught and charged with murdering Clara Suárez. He was locked away in Lecumberri for that one murder and was never linked to the others.

The survivors of Hiroshima and Nagasaki are known as *hibakusha*, bombed people.

I am a *hibakusha*.

I have written these pages with you in mind, Lucina, because I believe

THIRTY-TWO

Tuesday, September 17, 1985
13.08

After knocking on the door marked with a number 10, Elena hears approaching footsteps and the door swings open.

"Elena."

She nods. She doesn't know what to call the man who takes her cold hand in his warm clasp. Doubts had swamped her as she climbed the stairs. She felt torn between her desire to learn the truth and her dread of what the truth might be. She almost turned around and headed straight back to San Miguel. Why not just mourn him, forget all about the memoir under her arm, decide that it was the draft of another novel?

"Come in, come in." Ramón draws her inside, forestalling any attempt to flee. "Forgive the mess," he says, clearing newspapers from the table in the middle of the living room. He disappears into the kitchen, and from there asks if she would like anything to drink.

"Nothing, thank you."

"I'll bring you a glass of water and a beer. You must be thirsty, it's a long drive. I should make you a cup of coffee, you're freezing. But a beer will do you good. Would you prefer something stronger? Whisky? Rum? Cognac? A glass of wine? I've got everything, although to tell the truth I've always been a beer man."

Elena doesn't manage either a "yes" or a "no". He returns with the drinks on a tray, puts coasters on the table, sets out glasses of water and bottles of beer.

"May I . . . ?"

"It's there at the back," he says, and points the way. "I know women. I lived with three of them. After a long drive, the first thing my wife wanted was a bathroom. My daughters are the same."

"Thank you," she says uneasily, leaving her purse and the memoir on one of the armchairs.

After washing her hands and splashing water on her face, she says to herself, "Calm down, take it easy." She smooths her hair and feels more in control.

Ramón has Ignacio's memoir open in his lap. At her approach he closes it and puts it back on the empty chair.

"It's alright, señor."

"Ramón, call me Ramón."

She nods and sits across from him, picks up a bottle of beer and takes a sip, then a long swallow.

Ramón says, "I feel like I've known you for a long time. Manuel talked a lot about you." Elena makes a face and he corrects himself. "Ignacio. I never could call him that."

"He never mentioned you to me. He never said anything about his life here and the little he did say were lies."

"I don't know the whole truth either."

"I came to see you because I need answers."

"I know, and I'll try to give you some. What you told me about the manuscript," pointing at it, "surprised me too. I'm eager to read it."

Elena takes another sip of beer. She glances around the apartment, sees photographs on the wall, and gets up to take a closer look.

"This is . . . ?" She points at a picture of a woman with very pale skin, brown hair, and large clear eyes. The photograph is bigger than the others surrounding it.

"That's my wife Mercedes. She died three years ago."

"I'm sorry."

"Don't feel sorry, it's not your fault. Damned lung cancer." Ramón shrugs.

Elena examines photographs of Ramón with a number of Mexican and foreign celebrities from show business and politics. One has him with President Cárdenas. In the earlier ones, with Arturo de Córdoba, Pedro Infante, and Joaquín Pardavé, he looks like a kid.

"I interviewed all of them. Some became friends of mine." He gets to his feet. "These are my favourites." He nods at the photographs of María Félix and Natalie Wood. "Lovely women, but my treasures are these two." He points to several pictures of two girls as teenagers and grown women. "My daughters, Esperanza and Rosario."

Elena moves closer. "They're pretty."

"It's my good luck they take after their mother."

Elena smiles, feeling more relaxed and ready to broach the topic eating away at her. "It's very strange to be here. You're like a character in a book."

"Disappointed?"

"Why?"

"People are always better in our imagination or in the movies than in real life, don't you think?"

She smiles. "You're better in real life."

"I hope you aren't flirting with me. My grey hairs deserve some respect." He winks and laughs the very laugh Elena imagined when she read Ignacio's memoir. "You too are better in person," he says.

"Tell me about Ignacio or Manuel. Maybe I should hear about Manuel so I can understand Ignacio."

"I think I'm going to open a bottle of wine and bring out something for you to eat, because this is going to be a long conversation."

"Can I help?" following him into the kitchen.

"No, I've got everything ready."

In the kitchen she glances around.

"I know what you're thinking," he says.

"What?"

"That this house is rather tidy for a man living alone."

Her eyes widen in surprise. "Ignacio didn't say you could read minds."

Ramón laughs again, this time the giggle Ignacio described as a bird call. Everything about him reminds her of a bird.

"First of all, I can thank my wife for finding a terrific maid. Second, which ought to come first, my wife died because of all the cigarettes I smoked in her presence. The least I can do is keep the house the way she liked it."

Ramón hands her a glass of wine and picks up a plate of cold cuts, cheese, and olives. "Let's sit in the armchairs. We'll be more comfortable than in the kitchen."

Before sitting down, he raises his glass. "To Manuel."

"To a stranger," she toasts.

They clink glasses.

"I miss him, you know?" he says. "We'd become close again. My wife didn't like him, she said he had very dense energy. I've never understood this stuff about energy. Mercedes was very sensitive to it. Plus it really affected her when Julián killed Clara. She didn't want the brother of a murderer anywhere near her daughters. After she died, Manuel and I resumed our friendship. I'd wager I'm the only friend he had."

"I don't know what to think. I'm tired of turning it over in my mind. Maybe I should just let it go, maybe I shouldn't have even come."

"Don't worry." Ramón takes Elena's hand, and with a nod at her neck, "Manuel's medallion."

"I haven't been able to take it off, not even now that I know it belonged to a murdered woman. I should throw it as far away as I can."

"Elena, Elena, don't think about that. Relax."

Elena sighs, the air catching in her throat. She sips her wine, and again she sighs. "Tell me about Ignacio," she says, "about the Manuel you knew. Do you think he could have killed the girls in San Miguel?"

"No, I don't believe it. I'll tell you about Manuel, and then I'll tell you what I think about that. Alright?"

Elena nods slowly. Setting her wine down next to the beer and glass of water, she says, "You've given me too many drinks."

"It's going to be a long afternoon, you'll need them." Ramón hesitates, observing Elena sitting completely still, her legs crossed. He brings an ashtray close, pulls a pack from his shirt pocket, and offers her one.

"It's been a long time since I smoked a Kent."

He extends his lighter. "I don't smoke any other brand. I quit too late, after my wife got sick. Secondhand smoke, they call it. You could say she was a passive smoker." Ramón gets up and opens a window. "I noticed in the manuscript that Ignacio defined himself as a passive murderer. Passivity is a way of life, maybe the only way. I always suspected that Julián was behind 'the Saints' murders, as Manuel called them. But I didn't want to question what he wrote in his stories. That is, until Julián went to prison for killing Clara. We didn't publish anything about her death and we didn't let the other papers do it either. We wanted to spare Manuel that burden, despite the fact that his job was turning other people's sorrow into entertainment. In the end, our passivity is what defines us, not our actions. Maybe passivity is not inaction, but rather a concrete deliberate act."

"Now I understand why Ignacio said you were a philosopher."

"I'm no philosopher. I just like to use words to sweeten the experience of life and make us believe it's worthwhile."

Thinking about her own passivity, Elena finishes her cigarette and stubs it out in the ashtray. "I quit smoking too, until all this happened with Ignacio. You need company to deal with sadness."

"Some company that is."

"Better than nothing," she says.

"Another murderer."

"I guess I like murderers." Elena half-smiles, pushes a lock of hair that has escaped her ponytail behind her ear, and takes a sip of water. "So? Are you going to tell me about Ignacio? Is it true what the memoir says?"

Ramón picks it up and starts leafing through the pages. "Did you know Manuel wrote his books and stories by hand? He only used a typewriter once he'd settled on every word. And he never erased or crossed anything out. He would use brackets instead or start a new page. Did you ever see his handwriting? It looked like code it was so small. I don't know how he managed to read it. On the few occasions he let me have a peek I had to use a magnifying glass. He was very private about his writing. Of course, there was a lot he didn't want anyone to know."

"I agree. I never got to read his notebooks until after he died. They're obsessive."

"Meticulous in everything. Like his mother."

"Was she as bad as he says?"

"I don't know. The woman I met in prison was more pitiful than frightening. She was a midwife and an abortionist, what in the business we call a scarecrow for storks. I never saw Manuel or Julián emptying buckets of foetuses. And I can't confirm she killed a baby or chopped one up, only that he told me she did. There were foetus remains in the drainpipe, those I saw with my own eyes, but that's it. And that's nothing out of the ordinary for someone in her line of work, which society condemns so harshly. I interviewed her and I was present when she made her statement."

"You turned her into a spectacle," Elena says and helps herself to another cigarette.

"That was my job. Manuel gave me a story that was perfect for the paper. Maybe he made most of it up. I don't know."

He lights her cigarette.

Elena gets to her feet and goes to the open window. Children are playing ball in the park across the street. "Abortion is a crime," she says, blowing smoke out of the window.

"I'm not so sure. All my years on the crime beat gave me a different viewpoint. Many criminals come into the world because their mothers were raped. Others become criminals because they were raised by people who should never have been parents. Their mothers in particular lead miserable lives, beaten and mistreated in every way imaginable. Then there are the alcoholics and drug addicts who have children no-one wants."

"That's just a pretext."

"No, it's not a pretext. Julián and Manuel thought like you, and they waged war on those women. When you told me about the manuscript, it reminded me of one of the theories about Jack the Ripper."

"I didn't come here to talk about theories. I want you to tell me about Ignacio."

"That's precisely what I'm on about. Listen: Jack the Ripper lived in one of the poorest parts of London, the East End. Women sold themselves in dark alleys for two cents, anything to keep from starving. Jack murdered that sort of woman, wretched toothless prostitutes whose sin was selling the only thing they had so they could feed their children."

"Very touching, but I still don't see the connection to Ignacio."

"I'm getting there. Some say the Ripper killed because he wanted to free society from such women. That type of murderer is known as a 'missionary'. The name seems paradoxical, but in reality missionaries try to murder religions they consider evil. They murder one belief to impose another."

"You're philosophising again."

"Sorry. Another theory has it that Jack the Ripper was actually a woman. Not Jack, but Jill. What's more, some believe she killed other women for aborting their children. If what you say Manuel wrote is true, then Julián could be a missionary murderer."

"Why did Ignacio never turn his brother in? Maybe he and Clara would still be together, and I would never have met him. We'd all be happy," she says sarcastically. "I think he was as coldblooded as his brother."

"I don't know. He did have the sort of personality you need if you're going to write about crime. We crime reporters get very close to the evil in human beings, we live with it every day. And it makes us different. There's a saying: When you look into an abyss, the abyss also looks into you."

"What is that supposed to mean?"

"Over the years I met many reporters who couldn't bear being constantly exposed to the dark side of people. But for others, witnessing such things and writing about them was a drug. Most authors of crime novels are like Manuel. They're seeking the truth, trying to get to the bottom of crimes the police won't solve. We see corruption close up, people literally getting away with murder, all the squalid dealings of the justice system. That's why we're drawn to fiction. Manuel also had a real way with words."

"You think he was seeking justice?"

"Before, I would have thought so."

"Before?"

"Before learning about his memoir."

Ramón gets to his feet, sweeps stray ashes into the ashtray with the side of his hand, and wipes the table with his napkin. He refills his wine glass and stands by the window.

"The sun's about to set."

"Do you want me to leave?"

He ignores her question and sips his wine. "Dusk lasts longer than dawn. That's a metaphor we don't pay enough attention to. The dawn of our lives is over quickly. What's left is a long, long dusk. In my own life, night's about to fall and only now does this manuscript arrive. From the other world Manuel has put me in a bind. He did the same thing when we were young. He lived the dawn of his life in darkness, at best one long half-light, surrounded by the worst in people. Maybe the sun never came out for him. Maybe it was like being at the bottom of the sea with those creatures that belong in a horror movie. We think they're blind, and in our light they are. But they can see what's in the abyss, things that are invisible to us. Contact with evil gave Manuel and Julián that other vision. They're creatures from the darkness, who tried to live in the light."

"That's not it."

"It's not?"

"Not the reason why Ignacio didn't turn his brother in. You know why."

"Yes, I do. For the very same reason I told the story of the Ogress and many others. Ambition."

"That's right."

"He wanted to become a great reporter," Ramón says.

"Maybe to get out of poverty. To find a way to live."

"There are many ways to justify ambition."

"Maybe we shouldn't get caught up in this discussion. There are more urgent things," Elena says. "Julián got out of jail."

"When? How do you know?"

"Esteban del Valle found out."

"The pathologist."

"Esteban thinks Julián killed the girls in San Miguel. After reading Ignacio's memoir and learning Julián is free, he says he could swear to it."

"It's the same way 'the Saints' got killed so many years ago. But we can't be sure it was him. You know there were more murders after Julián was locked up? They were never investigated, since virtually all of them were women the justice system didn't care about. Prostitutes, poor people."

"How many more?"

"Maybe six."

"So in all there would have been nine murders?"

"It could be. Why?"

"I found a box of women's shoes in Ignacio's room. Nine shoes and none of them matched."

"I don't recall if all the women were barefoot or missing a shoe," Ramón says. "I can go back through the clippings."

"The day the girls were murdered, someone put photographs of the bodies under our door and on one of the pictures somebody had written, 'Look me up'."

"Really?"

"Ignacio got very upset and ran off and the next thing I knew he was in the morgue."

"Do you think Julián killed them?"

"I don't know. The case hasn't been solved because the girls had been on a date with one of the most influential men in San Miguel and the deputy public prosecutor."

"Did Esteban tell the prosecutor about Julián?"

"He was going to. I'll call him in a little while. Tomorrow I'm going to Ignacio's house in Colonia Roma. I want to see it. Though maybe his children have emptied it out."

"I'd like to go with you, but not tomorrow. I've got a couple of appointments that can't be cancelled."

"I need to see it tomorrow. We can go together another day if you want." Elena reaches for her purse. "I'll call you in the morning. Hang on to the manuscript, so you can read it tonight."

THIRTY-THREE

Thursday, September 19, 1985
10.47

The sound of barking awakens her.

She opens her eyes, sees nothing.

She tries to breathe in.

A coughing fit and a sharp pain in her chest.

"Elena?"

She attempts an answer, but what emerges is a sob. Her lips sting, so does her tongue.

"Elena, wake up. Don't go to sleep."

"Lucy..."

Elena was waiting in the hotel lobby when Lucina arrived at seven-thirty on Wednesday evening. She had slept in, then spent all day calling Ignacio's daughter, who was delayed, and trying to get up the nerve to go to Colonia Roma alone. Her last conversation with Lucina had been at four, and by six she was pacing the hotel room. She turned on a soap opera and stood in front of the television until the commercials came on. From the open window she could hear car horns, street vendors, pedestrians on Calle Isabel la Católica — what a contrast to the quiet at Posada Alberto.

"We could have lived in this city together," she said aloud. "I would have liked living here. Maybe I'll do that one day, leave the hotel, my mother, my aunt, not to mention her affair with my stepfather. Maybe I'll just lose myself in this crowd."

The television interrupted her thoughts and she turned it off. She went into the bathroom and peed for the fifth time in an hour.

"It's nerves," she said to herself. She washed her hands and painted her lips, then went down to the lobby. She considered having a drink. Anxiety coursed through her. Even her scalp tingled. By the time Lucina turned up, Elena was on her second rum-and-coke and her third plate of peanuts, and she had made three more trips to the bathroom.

"What could possibly have taken you so long?"

"Childbirth is not something you can schedule. Besides, this is the first time I've driven here by myself. My ex never let me do it on my own. I had to ask for directions three times to find the hotel."

"Well, here you are. Let's put your suitcase upstairs and get under way. I was thinking I'd wait only ten minutes more. I'm really nervous."

"Whoa," Lucina said. "Let's take a deep breath."

"Look, I'm going. You can stay here if you like."

Lucina stared at her, then nodded. "O.K. Let's go."

Neither of them wanted to drive in an unfamiliar city. They gave the taxi driver the address.

"I hope we have time to take a walk down Calle Mesones to see where Isabel lived. Maybe somebody there still remembers her."

"We didn't come for sightseeing," Elena spat out.

"How long do you think we'll be at Ignacio's house?"

"I don't know. As long as we need."

"Could you be a little less aggressive with me?"

"I'm not aggressive."

"Listen to your tone of voice."

"What about it?" Elena shrugged and looked out the window. "I suppose we can go tomorrow. Since we're staying downtown anyway." She kept her gaze on the street.

Out of the corner of her eye, she saw Lucina shift away from her.

It's not her fault, she thought. And out loud, "I think he stayed in San Miguel because of you, not me. He wrote that memoir for you. I know it's not your fault." She paused. "It's also not your fault I couldn't get pregnant," she added, surprising herself.

"Don't be so dramatic, Elena. We don't know why he stayed. We don't really know who the man was. And I wish I'd found a way to get you to conceive. I'm sorry."

Elena gave Lucina's knee a gentle pat. She sighed and became aware of the pine-scented air freshener hanging from the rearview mirror, along with two rosaries, one imitation pearls and the other wooden beads. On the dashboard, her back to the traffic and her hands in prayer, a small figurine of the Virgin of Guadalupe rocked to the beat of the Juan Gabriel song sputtering from the radio.

"What do you think we'll find at the house?" Lucina asked.

"I don't know."

"What do you hope to find?"

"Maybe nothing. His children probably cleared it out."

"I'd like to meet my brothers."

"Strictly speaking, they aren't your brothers. They're the sons of some Spaniard who put them up for adoption."

"One of these days I might look them up."

"What for?"

"Maybe they would like to know they have a . . . no . . . Jesus. You're right, what for?"

"I went to see Ignacio's friend Ramón."

"And?"

"He's quite the character. Ignacio didn't do him justice. He's warm, friendly, he's got a marvellous vibe. He confirmed nearly everything: that Julián is the brother; that he met Ignacio back when Ignacio called himself Manuel; that Julián did kill Clara. But he did not know about you, and now he wants to meet you. He gave me copies of all the articles he wrote in *La Prensa* about the Ogress. Your grandmother," Elena added with a wink.

"Ha-ha, very funny."

Elena touched her arm. "He also gave me copies of the articles Ignacio wrote about Julián's murders."

"Let's go and see him tomorrow, before we stop by the tenement downtown."

"Maybe."

"Elena, I'm nervous."

"Me too, Lucy."

The taxi stopped in front of 9 Cerrada de Salamanca.

Lucina reaches out in the darkness. "Elena. Elena. Answer me. Are you alright?"

Elena coughs to clear her throat of a mass of dust and saliva. "I don't know. My whole body hurts. I can't see a thing. I can't breathe! I can't breathe!"

"Easy, Elena. Try to stay calm. Don't let yourself go back to sleep."

"How long has it been?"

A faint blue glow from Lucina's watch suddenly shines. "Lucina, I can see you. Reach out your hand."

The two women stretch their arms and manage to graze fingers. "It's been almost four hours since the quake. You passed out."

What drew their attention when they got out of the taxi was the black garage door where the first-floor store used to be. The window bars and frames, also black, stood out against the whitewashed walls. From the balcony of the building next door, a dog barked and stuck his snout through the ironwork. The women looked at each other. Elena felt for the keys in her handbag.

"Which one would it be?"

"The one with the same brand name as the lock," Lucina said.

Elena's hands trembled. "I'm afraid."

The dog barked louder.

A woman loaded with shopping bags stared at them as she walked by, and a man came out to quiet the dog, hitting him twice with a leash. "Shut up!" he shouted. Then he noticed Elena and Lucina. "Who are you looking for?"

The woman with the shopping bags turned to listen. The dog whined. Elena struggled to get the key in the lock, her hands were shaking so. "Señoritas, excuse me," the man insisted.

The lock opened with a click. Elena turned the knob and in they went. The second door was unbolted, held only by the latch. Once inside, the two of them leaned against the closed door, breathing hard.

Groping for a light switch, Lucina nearly tripped over something. Elena found the light. The floor was strewn with books. "Should we leave?" Lucina said, not daring to move.

"Ignacio's sons must have been here," Elena said. "They left his room in the hotel a mess too."

They took a few tentative steps, trying to avoid the objects on the floor, but things crunched underfoot. Elena turned on a second light, which revealed a complete lack of furniture except for an easy chair and a wooden table with some of the veneer missing.

They advanced without speaking, hearts racing. Lucina ran her fingers across the dusty irregular surface of the table. They were still breathing hard.

In the kitchen they found dirty dishes and the remains of a meal. "Maybe a robber came in," Lucina ventured. Elena did not answer, fearing that if she opened her mouth her last bit of courage would abandon her.

"Shall we go up?" Lucina asked at the foot of the stairs. The two of them looked up and down the staircase.

"Let's do it."

They ascended slowly, every step an effort. At the landing, two doors. The first opened into a bedroom with a single bed and a stained mattress. No other furniture. The walls were bare, the closet empty. The second door led to the study where Ignacio wrote, or so they surmised. The bookshelves seemed to have been plundered and their contents spilled across the floor along with broken bits of his figurines of monsters and demons.

Elena had asked Ramón if Ignacio was part of a Satanic cult. Ramón laughed heartily. "That was my fault," he said. "To get more readers I wrote that Felícitas kept a skull and black candles, and held Black Masses. Years later, Manuel did a series for the paper on monsters and demons. He said he wrote it for me because of what I made up about the Black Masses. He said the least a demon-worshipper could do is write about demons. But no, Manuel did not believe in God or the devil."

Lucina squirms across the short distance that separates her from Elena. Though they can't see it in the darkness, they are lying under Felícitas' operating table. A steel beam from the collapsed building next door lies at an angle over them, holding off the rubble above. Elena is face up, almost seated. Her right foot is trapped under a chunk of concrete.

"I'm next to you. I don't want to move much, something else might fall," Lucina says, reaching out to touch Elena. "I can hardly breathe."

"I think I'm alright, doctor. It's just my leg and the pain in my chest." Elena coughs so hard she vomits. It's too dark to see the bitter liquid she spits up.

They hear a groan nearby.

"Elena?"

"Shhh."

*

A clean blow to the back of the neck had knocked Elena to the floor when she stepped out of Ignacio's room. She fell face-first.

Behind her, Lucina froze. Elena's collapse revealed a figure in the hall. Her gaze met Julián's.

"Hello, niece," he said.

She tried to run, but tripped and sprawled next to Elena. Julián kicked her in the face.

The first to come around was Elena. She was lying on her side, cheek down. She swept the floor with her gaze as far as the darkness allowed. A sharp pain brought one hand to the base of her skull. She wanted to sit up, but felt as if her face were stuck to the floor. Pushing harder with her hands, she felt dizzy. She heard a moan, almost a whisper, beside her. The room was dimly lit by a light outside the window. Lucina was less than a metre away. Face down, one arm under her body, limp like a doll.

Elena managed to drag herself closer. With a trembling hand she shook Lucina's shoulder, provoking a low groan. She shook her again.

Ignacio's daughter opened her eyes. All she could see was Elena's black jeans. With help, she sat up. Irregular spasms ran through her body. A face came to mind. "Julián," she said. Her lips were swollen and her mouth had a salty metallic taste. She spat and a wad of blood and saliva made a shapeless mark on the floor.

"So you're awake."

The voice was like a lash to the back. From the shadows a figure emerged and took on consistency and colour. The man was thin, tall, his hair in a buzz cut. He was wearing black trousers and a light blue shirt that Elena recognised as Ignacio's. "I never imagined I'd see you here," he said drawing closer. The two women backed up against the wall, one beside the other. "Make yourselves comfortable. We're going to be here for a while."

He went to Lucina, held her chin with one hand and kept the

other behind his back. He raised her face to the light. "You look like Clara." She tried to push him away. Julián pointed the pistol he had in his other hand. "Don't move. We're going to talk. You must have questions."

Julián dragged a chair over to the window. "I know the lies Manuel told you. Sometimes he would come to the prison and read out what he was writing for his daughter. And to give me the women's shoes he'd collected. I ended up with nearly a dozen. None matched."

Lucina squeezed Elena's hand.

"Manuel said I was his first reader, the one he wrote for. Fuck, did I ever hate him. I spent years planning what I would do to him when I got out of prison. But the bastard died before I got the chance. My fault, I've got to admit, idiot that I am."

Elena looked around, her eyes now accustomed to the gloom. The room was small, claustrophobic, as bare as the rest of the house. She recognised the place from Ignacio's description. It had to be where Felícitas attended to her patients. Apart from the chair the only furniture was the steel operating table. Like the ones in the morgue, she thought. Esteban crossed her mind, he had promised to meet up with them. She brought one hand to her neck, where her heart seemed to be pounding.

"Let me take a look," Lucina said to her.

"I'm alright."

"No point checking her out. Soon enough it won't matter. Nothing will."

THIRTY-FOUR

Thursday, September 19, 1985
11.06

A murky silence fills the darkness. The two women hold their breaths, focused on detecting another sound.

"Julián?"

They hear dripping, creaks they cannot decipher, rubble falling. Barking at first faint, then louder.

"Help!"

"In here!"

"Help!"

They yell to the dog, yell to the world lying who knows how many metres above them. The life force that Esteban's father tried to measure urges them to cry out.

"We're in here!"

"Help!"

They pause hoping for another bark, but the sepulchral silence settles in once more. Hot tears make their way through the dust and blood coating their faces.

"We're going to die," Lucina says.

"No, Lucy. Isabel did not keep you safe all those years for you to die in the house of the Ogress. That would be too ridiculous."

A giggle escapes Lucina's lips, then her body shakes with laughter. Elena starts laughing too, but it hurts. "You might not believe it," Elena says, catching her breath, "but Ignacio used to make me laugh.

A lot. That's why I liked him. Maybe that's why I didn't see who he really was. If I had, maybe my mother..."

"Don't go there, Elena. Let's not start blaming ourselves."

More barking.

"Help!"

They hear a man shout, "Here! Somebody's in here!"

"Over here!" The two women cry. "We're here!"

"I'm here too!" Julián's voice reverberates in the darkness.

"Let's go over the lies," Julián had said, crossing his legs above the knee in a way that was almost girlish. "Manuel was really good at telling them, the bastard. His whole life was a lie. He never even knew he wasn't my parents' son. A woman left him with them when he was two, my father told me about it, and nobody wanted to buy him. My parents reckoned it would be a good idea for him to stay, since I was a baby and he kept me company."

"He wasn't Felícitas' son?" Lucina said.

"Nope. The idiot never had the genes he worried so much about." Julián's voice was flat. "For years the bastard never visited. I figured maybe he was dead. But one day I got called down because someone named Ignacio Suárez was there to see me. 'Why did you kill Clara?' was the first thing he said. Not even 'Hello'. He had been savouring that question for decades before he finally got up the courage to ask it. I told him why: because she didn't deserve to be happy. I could have told him anything. I killed her because I hated him. He brought me a copy of his novel, the one that tells the story of the murders he committed. He told me his new name. I laughed. What a stupid name."

"It was you," Elena interrupted. "You're the murderer."

"The con job my brother did was impressive." Julián paused. "He killed them. I wasn't even there."

"What about Felícitas? Did you kill her?" Lucina asked.

"He said I killed her too?"

"It's easy to blame a man who can't defend himself." Elena realised she was repeating the words she had used with the detectives.

"It's also easy to blame a man in prison." Julián heaved a long sigh. He shook his head and without lowering his gun glanced out of the window. "It's too dark in here." He flipped on the light and it reflected brightly off the steel operating table. The nakedness of the room was even more evident, as was the swelling on Lucina's face and the dried blood on Elena's clothes.

"What are you going to do with us?" Lucina asked, squeezing Elena's hand. The words Isabel had repeated so often echoed in her mind.

"Manuel murdered the women he wrote about in the book and in the newspaper. I killed Clara, that's the only confession I'll make. And I've paid my dues."

"And you wanted to kill me," Lucina said firmly.

"You? No, no. I didn't want to kill you. I'm no child-killer."

"You killed the teenagers. They were practically girls," Elena insisted.

Julián went up to her, put the mouth of the pistol under her chin, and lifted her face. Their eyes met. Looking into that abyss made her dizzy and she averted her gaze. He forced her to look again. "That was a present for my brother."

"Killing two innocent girls was a present?" Elena said, defying him with her eyes.

"'Collateral damage', is what my brother called it in one of his books."

Elena twisted her neck, but Julián would not let her shake off the pistol under her chin. He glared at her, then took a step back. Again he glanced out of the window. The night was receding. A chorus of barks reached them.

*

A chunk of concrete gives way, causing a new collapse. Underneath the table they can hear bits hitting the steel.

"Help!"

"We're in here!"

They shout desperately, but this time no-one answers and the darkness is thicker than ever.

"Help me! Please!"

It's Julián's voice echoing off the rubble. The women's hearts jump.

"I'm trapped!"

Lucina breathes a sigh of relief. The monster can't reach them.

After he confirmed that he was the one who killed Leticia Almeida and Claudia Cosío, they had no doubt he would kill them too. What they could not know was that hell was about to open its doors. Julián was merely the threshold.

Julián returned to his chair. "Two years ago Manuel showed up at the prison for the last time. His visits were always a surprise." He again crossed his legs, the pistol dancing in his right hand. "He brought me his books, clippings of his articles, copies of his scripts, plus the shoes. I read his stuff because I didn't have anything else to do and I have to confess I liked some of it. The asshole was a really good writer. On one of those visits he told me about you." He pointed the pistol at Elena. "I thought he was gloating about his freedom, his sex life. I wasn't interested."

"I'm not interested in what you have to say either."

"The interesting part is coming, Elena. Don't be impatient. Manuel — Ignacio to you — wanted to tell me about your mother. That's right. He said she had gone into his room and read some pages of his, snooped around his clippings and photographs."

Elena's heart was pounding. For three years she had tried to keep Ignacio from seeing how much her mother disliked him. Impossible. Soledad made it obvious. She even tried to evict him several times.

"What your mother read was Manuel's version of the story of our family. The clippings were news stories about my mother and the murders of her patients. Well, my brother spotted her coming out of the room. Then he cornered her in the courtyard by the washstands. When I was at your hotel I saw the spot and it's very much like where my mother once drowned a cat in front of him. He punched her in the face, grabbed her by the neck, and held her head under the water in the tub where they soak the clothes. You should have heard him tell the story, all the details that stood out for him: the dripping water, your mother's struggle to raise her head, the startled birds flying off, the sound of a hedge-trimmer in the distance, his effort to keep her quiet so no-one would know. Then the rough voice of the gardener calling, 'Señora Soledad?'"

"What are you getting at?"

"Manuel tried to kill your mother, but he got interrupted."

"You're crazy. I don't believe you."

"That's just what your stepfather said when I told him about it. As fate would have it, precisely while I was telling him, Manuel pulled up in front of the hotel. Your mother's husband confronted him. They shouted at each other. I couldn't hear everything, since I didn't want Manuel to see me. I did hear him say, 'Julián? Julián is here?' But your stepfather would not let up. My brother took him by the arm, they got into the car and drove off. I don't know where he was planning to take him or if he just wanted to escape from me. Maybe that was it, and as fate would have it they crashed."

"You were in the hotel?"

"I was there several times."

Elena sprung up from the floor and leapt at Julián. "You lie!" she screamed at the very moment when her watch and the watches of every inhabitant of Mexico City showed nineteen minutes and forty-two seconds past seven a.m. Dawn had accompanied Julián's words like a curtain rising.

The ground began to shake. For a few seconds, Elena failed to register what Lucina was screaming: "It's an earthquake!"

Julián punched Elena hard and she fell back.

A loud crunch distracted him as he wound up to hit her again. The walls and roof were cracking. The window exploded. Julián struggled to get the door key out of his trouser pocket and into the lock. "Elena!" Lucina cried, scooting under the table and trying to pull Elena with her. As the door swung open, the building next door collapsed on its foundations and crushed the room that once was the maternity clinic of Felícitas Sánchez.

"It's just past seven o'clock in the morning. *Ay, Chihuahua!* Seven o'clock, nineteen minutes, forty-two seconds, central Mexican time. Everything is still shaking, but let's take this calmly. Hang on, let's wait a second before we speak..."

Ramón's television screen went black on the morning news with Lourdes Guerrero. He felt dizzy, but quickly understood it was the building swaying to the rhythm of the quaking earth. In the same instant more than three hundred buildings came crashing down.

Driving down Highway 57 towards the capital, Esteban crossed into Mexico State and switched on the radio. He had been on the road since six a.m., having barely slept awaiting a call from Elena and Lucina that never came. It was now after eight and a reporter was talking about an earthquake. He changed the station and on XEW heard the T.V. newsman Jacobo Zabludovsky describe the scene from his car: "Several floors of the Hotel Continental have fallen in. I am asking everyone, please, do not go out. The police and rescue crews are at work. I can't see more because of all the dust and smoke." Esteban continued listening and learned that the Hotel Regis, the Nuevo León, the Conalep, the Navy building, the headquarters of Televisa all had collapsed. Patrol cars and ambulances raced past him. Sirens wailed on all sides.

Elena tries to move her right leg. The latest landslide eased the pressure somehow and she manages to free her foot.

"My foot!"

"What is it?"

"I got it out, but it hurts like hell."

"Don't move, you could cause another collapse. Try to relax. I'm sure they'll rescue us."

"Lucy, I don't hear anything anymore."

"Wait, don't lose faith."

Once again a dog begins to bark above their heads.

"Here!"

"Help!"

Unseen by the two women, dozens of volunteers are removing stones and broken furnishings, chunks of concrete and wood, from the pile of rubble covering them.

"There's someone here!"

By now it is past noon.

"Help me!" Julián shouts. Elena's and Lucina's hearts tremble.

Every rock taken off the top causes a small landslide of earth, plaster, cement, glass.

"Here! Here!" Lucina shouts.

Twenty minutes later, light and air begin to make their way through tiny pathways in the rubble.

"Careful, go slowly," they hear.

"We're going to get out," Lucina says, bolstered by the oxygen she's breathing and the glimmer of light.

A sudden urge to retch takes Elena by surprise, forcing her to turn her head to the side. The pain in her abdomen is more intense.

"Elena, are you alright?"

"It hurts."

"Hang on."

A young man's face peers through a new opening.

"Help us! Please!" Lucina begs.

"We'll get you out, try to stay calm. How many are you? Are you alright?"

"Yes, yes, we're alright," Elena answers. "There are two of us."

"I'm here too!" Julián screams at the very moment the young man pulls his head back to tell someone outside about two trapped women.

The light filtering through the opening reveals Julián to be much closer than they had imagined. His leg is touching Elena's, but a piece of concrete lies across him.

"We're going to make the hole bigger." The young man is back. "First, we're going to give you oxygen."

A hose slides through the hole and they hear the hissing of gas. Slowly, Lucina squirms out from under the table.

"Lucina, what are you doing?"

Lucina does not answer. Taking advantage of the thin shaft of light, she makes her way through the debris. Stones sharp as knives slice into her arms, metal rods poke her. She moans, but does not stop crawling towards Julián.

"What are you up to?" Julián growls. Although the concrete slab has him pinned down, he tries to kick her, provoking a slide of sand and small stones. Lucina wipes her face with her forearm, feels the grit in her eyes. She reaches out and hauls herself up on the concrete lying across Julián. She can barely fit between it and the rubble above her.

"What are you up to?" Julián repeats. His voice is angry. With his one free hand, he pushes Lucina's head to get her off him. Lucina uses her left hand to defend herself. With her right she grabs a rock. The scuffle causes more debris to fall.

"Lucina! Lucina!" Elena struggles to edge closer.

"Enough! Cut it out!" Julián tries to fend off his brother's daughter, but Elena grabs his arm in time for Lucina to bring the rock down on his head. A long moan issues from the son of the Ogress.

As if a bubble had burst, the two women are suddenly aware of voices above, people working to widen the opening. The movement sends more debris down on them and on an unconscious Julián.

The young man again sticks in his head, this time shining a flashlight. "Do you think you can crawl out?"

"Yes," Lucina answers. "Yes."

The man works his way in and under the steel beam they had not been able to see in the darkness, which, along with the table, kept them from being crushed.

Another face appears in the hole. The light hurts the eyes of the two women, whose cheeks are furrowed with tears mixed with dirt.

"Lucina! Elena!"

"Esteban!" Lucina lurches towards the exit, helped by the young man.

Elena has half her body under the operating table. By some miracle a large chunk of marble from the floor of an apartment ended up next to the beam, protecting her from several protruding steel rods.

Esteban helps Lucina climb out of the opening, wraps his arms around her, then turns to wait for Elena. The young man, no more than eighteen, along with a much older man, manages to move several cinder blocks and free Elena. With their help she makes her way towards the opening. When she sticks her head out, the crowd of volunteers breaks into applause.

"Is there anyone else down there?" a fireman asks. No-one answers because the ground beneath their feet suddenly gives way.

"Landslide!" someone shouts, and everyone clambers off the pile of rubble before the hungry earth can swallow them. They reach the street safely as gravity sucks down the remains of the building — stones, concrete, cinder blocks, steel rods, marble, sand — along with broken bits of furniture, photographs, books, and more, things that once meant something to the people who lived there.

"Was anyone else with you?" the fireman asks again.

"No," Elena says.

"No-one else," Lucina confirms.

"We'll check," the fireman says, putting his arm around Elena to help her walk.

Elena and Lucina hear barking behind them and turn to see the dog from the balcony of the building next door, now reduced to ruins. He wags his tail and licks Elena's hand. She smiles and with a grimace of pain bends down to stroke his head.

"Max! Max!" a man shouts. "Leave the señorita alone."

The dog goes back to his owner and the two women watch, still smiling. Elena repeats his name, "Max."

ACKNOWLEDGEMENTS

Writing this book altered my body chemistry, sending me into a tailspin of anxiety and depression. I want to thank from the bottom of my heart the people who helped me out of that dark place:

To Luis and my children Ana, Luisga, Montse, and Juanpa, thank you for your love, your affection, your infinite patience, and your long, silent, nourishing embraces. Thank you for being my refuge and my anchor. I love you and I learn from each of you.

Puri, thank you for taking me for walks, for listening to me. I wish everyone could have a friend like you, Purificación. As your name implies, you purify the soul.

To my workshop buddies, my tribe, who would not let me go and insisted that I teach them, thank you for keeping me afloat.

To my girlfriends, each and every one, you fill my soul and clothe me with your affection. I understand how hard it must have been to stick by me through these dark times. Thank you for your unconditional friendship.

My uncles and aunts, cousins, family, I love you so much. Thank you to all the Llacas for keeping tabs on me day-in, day-out.

To the Anayas, thank you for making me feel like a daughter, a sister. Thank you for the many years of affection.

To my siblings: Mario, thank you for writing and calling me nearly every day, thank you for being there and for reading my work, even if you needed a push to get you to the end. Martha, thank you for taking charge during my mother's illness.

Thank you to Pablo Sada, Alicia Ortiz, Enrique and Sabine Asencio, Pachy Cambiaso, Carlos Galindo. All of your suggestions were invaluable. Thank you for your patience in answering my interminable questions.

Lili Blum, thank you for listening to me and encouraging me, and above all for your friendship.

Gretel, thank you for translating the first few pages and for all your affection.

Vero Flores, thank you for the path we walked together and all we learned.

To Sergio, Pot, thank you for being my reader ever since we were teenagers, for the many years of friendship and the unflagging encouragement.

Imanol Caneyada, thank you for your advice, suggested readings, company. Your messages helped me get to the finish line.

Thank you to David Martínez, my editor, for your passion and your patience. It was a marvellous experience working with you.

Carmina Rufrancos and Gabriel Sandoval, thank you for collaborating with me on a new project.

Anna Soler-Pont, my agent, thank you for listening to me so generously each time we met. Thank you for finding a good home for this novel, for your confidence and your friendship. On we go.

Thank you to María Cardona and the entire team at Pontas for your openness and professionalism. You make it a wonderful agency.

Thank you to my parents, who live on in each of my words.

During the long process of writing this book, a new member of our family arrived, Luis César. Thank you Ana Pau and César for making me a grandmother. Every day the baby fills us with light and happiness. I love you.

Thank you to my husband, Luis, for our thirty years together and for the family we have built. Thank you for your adventurous spirit, which forces me to go places I never imagined. I love you.